PR

"Strong and lyrical." —*San Diego Union-Tribune*

"A marvel, a fabulous trip . . . exciting, poignant, frightening and transcendent."
—Kate Wilhelm, Nebula and Hugo award-winning author

"Fascinating . . . Antieau deftly weaves together stunning imagery and powerful concepts . . . very highly recommended." —*House of Speculative Fiction*

"Erotic and profound." —*Science Fiction Age*

"Bet on this book to be a winner." —*Ann Arbor News*

"A powerful and impressive statement." —*Kirkus Reviews*

Kim Antieau, author of *The Jigsaw Woman,* has been published in magazines, anthologies, and *Trudging to Eden,* a collection of her short fiction. She is also the editor and publisher of *The Furious Spinners,* a reader-participation magazine exploring creativity, nature, spirituality, and more.

The Gaia Websters

Kim Antieau

A ROC BOOK

ROC
Published by the Penguin Group
Penguin Books USA Inc., 375 Hudson Street, New York, New York 10014, U.S.A.
Penguin Books Ltd, 27 Wrights Lane, London W8 5TZ, England
Penguin Books Australia Ltd, Ringwood, Victoria, Australia
Penguin Books Canada Ltd, 10 Alcorn Avenue, Toronto, Ontario, Canada M4V 3B2
Penguin Books (N.Z.) Ltd, 182–190 Wairau Road, Auckland 10, New Zealand

Penguin Books Ltd, Registered Offices:
Harmondsworth, Middlesex, England

First published by ROC, an imprint of Dutton Signet,
a division of Penguin Books USA Inc.

First Printing, June, 1997
10 9 8 7 6 5 4 3 2 1

LIBRARY OF CONGRESS CATALOGING-IN-PUBLICATION DATA:
Antieau, Kim.
The Gaia Websters / Kim Antieau.
p. cm.
ISBN 0-451-45511-8
I. Title.
PS3551.N745G3 1997
813'.54—dc21
96-49456
CIP

Printed in the United States of America

For Gaia,
where the wild things live,
and
for Mario,
my sweetheart

One

I am a soothsayer.

I admit this freely now despite all that I have learned. Or perhaps because of it.

In ancient times, it was said that a soothsayer was someone who claimed to foretell events, a prophet, or seer, someone who could calm or relieve pain.

I have never foretold any event. I do not see myself as a prophet or seer.

I have calmed and relieved the pain of many. I have also caused pain to many.

Perhaps this truthsaying, this story of mine, will calm or relieve the pain of some.

Perhaps not.

But it is all I know.

Ten years earlier, I awoke in a cave with no memory. I picked my name from the graffiti on the rock. The stone read: Sarah, Susan, Constance, Virginia, Bobby, Gloria. I chose Gloria. I liked the shape of the G, how it curved around into itself and then back out again. Like me in and out of that cave.

Although I did not remember anything about myself when I awakened, I quickly realized I must have been a healer. As I walked around the woods near the cave, I recognized too many plants and knew too much about their healing properties to be a casual student. Then I passed a little girl with bloody knees on my way into the town nearest the cave. We were both astonished to see the gravel cuts disappear when I touched her as I picked the stones out of her skin. She thanked me but ran away quickly. I turned and headed for another community, a ball of fear forming in my stomach.

I made the Washington Territory my home for a time. I worked as a healer, disguising my hands-on healing abilities as best I could. One year, I journeyed to the Arizona Territory. I got through immigration easily and was awestruck by the desert. All the prickly vegetation and seemingly stark landscape made me feel as though I had found a kindred land. I offered my services to the town of Coyote Creek and had been happily ensconced there until the day the man from the governor tried to follow me up Black Mountain to my home.

He kept tripping and falling on his way up the hill, pricking himself with every cactus that came within yards of the path. I hurried over the ridge to lose him. Cosmo stood on the trail watching the man, his head cocked in what I took to be an expression of puzzlement.

"Woman!" the governor's man called.

Cosmo's low growl carried up the hill to me. He did not like the man either.

"Gloria Stone!" the man screamed. "Get this mangy dog away from me!"

"*Coyote,* you idiot," I murmured, and hurried on. I could see my small house tucked into the next ridge, surrounded by saguaro and juniper.

"If the governor wants you, he will have you!" The man's whiny voice reverberated up to me.

I stopped. Who did he think he was? If the governor "wanted me," he would "have me"? I should go down and take his shoes and make him walk back barefoot. Or maybe I should rip off his clothes and let Cosmo chew him all over.

No. Too much trouble. I had had a long day, and I was tired.

Then I heard the sound of scree rolling and the man's cry as he tumbled down the hill like the useless little weed he was.

Cosmo yelped.

"I'm coming," I grumbled.

Lucky for the man, a magnificent saguaro had stopped his descent, and he now lay sprawled against it.

Cosmo waited on the trail until we met. Then he followed me to the saguaro and the injured man whose face and hands were bloody from the prickly pear he had rolled into.

"This is your fault!" he said.

Cosmo yelped. The man shut his mouth.

"What's your name?" I asked.

"Primer," he answered. "I'm from the governor."

"Yeah, yeah," I said. I reluctantly knelt and felt his legs.

"Stop that," he said. "You are to come with me at once. That hurts!"

"It ought to hurt," I said. He had a bad sprain.

I did not have any herbs or lotions to apply to distract him from my hands-on healing.

"I can fix it if you'll shut up and let me," I said. I had to have his permission; it was an ethical thing with me. "If not, I can leave you here with Cosmo. He's not a vegetarian. Or a scavenger. He kills his meals."

The man grunted and nodded assent. I put my hands on his left ankle.

"Listen," I whispered. Dazed, he looked away from my hands and up at my face. Some. Thing. Was wrong. I connected. Felt dizzy. Could not sense. Then a little. Peculiar.

My hands moved slowly over the torn muscles. Something was different. I could not find. Him. Then suddenly, his muscles healed quickly.

"There," I said, moving back onto my heels and away from

him. My dizziness disappeared. "I guess it was just bruised." I scratched Cosmo's neck.

The man touched his ankle. "It feels fine. You *are* a soothsayer."

He got up and dusted himself off.

"No," I said, "just your local health-care provider."

"Will you come with me now?" he asked.

"I've relayed this message to the governor before. I'm too busy. This community needs me. Maybe if things slow down in the summer." I started up the trail again. The huge old saguaro waved at me with both arms.

"Summer! That's next year!"

"You better get down the hill before dark," I said, without looking back. I suspected he feared the dark. "Do you want Cosmo to take you?"

"No! I know the way." I heard the stones rolling under his feet again as he started down. He would be lucky if he did not break anything before he reached the village.

Cosmo ran up beside me.

"I wonder why the governor sent someone like him to get me?" I said, as we went over the ridge again.

I reached the low twisted juniper which signaled level ground and my home just as the sun was going down over the mountains, changing the land from gold to rose. Cosmo yelped and went to run with the dusk, as was his habit. He ran straight toward the receding light. To hurry it on, I often wondered, or to try and catch the curtain of light and pull it back? Either way, he had fun.

Once inside my house, I kicked off my shoes and walked across the cool stones to the table in the middle of the large airy room which was my kitchen and living room. A vase of fresh flowers stood alongside my covered dinner and a glass of lemonade. I took off the ceramic lid and steam rose from rice, beans, and vegetable burritos. The smell of cilantro filled me with anticipation. I picked up the plate, flatware, and lemonade and went outside to watch the sunset.

This was my payment for staying in Coyote Creek: this

house which they cleaned and kept up; my clothes, which I got to choose; and three meals or more a day, mostly cooked by Millie and brought up to me by a variety of people. In exchange, I was supposed to keep the inhabitants healthy, or at least to heal them when they fell ill.

I sat on the gravelly Arizona dirt. Cosmo howled in the distance. For a moment, I imagined I could feel the ground beneath his padded paws. "Go, Cosmo!" I called and laughed. I stared into the bloody light, noting but not really focusing on the hills, rocks, cacti, junipers, and Joshua trees which surrounded me. A kind of jumble of disparate struggle in this desert, so silent and still. I longed for this spot all day as the people came to me. I touched them, healed their bodies, and sometimes their spirits, and did not feel touched by them or connected to them. I was more comfortable with scorpions, rattlesnakes, and coyotes than I was with people. However, the scorpions and rattlesnakes did not feed and clothe me.

I gulped the lemonade. My face puckered in sourness. It was just the way I liked it: only a touch of honey.

Coyote Creek was a nice community. Arizona Territory was well organized. Most people had enough food and shelter. Trading with other territories went well, and the governor seemed to be good at keeping out plagues and other undesirables. The communities in Washington had been more isolated and paranoid toward outsiders like me.

The governor here was relatively new. His mother had died a few years back. Soon after her death he had started sending out messages that he wanted me to come to the Grand Canyon and meet with him. Thus far I had successfully avoided our meeting. I suspected he wanted to see me because he believed, like everyone else, that I was a soothsayer.

He was wrong. I had heard all the stories: soothsayers were extraordinary healers, inheriting their abilities from a long line of illustrious healers. They had great compassion, wisdom, and empathy. I had no lineage of great healers that I remembered; I certainly was not compassionate or wise. Supposedly soothsayers could not lie. They were always "truth sayers."

Although I did not do it very often, I could lie quite easily and convincingly. No, I was not a soothsayer. I just had the heat or energy or whatever it was in my fingers to put disease at ease.

I finished off the burrito as the rose sky was replaced by a gray one. Now Cosmo would be indistinguishable from anything around him. A gray ghost. This was his time of day: the between and betwixt time. Magic time. I smiled. What would our good Reverend Thomas Church think about my magical musings? He had already asked me if I was a witch. Was he preparing a bonfire in my honor? The Rev made me nervous. Or else the supposed comeback of Christian churches made me nervous. Rumors were circulating that some congregations were using soothsayers as their latest scapegoats, accusing them of being the devil or witches, or worse, tech violators.

Of course, I really did not know Church well enough to judge him, even if I had found him snooping around my clinic more than once. I did not know how he felt about soothsayers or healers or anything. I hoped he would not cause any problem so that everything could remain the same. I liked the town and this piece of land where my house sat and Cosmo and I roamed.

The land was not mine, of course, but it felt like home.

"Of course this land is home," my friend Kara told me once. "When a woman bleeds on a piece of land, she becomes a part of it and it a part of her."

I did not tell her I did not bleed. In the ten years since coming out of the cave, I had never menstruated. I did not know my age. Judging from the other women I had met, I was somewhere between thirty and fifty, so maybe I had already gone through the 'pause.

One day Cosmo and I were roughhousing outside and my wrist got caught on his incisor and started bleeding. I watched in fascination as the red dripped onto the beige ground. Color. Life. After a time, Cosmo whined and I covered the wound with my other hand so I would not bleed to death. A moment later, not even a scar remained as a reminder. But I knew. I was now a part of this land, and it was a part of me. I liked the feeling.

It was dark, and I was reminiscing too much.

I went inside to the bedroom where I fell asleep to the sound of coyotes serenading the rising moon.

Later I half awakened to milk light and the smell of something feral or musky.

"Cosmo?" I whispered, turning into sleep again.

I felt lips on my earlobe, warm breath on my neck.

"Benjamin." Kara's brother, fresh from the desert night.

He caressed my back and shoulders, kissed the back of my knees, massaged my calves, put my toes in his mouth: first one and then the others. Sleepily, I turned over and held out my arms to him. He was a shadow leaning down to put his mouth over mine.

"I thought you were Cosmo," I whispered.

"He kisses you like this?"

"I never have seen the two of you together."

He laughed, leaning his head back just as Cosmo did when he howled at the moon. Benjamin's hair slipped over his shoulders and brushed my cheek. "I guess you've found me out."

I pulled him down against me. "I don't care who you are. You smell good, and I'm awake."

Benjamin was gone when I awakened. I went outside. Cosmo lay near the door, his fur blushing with dawn. All was touched with pink and gold, nothing in shadow yet everything partially black. I sat next to Cosmo, and he put his muzzle on my bare thigh.

"Good morning to you, too," I said.

A rabbit ran out in front of us. Cosmo twitched but let the animal pass. I laughed. Cosmo had been my friend for five years or more, since I came to Coyote Creek. I found him in the desert tangled in an old trap with its rusty teeth embedded in his leg. Broken bones were easy to fix; systemic illnesses were more difficult. After I relieved him of his steel accessory, I carried him to the house. I lay with my hands on him all night. I fingered old barbed wire scars on his flanks and the extra toes on his front paws. Through that night, Cosmo watched me, his breath shallow. Then around dawn, he shook himself, got off the bed, and went outside. He returned to the house a day or two later and stayed. Coyote Creek was known for its proliferation of coyotes—thus the name—so Cosmo was even welcome in town. Of course, basically, anything I did was tolerated. Thus far.

Now I kissed the top of Cosmo's head and got up and went inside. I put on shoes and slung a towel over my naked body. Cosmo and I raced to the stream below my house. Surprisingly, it still ran strong even though it was autumn. Usually the sun sweated it all away by this time, but the summer had been mild. A few aspen grew near the banks of the stream. I threw my towel over a low branch of one and dipped my right foot into the clear shallow water. Not too cold. Cosmo chased a blue dragonfly away from the river as I squatted and splashed water over me.

I was just about to reach up and wash Benjamin out of me when I noticed Reverend Church standing on the other side of the stream watching me. He was good-looking: blond, green-eyed, with a slight build.

I stood and put my hands on my hips.

"Gee, Church, if you wanted to see me naked, I could have arranged a more convenient location."

He had the good graces to blush.

"I was on my way up the hill."

"Yeah, well, the path is that way," I said, pointing to my right. A cool breeze shivered across my breasts, puckering my nipples. Great, I was becoming the religious pervert's wet dream.

"I got lost," he said, looking at his feet. "I need to talk with you, but I'll wait until you're dressed."

"That's right," I said, stepping out of the water and reaching for my towel. "Your religion thinks the human body is dirty." I patted myself dry, then wrapped a towel around me and put on my shoes. I was annoyed that this man could actually embarrass me. I was not naturally modest.

"I'm afraid you are repeating ancient rumors," Church said. "We have nothing against the human body. God made it in his image."

"In *his* image?" I shook my head. It was too early for a thealogical discussion. "Listen, if you want to talk with me, wait until I get to town."

"I thought you might be too busy there."

"Never too busy for you." I smiled and walked away. Two irritating men in less than twenty-four hours. These were not good omens.

When I reached my house, the sunlight was full on it. I went inside, got dressed, and ate a bowl of granola with raisins, nuts, and soy milk. Cosmo yelped once when he returned from dragonfly chasing and once when Church came up the path.

I stepped outside. The sky was azure, not a cloud anywhere, unless I counted Church, who stood away from Cosmo with his hands folded in front of him.

"Cos," I said, snapping my fingers. Cosmo relaxed and moved off to the side. I hurried down the trail.

"We can talk on the way," I said. Maybe now I would ask him why he kept hanging around the clinic. A few days earlier, when I caught him alone in my clinic, he had been holding a bottle of dried rosemary and peering closely at it. I had stood silently until he turned and saw me, blinked rapidly, and set down the bottle.

That was when he asked me if I was a witch.

The question sent a thrill of fear through me. "Define witch," I said.

He nodded, as if my answer satisfied him, and then he left.

Now he matched strides with me. "I wanted to talk to you about the man from Governor Duncan, Mr. Primer," he said. Cosmo whined behind us.

"He was here last night," I said. "What about it?"

The Rev deftly stepped over scree and around a prickly pear that reached for him.

Overhead, a turkey vulture roamed.

"We're concerned he could create problems for the town," he said.

I glanced over at him. "We?"

"Yes. The town council. Didn't you know I'm on it now?"

I shook my head. I recalled no election.

"Santana Janis resigned, and I was appointed by the council to fill her seat until the next general election."

"I've got to start going to those meetings again," I said. "How can Primer cause problems? He's gone, isn't he?"

"No. He's staying in the refectory."

"Then he's your problem. You gave him a place to stay."

The path curved around and there was Coyote Creek comfortably slouching into the desert. Cosmo sprinted ahead of us, joining other gray ghosts for a run along the ridge. From here, the town seemed little more than a bunch of wooden shacks, some with tin roofs catching the morning sun. Coyote Creek probably looked the way it had three hundred years ago, except now no automobiles roamed the streets, no jet planes left their marks in the sky overhead.

"The council gave him a place to stay," Church said. "It is our obligation to the governor."

"What's this got to do with me?" I asked. A goat bleated below. Cosmo yelped. I hoped the goat had a place to hide.

"He's here for you," Church said.

We got to level ground via a path around the shady back of Millie's Cafe. Herb, Millie's husband, waved as he dumped scraps onto the compost pile.

"You going to the dance over at Freedom?" Herb called.

"Absolutely," I said. "Maybe someone will get me drunk, and I can take advantage of them."

Herb laughed. Church and I went single file down the tiny alley between the two buildings. I swung the wooden door open, and we stepped into sunlight and onto Coyote Creek's dusty main street. A park of gambel oaks supposedly planted soon after The Fall shaded part of the street. Today several children rolled under the trees together, each trying to wrestle a ball from another. What a wonderful way to first encounter the bodies of other people, to know what they feel and smell like. I closed my eyes for a moment, remembering Benjamin pressed up against me in the night.

"There's a dance?" Church asked.

I opened my eyes. "Is dancing against your religion?"

"You really are very intolerant," he said evenly. "You know nothing about us."

I looked at him. He was right. I remembered no encounter with people of his religion, yet something about him made me uneasy. Perhaps in that vast unremembered part of my past a Christian or two lurked.

"I apologize," I said. "I just don't like people following me or watching me bathe. It kind of gets on my nerves. It would be like me say . . . watching you flagellate yourself, or whatever it is you do in church."

The Rev smiled. The expression did not quite reach his eyes, which looked at me intently.

"Why don't you come to church sometime and see?" he said. "As far as this Mr. Primer from the governor goes, the council would like to speak with you."

"Anytime, at my clinic. Now, I've got to get to work."

He nodded, and we parted. I walked a couple of doors down to my cozy little place of business: a little cottage set back from the street. I kicked off my shoes to walk on the bare stone path that curved through the courtyard to the wooden door of the clinic. Cosmo lay alongside the walkway, panting. Apparently the goat had made good its escape. I pulled on the antler that was the door handle and went inside.

As always, I was greeted with a melding of aromas; this morning lavender and rosemary distinguished themselves. A pot of rose hip tea awaited on the rickety table off to the side of my examining table. A piece of corn bread slathered with butter lay next to it. I grinned and sat at the table. As I bit into the corn bread, I looked around the room lined with shelves of herbs, roots, barks, tinctures, and potions. Sometimes life was grand.

* * *

I treated a child with breathing problems by laying my hands on her chest and giving her mother mullein tea to take home with her. Later, someone came in with a sprained ankle. A tick infection. A touch of depression. A cold. I helped each with a little smoke and mirrors, laying on of hands, and a story or two.

At lunch, Millie dropped off roasted prickly pear and a light stew of corn, pinto beans, rice, spices, and herbs. I went outside, sat, and leaned against the palm tree in the clinic courtyard.

Georgia came up the walk and sat with me. She reveled in chokeberry cobbler while I chewed vegetables. When I put down my empty bowl and looked at the older woman, she grinned as if she knew what I was going to say. I said nothing.

She laughed. "I told you you need to come to all the council meetings. I'm just mayor. I can't control everything! Church is persistent."

"He's a religious kook. How could you?"

"It's harvest and party time. No one wanted the job. And he's really a nice man."

I shook my head. "Then the seat should have been left empty. He does not represent this community."

"He is part of this community," Georgia said. "Why don't you like him?"

"It was religions like his that caused so much havoc after The Fall," I said.

"That was a long time ago," she said. "Besides, don't they blame soothsayers for The Fall?"

I glanced at her. "I'm not—"

"You're not a soothsayer. Yes, we've all heard it before. Why don't you just go visit the governor?"

"The council wants me to go? You may never see me again."

Georgia laughed. "You believe all that rubbish about governors kidnapping soothsayers for their own sinister use? Please."

"No. I believe they probably offer the healers the easy life so they never want to go back to their communities."

"Hah!" Georgia said. "You couldn't get it much easier than you have it here."

"Except I probably wouldn't have to put up with religious radicals snooping around the clinic."

"Gloria, what are you talking about?"

"I came back from lunch one day, and Church was in the clinic handling my stuff."

"I've gone in the clinic when you're out dozens of times and handled your stuff! I've even used some of it! Why don't you take me out and hang me?"

"That's different."

"What's different is he unnerves you." She stood. I reached my hand out, and she pulled me up. "Which reminds me. We're having a special open meeting this afternoon. Weapons and technology violation."

"Who?"

"Stempler Jones."

I shook my head. "So we'll break up his gun again. What's the technology?"

"A fuel-burning generator."

"Stupid jerk. I suppose he says it's a collector's item."

Georgia nodded.

"Then fill the fuel tank with cement."

"That's not very authentic," Georgia said, imitating Stempler's drawl. "Besides, cement-making is outlawed in some territories, and generators are lawful in some."

I put my hands on my hips. "Not fuel-burning generators. And he can just move to one of those places if he doesn't like the rules here."

"My feelings exactly."

She leaned over and kissed me on the lips and patted my butt. "I hope you come to the meeting. Church will be there. Maybe you should just have sex with him and ease the tension a bit. It worked with us." She laughed and left the courtyard.

"He doesn't believe in sex!" I called.

Benjamin passed Georgia. I smiled. He was so beautiful, he took my breath away each time I saw him. His shiny black hair was pulled back into a braid now, and his face was all gorgeous brown angles. He kissed my lips.

"Who doesn't believe in sex?" he asked. He pulled me down onto the ground under the tree.

"The Reverend Thomas Church."

"Oh? He seems fairly normal to me."

"Why did you leave before I woke up?"

"I was there, watching the sunset."

"*Cosmo* was there."

Benjamin kissed me. "Remember last night, you discovered the ancient Native secret of shape-shifting. You've heard of werewolves. I'm your werecoyote."

I turned around and straddled his lap and linked my hands behind his neck. "As if you didn't have anything better to do than follow me around all day and chase butterflies and goats."

"We're soul mates," he said. "You just don't believe it."

I moved off him. He kissed my neck. "Someday you're going to have to believe in something."

I brushed away his kiss and stood. I was becoming tired of everyone telling me what I had to do.

"I have to go back to work," I said.

"I came to see if you wanted to quit early and go to Freedom. The best festival food is the first food. Kara and Grandma Macha are cooking."

"I want to go to the tech meeting, and then we can leave."

He stood. "I'll meet you after. Right now I think I'll run with the other coyotes."

We sat under the tallest oak for the meeting. Children played behind us. I sat near the back, glancing around for Cosmo. Stempler Jones talked endlessly. Several people looked longingly at the meeting hall behind the oak. It would be hot and stuffy, but the discomfort level would keep discussion short and to the point.

"Under the Constitution of these here United States," he said, "I am entitled to bear arms."

"Please don't bare anything," someone called out. "We've seen enough of your old white body."

Everyone laughed, except Stempler.

"Mr. Jones," Georgia said, "if that is your final argument, you don't have a leg to stand on, so to speak. We haven't been these United States for centuries, and we do not live under the rule of that Constitution."

Millie leaned toward me and whispered. "Quoting the Constitution as a legal argument is as bad as quoting the Bible."

I nodded and glanced over at Thomas Church. He caught my gaze. We looked at each other for a moment before he turned his attention to Stempler.

"Mr. Jones, you can't honestly say you wish to return us to the tyranny of war and consumption," Church said.

"I just want my rifle! The gophers are driving me crazy!"

Several people gasped. Overhead a hawk screamed. I looked up. Something twitched for freedom in the raptor's claws.

Herb cleared his throat, glanced at Georgia next to him, and said, "You've been shooting gophers?"

Stempler hesitated, then said, "Yes."

"Did you eat them?" Jeri asked. She was another council member, along with Herb, Church, Doris Canyon, and Maria Rio.

Stempler shook his head. "I didn't hit nothing but dirt."

Everyone laughed again, and the tension evaporated.

"You know the rules," Georgia said. "Anyone need more discussion?" She looked around. "All right. Let's take a hammer to the rifle."

"Wait a minute!" Stempler cried. "Why isn't a hammer bad technology?"

I groaned, along with several others, and plopped backward onto the ground. Stempler could have us here for hours arguing over what was acceptable technology and what was not.

"Stempler," Millie said, "I am tired of you trying to throw us back into the dark ages. You have a right to your views and opinions, but we've made our laws, and we've all agreed to live by them. You never come to the technology review meetings and say your piece then."

I sat up and saw Primer standing at the periphery of the group, kitty-corner to me. He nodded when he looked at me. I tried to smile but grimaced instead.

"My family lived on this land long before you or any of your laws existed!" Stempler said.

Doris rolled her eyes. Her family had lived on the land centuries before Stempler's family crossed the pond and settled where they were not wanted. I hoped this meeting would not degenerate into us against them, or who was here first, second, and last.

"Stempler, either you destroy the gun, or we will," Herb said. "Now let's discuss the generator."

I got up, stretched, and walked across the street and sat on Millie's porch. A breeze brought the smell of piñon with it; it also carried away Stempler's argument about the generator. Church glanced over at me and smiled. It was a coconspiratorial smile: we both knew Stempler lived to create problems. I gave him a quick smile.

Just then Stempler picked up his rifle and smashed it against the ground. It cracked easily and fell to pieces, its usefulness long ago ended. Georgia called the meeting to an end. People got up and stretched. Some walked away. Primer went to Church and the other council members. As they talked, several glanced over at me.

Cosmo came and nudged me. I jumped up. "Great timing. Let's go!"

By the time I reached my house, Cosmo had disappeared. Benjamin waited inside for a little afternoon delight. Afterward, I slipped on a skirt, and then we headed for Freedom, the village around the mountain and down the hill from Coyote Creek: Benjamin and Kara's home.

We smelled and heard the celebration just before we reached the village. The small adobe and wooden houses were scattered here and there, some semicircling a large open area where picnic tables were now piled high with food. Off to the side, several men and women sat around a huge drum practicing for the evening of ritual and dancing. A short distance from them was a pile of wood and brush for the bonfire.

"Ria, honey!" Kara came up and embraced me. "We could use your help! You're *such* a good cook."

She giggled at the joke and led me to one of the huge underground ovens. Macha, Kara's maternal grandmother, nodded a hello and handed me a winnow tray.

Kara poured seeds and dropped hot coals into it.

"Now, shake, honey. Not you—the tray." Then she and Grandmother Macha turned to more important things. I had been given the no-brain job. Benjamin waved and left me shaking.

At sunset, we said prayers to the directions and chanted blessings to all. Then we ate. I consumed my roasted seeds, cactus fruit, wild rice and herbs, and piñon nuts. I sucked on sweet yucca and got string in my teeth and then went on to corn and beans with chillies, shortcake, paper bread, baked corn mush wrapped in corn husks, squash, and chokeberry cobbler. All washed down with sweet water and a dry wine.

The fire was lit, and the drumming began. Several elders told stories. The men danced, and then the children, and then the women. My body throbbed with the desert: the food, water, wine, and music. The whole night seemed to undulate with desire. The fire shook the shadows. Moans of ecstasy came from all directions.

Georgia whispered in my ear, "You wanna get laid?"

I laughed, turned my mouth to hers, and opened it to her tongue.

When the kiss ended, I said, "I've got a previous engagement." Benjamin now danced with the men, dressed only in a loincloth. The muscles in his butt and thighs bulged and relaxed, bulged and relaxed as he moved.

Georgia kissed my ear.

"I don't know what you see in the opposite sex. Look me up later if you can't get any satisfaction." She waved and left.

Millie and Herb came over.

"It's going to be one of those nights!" Millie said, shaking her hips. "When can we dance?"

"Soon, I think."

Millie sat next to me on the bench and elbowed my side. "Guess who's here?"

I shrugged. She raised her eyebrows and looked to her left. I followed her gaze. Reverend Church stood with his hands in his pockets, his face bathed in firelight.

I groaned.

"Is it true his religion frowns on lovemaking?" Millie asked.

"That's what I heard," I said, taking a sip of wine—or whatever it was Kara had poured into my glass. "Though the good Rev says I'm ignorant, or intolerant, of his religion."

Herb sat on my other side. "I'll tell you this much: he has his eye on you. He's always watching and asking about you."

Millie said, "The Rev has a crush on the soothsayer. Watch out!"

"I'm not a—"

"You're not a soothsayer. Yeah, yeah," they both said at once.

"You're drunk, and we're not," Herb said, standing again. "Millie, my love, let's go catch up."

In the background of the drumming, I thought I heard coyotes howl on the ridge. I looked behind me, but all was black.

Benjamin's dance ended, and he wove through the people to find me. Without a word, we walked away from the circle and houses and went under the ridge where the coyotes howled. My skirt became our bed as I opened to him. He whispered something in my ear, but I heard nothing except the drums and the coyotes. Or maybe he was the drumbeat. All seemed dreamy and unreal, magical and perfect.

When our bodies stopped undulating, Benjamin sucked the sweat from my earlobe and went back to the dance. I curled up on the warm desert floor and fell to sleep.

The drumbeat tattooed numbers and letters in a line across the inside of my brain. Someone screamed.

My eyes snapped open.

A shadow covered me. I did not recognize the scent.

"Are you all right?"

Church.

"You're blocking my light," I said, sitting up. My heart raced.

Church stepped to the side of me. I could see the fire and dancers again.

"May I sit?"

"It's a free territory." I tried to breathe deeply. My heart slowed.

"I thought I heard you scream." He sat next to me but not close.

"I didn't scream. You must have heard the coyotes. I fell asleep and had a peculiar dream. I don't usually dream."

"Oh."

"*Oh?* Have I given you another indication that I'm evil incarnate?"

"Why do you suspect everything I say?" he asked, watching the festivities.

"Because you seem to be following me everywhere."

"Perhaps I'm trying to convert you."

"Well, don't. I do *not* look at the world the way you do. We are not evil because we came onto this Earth through our mother's vagina."

"You do have a way of saying things," he said. "I am just trying to be a spiritual advisor to the community. I'm trying to do the right thing."

"We are each our own spiritual advisor," I said. "And we have elders who conduct the rituals and blessings. We don't need you. Advise your own people, whoever they are."

"I make you angry," Church said.

"And I make you nervous," I said.

His jaw clenched. I had not touched him yet, but I suddenly knew Millie was right: the good Reverend was attracted to me. Fascination with the abomination?

The wine pulsed through my veins, dancing with the drumbeats. I was not going to let this man spoil the celebrations. It was a night of sensual pleasures.

"Rev, you know what this dance is about, don't you?"

"A celebration of the harvest in preparation for winter."

"Yes, the harvest and each other. We honor the Earth, our Mother. It is a time of lovemaking, drinking, and eating. Can't you feel it in the rhythm?" I leaned close to him so he could feel the warmth of my body. It was nasty of me. I should have stopped. He leaned a bit closer to me, against his will, I was certain, and our arm hair meshed.

He shifted away, and I laughed, my annoyance with him suddenly gone.

"Sorry, Church, I was feeling a little wicked. You bring that out in me. Come on. You want to dance? No sex. Just a little rhythm." I hopped up and reached a hand out to him. If we were going to live in the same town, I supposed I would have to learn to get along with him.

He gripped my hand and I suddenly saw a part of him, like a piece of shattered mirror, and reflected in that shard was a fragment of me. For a moment, I felt as if I were sinking into him.

I quickly pulled him up and immediately released his hand.

When we got back to the others, I purposely lost Church in the crowd. It was one thing for him to be sexually attracted to me, another to have me as a part of his internal structure, his story, or whatever it was I saw or felt when we touched. He made me a little dizzy. Or maybe the wine did.

I stumbled to Kara's house. I tripped around in the darkness until I found her couch, upon which I fell to sleep.

Two

Things seemed to settle down again after the celebration. Primer went to Phoenix for a couple of weeks, so I did not have to worry about him lurking around. The weather cooled. I forgot about the number dream and Church's peculiar handshake until he came to the clinic a few days later with a young woman.

"Hello, Gloria," Church said. "This is Angel Woodbury." She was blond and sweet-looking, maybe twenty years old. She smiled and held out her right arm. A small second-degree burn bubbled near her wrist. She glanced at the Reverend. "She burned it on the oven door in the church," he said.

"I'm not very coordinated," she said quietly.

"Don't you have any aloe at the church, Rev? You don't need me for this."

Angel looked disappointed. I smiled and went to the windowsill and got a small aloe plant.

"Okay, Monsieur or Madam Aloe, I ask for your help with this little angel." I broke off a piece of the plant, squeezed the unbroken end, and gently spread the clear gel across the burn.

Angel smiled. "That feels cool."

I handed her the plant. "Put this in the window of your kitchen, just in case you need it again."

"Thank you. It was nice meeting you. Reverend Church speaks very highly of you."

"I'm sure he does," I said, glancing at Church.

She gave Church a radiant smile.

"I'll catch up with you," he told her.

She nodded and left the clinic.

"Why didn't you heal her?" he asked.

"What are you talking about? The aloe will help her."

He held out his right palm. "On the way to Freedom the other night, I fell and scraped my hand. After you touched me, the cuts were gone. You healed it."

Was that why I had glimpsed part of him? I had been healing him and had not realized it. The thought flashed through my brain that he had had Angel burn herself on purpose so he could catch me in the act of healing. I shook my head; that was ridiculous. I was too paranoid.

The clinic felt suddenly stuffy. I went outside and sat on the porch. Church followed.

"You have a tremendous gift." He sat next to me.

"Church, it was dark. How could you see? You probably just heal quickly."

He held out his hand again. Not a mark on it.

"Maybe your god did it," I said.

"He does have a hand in everything."

"Was that a joke?" I asked. "A hand in everything?"

Church frowned and then smiled. "No."

"Why do you always call God a he?" I asked. "How do you know God isn't a she?"

"I suppose historically we have called God a he because he was portrayed as such in the Bible."

"Do you see God as a he up in the heaven orchestrating our every move while humans—men—are at the top of the hierarchal heap here on Earth?"

"No, personally. I don't think of God that way. Is that why you don't like me? That old dominion over nature argument? I don't believe in that. We are guardians of the Earth and should treasure it and its creatures."

"*Her* and *her* creatures, thank you very much."

He was quiet for a moment. "I have heard that soothsayers heal by laying on hands."

"Have you also heard that in some communities the church has tried to hunt down soothsayers to get rid of them?"

He looked at me. "No. Why would they do that?"

"You tell me."

Now he stared at me.

"Where's Angel from?" I asked, changing the subject.

"Down south where I grew up. Everyone thinks we'll get married."

"Congratulations."

He shook his head. "She's very young. I believe in the sanctity of marriage, and I want to make certain she's the one I can truly give myself to for the rest of my life." He stood.

Cosmo ran up to me and licked my face, a coyote's French kiss.

"You mean you don't know if you can love her the rest of your life?" I asked, looking up at him. "Or you don't know if you can practice monogamy?"

He looked at me. "Both."

I shook my head. "You're entitled to your beliefs, Rev, but monogamy was basically practiced first when men virtually owned women and secondly when sexually transmitted diseases were killing millions. It's outdated now, in my opinion."

Church squatted so he was level with me again. "Haven't you ever loved anyone enough that you wanted to be only with that person forever?"

Cosmo. But he was not a person. If I let anyone else stay around for long enough, I was sure they would discover who I really was—and then leave. I did not allow anyone too close for very long. Maybe in the time before I remembered I had loved someone that way.

"That is a very personal question," I said.

Church laughed. I had not heard him laugh before. He sounded so normal I was thrown a little off-balance.

"The few discussions we have had are always very personal."

I slapped my thighs. "You've got me there. But, right now, I've got a date with Cos."

We both stood.

"Why don't you stop by the church this Sunday?"

"My church is under the great blue sky and on the desert floor running with Cosmo or making love or eating sweet, sweet yucca. And I don't just go to my church on Sunday."

"That sounds nice," Church said quietly.

"Besides, I'm going on my rounds this Sunday," I said. "Every month or so, I go out in the country and see if anybody needs any healing."

"Then I'll talk to you when you return."

I watched him leave and realized I looked forward to seeing him again.

"That's all I need," I said, and went back into the clinic.

I could have taken the town solar buggy, but I was not going too far out this time. We walked, Benjamin and I, each with a small backpack filled with salves, ointments, and herbs as well as our food and water. The desert was pleasantly cool and flat. We avoided rocks and any crevices and made enough noise to let the rattlesnakes know we were coming. We were silent the first part of the morning. In the distance, Bear Butte rose. Beneath it, presently unseen, was the Eden settlement. They were without a full-time healer, although a nearby medicine woman stopped on the months I did not come.

"I heard this spring there is going to be a gathering in Red Bluffs," Benjamin said. A horny toad dashed in front of us. Ahead, a roadrunner stopped, looked at us, then raced away. Benjamin had once said I was like a roadrunner: you could not tell from my tracks whether I was coming or going. In some societies, the roadrunner was considered magical, so I took his observation as a compliment, whether it was meant to be one or not.

"What kind of gathering?" I asked. Benjamin never told a story all at once.

"Soothsayers and other healers."

"Uh-huh." Our feet crunched over the earth; the sound made me hungry for popcorn.

"Just thought you'd like to know. I believe it's May first."

"Sorry. I'm usually making mad passionate love that day."

"Maybe it was spring equinox," he said.

I shrugged. "Maybe I'll go."

"I'm leaving pretty soon for the dances at de Chelly. Do you want to come?"

"I'll think about it."

"It'd be nice if we could spend a few weeks together."

"You're the wanderer," I said.

"In what universe?"

I glanced at him. He looked away.

An hour or so later, we reached Eden. Sandstone-and-mud houses nestled up close to the butte, whose shadow shielded them from the midday sun.

The dog barked once until she recognized me. Then she ran to us, wagging her little butt until she nearly turned herself around. Paula followed, extending a hand to both of us.

"We're so glad you're here," she said. "I've got kind of an emergency if you wouldn't mind starting right away."

"Of course not," I said.

She escorted us to the quarantine house on the edge of town.

"We have a new family," she said. "Tricia and Timothy Booth and their two girls. All of them are ill. We're not certain whether it's contagious or not. We've taken the necessary precautions."

I nodded. When we reached the house, I went in alone. The single room was bright, the walls painted white—the one house in town with washable walls. A man sat in a rocking chair looking out the window. A woman sat near him on the floor, her head on his knee. He gently stroked her hair. Two children, probably seven and ten years old, lay on two of the four cots.

"Don't get up," I said quietly to the couple. "Let me tend to the children first."

They nodded and did not watch me go to their children.

I knelt on the floor between the cots and looked at each child. Then I felt their pulses. The older child was the sickest.

"Hello," she whispered.

"Hi, darlin'," I said. "I'm here to help you if that's all right?"

She nodded.

"What's your name?"

"Lizbeth."

"Okay, honey." This time I used no smoke and mirrors. I put my hands on Lizbeth's head. Immediately, I felt a connection and saw a huge blinding white light. I tried to close it, or fill it, but I could only jump beyond it.

"All right, Lizbeth," I said. "There was once a little girl who was as bright as the sun and as quick as a roadrunner. She never liked to be still. She was born with invisible wings on her feet." I moved my hands to her chest. "No one saw the wings, but everyone knew they were there because she was so fast. And never still. One day, she came across a castle fortress with an invisible monster in it. She didn't know about the monster, and she thought the castle was very beautiful. But the monster attacked her." I touched her abdomen. "She was very fast and never still, so she made her escape. He had hurt her badly, but she ran back to her village and told everyone about the invisible monster. No one ever went near the castle again. The little girl saved all the villagers, and she got all better." I held her legs and then her feet.

"Is that true?" she asked.

"All true," I said. I laid my hands on her chest again. "She still runs to this day."

Lizbeth closed her eyes. Inside, almost all was healed.

I kissed her nose. "Now for your sister." I turned around. The smaller girl smiled.

"You are magic," she said.

I laughed. "So are you. May I help you?"

She nodded. "My name is Amy."

I put my hands on her head; they seemed huge compared to Amy's tiny skull. We connected. The white light pulsed.

"Ah, Amy, the beloved. You are the fairy child. Did you know that?"

"No," she said, her voice surprised and excited.

I smiled. Unlike adults, children did not seem to become hypnotized when I healed them, or perhaps they were just more verbal in their hypnotized states.

"Yes! Long ago, fairies traveled freely between their world and this." I put my hands on her chest. "Then some got lost and could not find their way home. Soon they forgot they were fairy folk. But one little girl—maybe you're that girl—she did not forget. She still travels between both worlds because"—I went down to her legs and feet—"because she knows both worlds are one."

"So it's okay?" Amy asked.

"Yes, sweetheart, it's okay. But I want you to sleep now." I reached out one hand and held it over Lizbeth's eyes and then the other over Amy's. "Sleep."

They would be out for hours while their bodies continued healing.

I went to the parents.

"They'll be fine. Now may I help you?" The man, Timothy Booth, nodded lethargically. The woman, Tricia, scooted back while I stood in front of Timothy and put my hands on his shoulders. For a moment, the white light was all, eating him and coming after me. I breathed deeply to quell my panic and went beyond the light again. I found no story. I moved my hands over the man. When I finished, I dropped my hands to the woman's head. With her, I saw lights and heard laughter. So I laughed. And then I felt a field of Queen Anne's lace. Tricia ran and ran, laughing through this memory at the sound the flowers made snapping against her legs.

When I was finished, the parents were totally changed. Their lethargy was gone; their faces had color.

"You need to sleep, too," I said, "but I'd like to ask you a few questions first, if that would be all right."

The three of us went outside. Paula and Benjamin greeted us.

"You look much better," Paula said to the couple.

"I feel a thousand times better," Timothy said.

"I don't really know what was wrong with you," I said. "I've never seen anything like it. Can you tell me when it started?"

Timothy said, "The girls got lost near a restricted area a few days before we got here. At least we think it was only a few days."

"Weren't there signs? A fence?" I asked.

"There was a fence," Tricia said, "but it had breaks in it. Naturally, the kids found it interesting."

"Was there anyone else around?" Benjamin asked.

Timothy shook his head. "Not at this one. It wasn't immigration. Maybe a toxic dump. We went in after the girls and then—" He stopped and frowned. "We don't remember what happened after that. In fact, we sort of came awake near Eden, which was our destination."

"But we don't remember how we got here," Tricia said.

"Go get some rest," I said.

The couple nodded and went back inside.

"Come on," Paula said. "Let's feed you two."

Paula took us to a tall juniper. Benjamin and I sat beneath it while one of the teenagers served us pumpkin and zucchini soup with bread covered in seed butter. I looked off to where we had come from. The intense sunlight which overwhelmed the landscape with blue sky had dimmed, and the desert seemed more dimensional, softer, with the horizon shifting from beige to red to purple. The community itself was late-afternoon quiet.

Paula came and sat with us. "I'll send someone to the governor," she said, "and have them repair the fence in that restricted area. I imagine the Booths must have stumbled into some toxic waste or something, don't you?"

I shrugged. I hoped I had fixed whatever was wrong with

them, but I was not sure. It had been an unusual experience, almost like healing their bodies without touching their minds.

"Well, if it happened near a restricted area, it's the governor's responsibility," Paula said. "He'll take care of it."

Benjamin said, "The only thing that will really fix it is time."

"We're lucky," Paula said. "I heard near Santa Fe, stuff is leaking into the groundwater."

"And people like Stempler Jones are nostalgic for those times," I said. "I don't understand."

"He's not really like that," Benjamin said. "He just wants his toys."

"Anyone else need my services?" I asked Paula.

"Sure," Paula said. "We'll set up the clinic in my house since the quarantine house is occupied."

I drank the rest of the soup. "Don't forget to destroy their clothes or any other objects the Booths had with them in the restricted area, just in case it is contagious."

"Of course," Paula said. "You look a little tired. Are you sure you want to see people today?"

"I'm fine. I'll start seeing people in an hour."

Paula got up. "I'll take care of it."

When she left, a bluebird perched on the juniper began singing. I leaned against Benjamin.

"I am a little tired," I said, closing my eyes.

The next thing I knew the number and letter sequence was flashing on and off in my sparse dream landscape. Someone screamed.

I opened my eyes and lifted my head from Benjamin's shoulder. My heart raced.

"What is it?" he asked.

The bluebird still sang; the village was still quiet. I must have dozed only for a few minutes.

"Nothing," I said as I sat up. "Do you dream?"

"Yes."

"Do you ever dream of numbers or letters?"

He brushed a strand of hair off my face. "I don't think so.

Usually I dream of running in the desert or sitting on the mesa top, howling at the moon." He grinned.

I looked out in the desert again. The purple horizon had changed. Storm clouds were moving across the Earth. Even from here I could see the shadows the clouds cast. A zigzag of lightning joined the sky and Earth for a shattering moment.

I slowly stood. "Come on, love. Let's go heal these people."

I had only a few cases. One was chronic. I had healed her before, but it did not always take if the body's own systems were unable to kick in, or if it was time for someone to die. People, animals, trees all died. I could not stop the process.

When I finished, I checked on the Booth family. The scene was much livelier than it had been earlier, even though they all slept. When someone was sick, their energy was different; when they were healing, it was different still. Health just seemed to radiate from the newly well, as if they had just had a grand holiday. I laid hands on each family member again and then went outside into the stormy dusk.

The village was lively now, too. Children ran about laughing and screaming. The dog growled and snapped at one boy's heels. Swifts swooped about, their black-and-gold wings whistling as they dived from place to place. A cool wind brought the smell of piñon and the taste of minerals. The storm was coming.

"You did good here today," Benjamin said, putting his arm across my shoulders. "You are amazing."

I loved thunderstorms. The pure natural state of them excited me, made me want to be a part of it.

"It's my job," I said. "And I happen to do it well."

Benjamin said, "You see what you do just as a job?"

"Everyone has a role."

"I don't have a role," Benjamin said. "I have a life. Do you see your life as a role you put on and take off?"

I looked at him. Mostly when I was with Benjamin or Cosmo, I was relaxed and comfortable. Other times, I felt as though the truth about me would be found out any moment—whatever that truth was. I never liked meeting strangers. I always wondered if they had known me before. Maybe that was why I did not trust Church and was drawn to him at the same time. He looked at me as if he knew something about me that I did not know. I wanted that knowledge of myself and feared it, too.

"I'm glad I can do what I do," I said. "I wouldn't know how to survive otherwise."

"You like your life now because you think you are in complete control."

I laughed. "You betcha."

We ate outside in the community center, slopping up chili with flat bread along with about twenty-five residents of Eden. The storm ran the last of the meal and the storytelling inside. I stood outside, watching the lightning snap at the ground as if looking for something. The wind pushed the rain almost sideways, whipping up dust and tumbleweed. Thunder shook the ground. When the rain reached Eden, I let it drench me. I wanted to be the connection between sky and Earth: *She who is the drawing force.* Of course, if lightning hit, I would be no force at all, probably just dead.

Reluctantly, I turned away from the storm and went inside.

After the thunderstorm had passed and a half-moon rose and silvered the desert floor, making it look like the ocean it once was, Benjamin and I climbed partway up the mesa and made love. In the morning, we said good-bye to the residents of Eden and headed back.

As we walked, I gazed about me. Something about the desert often left me inarticulate. I was stripped. I existed as part of the land. Or on top of it. Like an ant wandering the body of some huge being.

This morning, the desert smelled sweetly of creosote. Canyon wrens sang from saguaros. We wandered around pink verbena and thickets of devil's claw, their fuzzy yellow flowers accessorized with woolly leaves that looked almost like feathers. We went down into a wash and ate the dark red berries of the swanpaint. And up out of the wash, I smelled desert sage—chia—and walked through cleavers which stuck to my pants. I pulled them off and put them in my backpack: Millie roasted the seeds. All this we did in silence, except for the sound of our feet and the songs of birds. We wandered the desert with deer, rabbits, quail, and roadrunners. Turkey buzzards and hawks rode the thermals on a clear blue sky washed clearer by the storm. Today the blue was darker, more intense, the color, I imagined, of sapphire.

On Stern Mountain, we visited Barbara and Louis and their three children. Everyone was happy and healthy. They fed us bread made from hops and spread with chia butter and canyon grape jam, followed by squash soup, some juicy red hedgehog cactus fruit, roasted wild potatoes, and bearberry cider. We napped after the feast, then walked on up to Stempler Jones's place. Snow powdered a ridge in the near distance.

Stempler's house seemed to be a part of the mountain, like mine, except his was large and made of glass and steel. Inside, the house was open and sparsely decorated, a Frank Lloyd Wright knock-off, if not the real thing. Stempler had one of the best views in the area. In the spring, his front yard was covered with poppies that fell down the mountain like a huge orange comforter. To the south stood Black Mountain and my home, Coyote Creek, and Freedom. To the east lay Beauty Valley, an enclave of low red-and-orange hills with crevices in each that looked like veins, or skeletal fingers reaching up, up. Legend was a many-breasted priestess slept in the valley, and there she awaited the new age when laughter and beauty would prevail. Every time I looked down on the valley, I smiled, so perhaps a new age was not too far off.

"Stempler!" I called. His front yard was littered with tools and gadgets.

"What?" He came out the front door, ready for bear.

"Just stopped by to see how you're doing," I said. "You need any salves or ointments?"

"No," he answered. He sat in one of the low wooden lawn chairs amidst the clutter. He crossed his long legs at his ankles in front of him and stared at us. It was a long way back to my house, but Stempler, as usual, was not very hospitable.

"All right. We'll see you later," I said. Benjamin shrugged, and we started to leave.

"There were some G-men snooping around here earlier. You with them?"

Benjamin turned around. "Stempler, you know who we are."

"I also know I get called in for tech violations after she visits."

"*She?*" I said. "I'm standing right here, you old fart! I have never turned you in on a violation, but I certainly would if I thought you were breaking the law."

Stempler nodded. "The G-men were asking about my technology and about Coyote Creek."

"Are you sure they were from the governor?" Benjamin asked.

"Yes." He looked out across Beauty Valley.

"Was one of them called Primer?" I asked.

"Didn't ask."

"The governor has no jurisdiction in technology violations," I said. Unless there was a network or a conspiracy. "Why would he be fussing with you?"

"I wondered that myself," Stempler said. He sat up and put his elbows on his knobby knees. "I could use some burn salve. And I've got some beans cooking."

Benjamin flashed me a grin, and we stayed to supper. At dark, Stempler even threw us a couple of sleeping bags, and we slept on the hardwood living-room floor while he slept in the loft. Although we considered ourselves lucky, I longed for my own bed and Cosmo's howls.

I dreamed the number and letters sequence again, but this night no one screamed.

We were up and out when the night and day met, melting into that gray tension which becomes dawn or dusk. Stempler was gone before us.

On the homeward trek, Benjamin entertained me with a series of bawdy coyote stories, and we giggled through a cloud-filled gray morning, eating goodies Paula had packed for us before we left Eden. We also palmed a few pink mistletoe berries and found more swanpaint. Scrub jays screeched at us, but we pulled the berries off anyway.

By midday, we walked up the foothills of Black Mountain and into my house. I was tired and invigorated at the same time. I called to Cosmo and got no response. Benjamin and I bathed in the stream, and then together we made bean and rice burritos and salad from some parsnip and lovage greens we had gathered on the way up. We ate outside.

I leaned against Benjamin as we sat outside, eating. I was glad he was next to me. Glad about everything. I was alive and happy.

Three

A few minutes later Georgia appeared, her face red from the climb.

"I've got to get out more," she puffed as she sat next to us. I handed her my cider.

When she emptied the cup, I asked, "What's up?" Georgia had not been to the house for years, since before we stopped being lovers.

"I lost the toss," Georgia said. "We were hoping you'd gotten back. Millie, Herb, and Josh are all sick, and some others, too. We tried echinacea, garlic, and a few other things, but it hasn't helped."

"Well, I better get down there," I said.

Benjamin and I stood. Georgia groaned, set the cup down, and pushed herself up.

"Do you need me to go with you?" Benjamin asked.

I shook my head.

"I'm leaving for de Chelly in two days unless I hear from you," Benjamin said. "I hope you can come."

"Me, too."

We kissed. I gazed at his face. He looked the same, the

quiet man who ran with me through the desert, held me in bed, and sometimes asked me to reveal my deepest feelings. When I couldn't, I often wondered if he wished I was less of a desert creature with my protective gear always in place. I kissed him again.

"Good luck," he said.

Georgia and I hurried down the mountain. I glanced up once and saw Benjamin, a desert shadow who disappeared behind a saguaro as I continued on.

I found Millie, Herb, and their son Josh in their apartment behind the café. Millie sat up groggily when Georgia and I approached her.

"If I didn't know any better, I'd say it was something we ate," Millie said. "But don't repeat that to anyone."

I smiled.

Herb stirred on the couch next to her; Josh continued sleeping in a cot against the wall.

"What are your symptoms?" I asked.

"Nausea, vomiting, headaches. I think Josh has a little fever."

"I should check on the others," Georgia said. "Do you need anything from the clinic?"

"Not yet," I said.

"I'll be back."

I took Millie's hands in mine. I felt a connection and the memory of golden sunshine spreading across wheatfields. The smell of baked bread ran through a generation or more.

"The green green grass of home," I sang. Millie laughed.

"You say the strangest things," she said. "What's wrong with me?"

"I don't really know." I let go of one of her hands and reached into my pack and pulled out a eucalyptus lozenge. "Suck on this."

Something felt strange. I did not know what ailed her. I did not have to know in order to heal, but my ignorance surprised me. It was happening too often lately.

"I am feeling better now," she said.

I put my hands on Herb and then Josh and had them take the lozenges.

"All of you drink lots of liquid," I said. "I'll have someone make soup."

Georgia came back just then.

"We've got three more families ill," she said.

Josh vomited up his lozenge.

"I don't know what's wrong with them," I told her. "Have soup made. Millie has the recipe in the café. The one for colds and flus. Also make ginger tea."

Georgia nodded.

"Whose house is next?" I asked.

"Church is outside," she answered. "He'll take you. All the other council members are sick. Except Jeri. She's tending to Doris Canyon's family."

I left Millie with Georgia and hurried through the empty café outside to Church.

"Hello, Gloria." He smiled. "It's nice to see you."

"Hello, Reverend," I said. "Lead the way."

We went to Maria Rio's house next. She was ill, along with her brother, sister, and two sons. I laid hands on all of them, and again I could not really diagnose what was wrong. They all began feeling better before I finished. I instructed Church to have Angel—or someone at the church—make the flu soup, too. Next to Millie's, the church kitchen was the best in town.

I went to four other houses. Almost every member of the household was ill with similar symptoms. I was baffled. I had never seen an influenza epidemic take out this many people this quickly.

I opened the clinic so any new cases could be brought to me there. The sky was still gray, and the day had gotten cold.

Cosmo ran into the courtyard and howled. I fell to the ground, and we rolled around together. He lightly bit my shoulder.

"Where have you been?" I asked.

I hugged him as he excitedly growled.

Someone cleared his throat. I looked up.

Church.

I kissed Cosmo, and we released each other. Cosmo sniffed at Church's feet, then sat on his haunches and stared at the Reverend. Church looked extremely uncomfortable. I suddenly wondered if he had ever had sex.

I was about to ask him when he said, "The soup is being distributed along with the ginger tea. I brought a pot of tea for you."

"Good, thanks. How are you feeling?"

Church shrugged. "Never better, thank you. Angel is fine, too."

Jeri came up the walk carrying one of her young children; her husband Raoul carried the other.

"We just started having symptoms," she said.

We all went into the clinic, and they put the children on the examining table.

"Hi, sugar," I said, taking the girl's hand. I felt an instant connection, a quick healing. She smiled and touched her stomach. "Yes, I know. Church, could you pour her a bit of tea?" I leaned close to the girl and said, " 'Twas brillig and slithy toves." She laughed. Church handed her a cup, and Jeri helped her daughter drink the tea.

"She'll be fine," I said. "Now for the other little one."

Until evening, I treated the ailing townspeople. Church came and went and did not seem to watch me as closely as he had in the past.

When dusk fell, Georgia brought me news that Millie and her family were ill again. I gathered some herbs and syrups together and started to follow her back to the café when we nearly ran into Primer on the darkened path leading out of the courtyard.

"Now isn't the time," I said, trying to edge past him.

"Now is exactly the time," he said. "It is my duty to inform you as mayor and you as healer that the town of Coyote Creek is being quarantined."

"What!" I said. "I have not requested a quarantine!"

"You should have. A highly contagious epidemic is obviously sweeping the town. No one can be allowed in or out."

"I am not convinced it is contagious," I said. "Too many people are ill."

"Your logic evades me," Primer said.

"In most contagious illnesses," I explained, "only a percentage of people actually get sick."

"Epidemics are different," Primer said. "It is too late to argue statistics. The governor has given me complete authority in these matters. I have already posted sentries."

Georgia and I looked at each other.

"How did you arrange this so quickly?" Georgia asked. "People just started getting sick yesterday."

"I told you the governor has given me full authority in these matters."

"How far does the quarantine extend?" I asked.

"Your house is not included. You will have to stay in town."

"That's not what I asked, you weasely little—"

Georgia held up a hand. "We haven't time for this. Come on, Gloria."

"Cosmo," I said. "Stay here. Don't let this . . . this man into the clinic."

Georgia and I went to Millie's again. The brew in huge soup pots smelled great, and I realized I had not eaten since Benjamin and I had at my house. Benjamin. I had forgotten he was leaving for the dances. I would not see him again for weeks. Stupid quarantine. No town liked them. Even after one was lifted, traders and the like stayed away for months. And now it was separating me from Benjamin. He would probably think I had not wanted to go with him, which was true, but I resented not being able to make the decision myself.

I went through the café to the residence. Millie and Herb were in bed. I laid hands on them and used no pretense that I was doing anything else. I should have given up the charade years ago. The townspeople did not care how I healed. They trusted me.

Millie and Herb were ill with the same thing they had had earlier. Either my original healing had not taken, or they had gotten sick again. Fortunately, their illness—and everyone else's in town—was not life-threatening.

When I finished healing, they were better, and I was tired.

"When did you start getting sick again?" I asked.

"A couple hours after we ate," Millie said.

Perhaps food was not a good idea.

"Then lay off food until you're stronger," I said. "Or until I have this figured out."

I left Millie's and reluctantly went to the church. I had not been inside since the Rev had taken it back from the town nine months ago. Before that, we had used it as a town hall; the stained-glass windows and high ceilings kept it cool in the summer. As I stepped into the body of the church, the floor creaked. I touched the wooden pews. All of our Southwestern decoration was gone. The building now seemed barren, decorated only by a huge wooden cross with the body of a dead man nailed to it. A crown of thorns pierced his skin. I turned away quickly. How could they worship such cruelty?

I walked out and then down the stairs to the basement. Many of the chairs and long tables were filled with townspeople eating the soup I had asked Church to prepare. Jeri and her family sat at one table.

"We're much better," Raoul said. "Thanks, Gloria."

I smiled and walked to the back of the room where Angel stood ladling soup into bowls.

She smiled when she saw me. She put the ladle down and kissed my cheek. "Hi, Gloria."

"Hello, Angel. How's it going?"

"Everyone here seems to be doing fine. Maybe the worst is over."

Church came out of the kitchen carrying another soup pot, followed by a little girl, who put baskets full of steaming bread down next to the pot.

"Hello again," Church said.

Angel smiled radiantly at both of us. How was she able to project such light and warmth?

"You've got a good crowd, Rev," I said.

"Have no fear. Most are not worshipers."

I glanced at him. This time his smile reached his eyes. He handed me a bowl of soup and a piece of bread.

"You probably need to eat, too," he said.

"And you, Reverend Church," Angel said.

I took the proffered food and sat at one of the empty tables. Church sat next to me.

"If people keep seeing us together, they might start to talk," I said.

"About what?" he asked. "That I've converted you?"

I laughed. "No. That I've converted you."

He smiled.

I was bone weary and barely tasted the soup.

"Is Primer still staying with you?" I asked.

Church nodded.

"Did you know Coyote Creek is in quarantine?"

"Seems like a good idea."

I glanced at him.

"Though Mr. Primer should have discussed it with the council beforehand," he said, "and with you, of course."

"Are you trying to kiss up to me?" I asked.

"Pardon me?" He put his spoon down and looked at me.

"I asked if you were trying to kiss *up* to me, not kiss me. Listen, Rev, Primer is a slimy little bastard. Take my word on it. I'm usually a pretty good judge of people."

"I did think it strange he had sentries set up so soon."

"Exactly."

We finished our meal in silence. Then I said good-bye to him and the others and left the church. I was exhausted and needed rest.

I slept on the floor of the clinic. Cosmo beside me. Once or twice, he growled and I thought I heard someone walk away. Just before dawn, Cosmo left. I fell back to sleep and dreamed about Church. We were inside his church. In the middle of this rectangular building was a circle with sand in it. Church and I stood in the sand, our feet bare, and got married. Just as we were taking off our clothes, I felt a hand on my hair.

I opened my eyes. Church came through the doorway carrying a tray. I sat up and looked around. Just me and Church.

"What are you doing here?" I yawned.

He knelt beside me and put the tray on the floor: eggs, potatoes, salsa, ginger tea.

"The way to my heart is definitely through my stomach, Rev," I said, popping a tiny potato into my mouth.

Church hesitated, seemingly embarrassed.

I patted the floor, and he sat next to me.

"I thought you might need a good breakfast," he said. "Some of the people you treated yesterday are sick again. And there are new cases."

I sighed. What was going on?

"If anyone else on the council is well," I said, "I want you to try and figure out what the people who are sick have in common and what the people who are not sick have in common. We all drink the same water, so if something was wrong with the water, I think we'd all be sick, wouldn't we? Also see what those who have gotten ill again have in common."

Church nodded. "That's a good idea. You don't think it's a flu of some kind?"

"It just doesn't feel like it." I yawned.

Church cleared his throat.

"What? What else?" I was eating too quickly.

Cosmo came to the door, panting. He whined when he saw Church and then flopped down in front of the open door.

"Why doesn't he like me?" Church asked.

I shrugged. "He's just overly protective, and you're new. Now, what else is happening?"

"Primer wants us to put all the sick people in one place."

"Quarantine them further?" I asked. "It's not practical or warranted. What is his problem?"

"You, apparently."

I put the empty plate on the tray and stood. Church quickly turned away; I was wearing only a T-shirt and underpants.

"You've already seen me naked," I said as I pulled on my slacks. "Besides, in my dream, you were taking off my clothes."

Cosmo followed us into the courtyard and a clear cool blue autumn day.

"You dreamed about me?" Church said.

"Yeah. Pretty weird. I don't usually dream—except . . ." I stopped and looked at him. He had a sweet-looking face and a nice smile. My distrust for him had evaporated in the last days as we worked together. Now I stared at him and remembered what had happened the first time we had touched, and suddenly I longed for that feeling again—a complete connection with the familiar.

He smiled. "What about your dream?"

"Never mind," I said. "Let's get going."

The day was a blur of healings. Over and over. Some people got sick again, some did not. By evening, I could hardly move. I stumbled into the courtyard of my clinic, exhausted beyond anything I could remember. I dropped to the ground and pulled myself up to lean against the palm tree.

Suddenly Primer was there, towering over me like some bent shadow out of a nightmare. "I told you you should have come with me."

"What are you talking about, Primer? Leave me alone. I'm exhausted."

"I said if the governor wanted you, he would get you. You belong to us."

"What?" I wished I could see his face. "Are you saying you had something to do with what's happened here?" I could not move, I was so tired. I had no adrenaline left. I closed my eyes.

"I'm telling you that if you care for these people, you will come with me back to the governor."

My stomach twisted with unfamiliar fear. Where was Cosmo? There. On the porch, sleeping. Was this all a dream?

"Will you come?" Primer growled.

Had Primer poisoned the entire town? Killed Cosmo? Just to get me to visit the governor? I had healed Primer's ankle; I should have known he was capable of this.

"Yes. I'll go."

"When?"

"As soon as everyone is well."

Suddenly the numbers and letters flashed in front of me. Someone screamed. I floated away.

I awakened to a starry sky. My body creaked as I sat up. Then I remembered Primer. Had he really been there? I got up and went to Cosmo on the porch. I touched him; he did not move. My heart raced. I put my hands on his head. He was alive, but drugged. Or poisoned. Like the townspeople?

I would kill Primer. No. But I would make certain he made restitution. I was exhausted. I needed rest before I could do anything else. I needed Cosmo. My hands finally felt a connection. After a minute or so, Cosmo yawned and opened his eyes. He whimpered.

I hugged him. "Don't let that man near you again, Cos."

I went inside the clinic with Cosmo, bolted and blocked the door, and fell to sleep again, one hand on Cosmo. I had coyote dreams and awakened late morning to Georgia pounding on the door. Cosmo yelped. I put my hand on his head and gave him a quick healing. He seemed his usual self.

Then I unblocked the door and let Georgia in.

"What's going on?" she asked. "I've never seen this door locked!"

"Primer poisoned Cosmo," I said, "and I think he might be responsible for everyone being sick."

"What?"

I shut the door again, motioned Georgia to a chair, and sat across from her.

"When I came back last night, Primer was here. Cosmo was on the porch out cold. Primer said he'd warned me I should go with him and that if I really cared about you all, I'd better go with him now."

"How could he have made so many of us sick and why? That just keeps you here."

"It was a way of threatening me. 'See what I can do, and I'll do worse if you don't come.' "

"I'm not convinced he poisoned us," Georgia said, "but he has, at the very least, used a bad situation to his advantage and he was wrong to threaten you."

"We still need to figure out why everyone is sick."

"Church and Jeri interviewed everyone to gather the information you asked for. They're in the church basement."

"Come on, Cos," I said. "I don't want you out of my sight."

As we started to leave, I noticed a bowl on the porch, empty except for a tiny pool of water in the bottom of it. I picked up the bowl and smelled it. Nothing. I tossed out the water, turned over the bowl, and followed Georgia to the church.

"Doesn't this place give you the creeps?" I asked her, as we stepped inside.

"No. Why? I've been coming here my entire life."

"Yeah, but there wasn't a dead man hanging from a cross."

"That is bizarre," she agreed.

We walked downstairs. The place was nearly empty except for Jeri, Church, and Angel. Angel kissed me and handed me a bowl of nuts, seeds, and currants.

Church and Jeri greeted us.

"Good morning," I said, as we sat with them.

Cosmo sniffed around behind me.

"What a sweet dog," Angel said. She crouched near him, and he stuck his muzzle in her face.

"He's a coyote," I said. "Cosmo."

Church watched their friendly exchange, so unlike his own encounters with Cosmo.

"He's a sucker for a pretty face," I explained.

Georgia told Church, Jeri, and Angel what had happened last night between Primer and me. Jeri paled.

"We need to hold a public meeting as soon as possible," she said.

"First, we need to get everyone well. What did you figure out?" I asked.

"Approximately eighty percent of the town's population became ill," Jeri said. "Of those eighty percent, sixty percent were reinfected, or got sick again. As far as we can tell, everyone is eating the same food and drinking the same water."

"The soup seemed to help some people," Church said, "but others got sick after eating it."

"Was there any difference? Like where they ate it?"

"Not where they ate it but where it was cooked. The people who ate the soup here generally got better or took longer to get sick again. Those who ate the soup from Millie's all got sick again."

"What's the difference?" I asked.

"The water," Georgia said. "I just remembered the church and a few of the houses have well water while the rest of us get ours from the reservoir."

I thought of the bowl on the clinic porch. Primer must have put poison in the bowl of water and hoped Cosmo would drink it. And in the reservoir.

"All right," Georgia said. "We'll need to make certain everyone gets their water from the church for a while. Also, we'll appoint someone to watch Primer until the town meeting. Gloria, you'll have to heal these people all over again. Are you up to it?"

I hoped so. "Sure," I said.

Jeri and Georgia left. I stayed to finish eating.

"I-I didn't know Primer was like that," Church said. "Threatening you. I thought—I don't know what I thought."

"You thought I was just being stubborn and pigheaded," I said. "Well, I was. I didn't know what he was like either. People sometimes surprise you."

"Do you need anything today?" he asked.

"Strength," I said. "I'm about out."

"I'll pray for you."

"Yeah, you do that."

I spent another day performing almost nonstop healings. By lunch, I was near tears, a rare occurrence for me. Jeri brought me lunch. When I finished, she led me to the next sick person. Cosmo followed me most of the day, but by afternoon, he was completely back to his old self. I hoped he stayed out of Primer's way. Once when I had a momentary breather, I thought of Benjamin and wondered if he had tried to get into town; if not, he was on his way to de Chelly. I had heard Louise Mayhi had her eye on him. She would be at the dance. She was probably ready to have babies and share with him her deepest darkest self. Or maybe she did not have a dark self. Maybe only I did. I placed my hands on the next patient. And the next.

As the day went on, my thought processes seemed to short-circuit. Each time I touched a patient to heal, I connected for a moment with their souls, like always. And then disconnected. In my exhaustion, I started to believe each time I touched someone I was connecting with some great cosmic truth, only to have it yanked away when I withdrew my hands. I had no stories to tell, no lines of wisdom, not even nonsense words to babble.

When the last patient left, I was nearly blind with exhaustion. Tears streamed uncontrollably down my cheeks. Then someone—two someones—came to each side of me and led me outside. I noticed it was cold, but that was all. Then I was inside. Warmth. Softness. Cosmo's furry face. Then all blacked away.

Someone touched my hand, and I shattered. One of the shards mirrored me shattered into a million pieces; another piece mirrored Church.

"Shhhh." A whisper. The glass froze into sand again and the wind blew it all back into the ocean, including all those broken pieces of me.

Still someone held my hand.

My body trembled. I felt as though lightning kept lacing through me, trying to connect heaven and Earth.

A kiss awakened me.

Like Sleeping Beauty. Or the woman in the glass coffin. Or the woman who was the glass coffin.

I opened my eyes. My face was awash in tears. My own?

"Hello." Reverend Thomas Church smiled.

"You?"

His fingers squeezed mine. No more shattering.

"Where's Cosmo?" I asked.

Church released my hand as I carefully pushed myself up. I was in bed. The room was dark, like one of the Spanish missions. The refectory.

"Cosmo wanted to take a run," he said. "I left the door open so he could come and go. He doesn't growl at me anymore."

"Wonders." I sighed deeply. "I've never treated that many people. I am really tired."

"You've been asleep for a day and a half."

"You're kidding?"

Angel knocked on the open door and then carried in a tray.

"Hi," she said shyly. She kissed my cheek. I felt a momentary shatter, as if I were going to split again, but her lips moved away and I was still whole.

"I'm not hungry," I said. "But thank you."

"They all said you're always hungry," she said.

I smiled. "I guess they were all wrong. But you can leave it. Maybe I'll get hungry again."

She smiled and put the tray on the table next to the bed. She glanced at Church, who was watching me, and then she left us alone.

"Are you going to marry that girl and put her out of her misery, or what?" I asked. I glanced at the food. It blurred into a mass of slop. I turned away.

Church moved the tray out of my sight.

"We talked to Primer," Church said, not answering my question. "Of course, he denied everything. No one else has gotten sick, and we've kept a few teams patrolling the river and reservoir. Primer lifted the quarantine, and he's left town."

"What did he say about me?"

"He said he never threatened you. He denied ever speaking to you that night."

I slowly stood. "I guess I have to go visit the governor."

"But Primer's gone."

"He's unseen. That doesn't mean he's gone. I don't want him coming back and causing more trouble. Is everyone feeling better?"

"Yes."

"Good. I'll get ready to leave soon." I suddenly felt woozy. I dropped down on to the bed again. "Maybe I'll eat a little first. Hey, Rev, is this your bedroom?"

"Yes."

"Very romantic. Where'd you sleep last night?"

"In the bed with you."

I grinned. "Yeah, right. So you do have a sense of humor."

"Apparently." He handed me a bowl of something that looked like gruel.

"Maybe I better go to Millie's Cafe," I said. "But don't tell Angel."

Eventually, I made it outside. At Millie's I was treated like a returning hero. Half the town seemed to be packed inside the café. I was first given ginger tea. And then apple pie, hot currant bread and butter, pumpkin pie, pinto bean soup, corn on the cob. Cosmo lay at my feet, snapping at the crumbs. I did not have the heart to tell them I was not hungry, so I ate as much as I could.

Four

The council decided I should not travel alone to the governor. Reverend Thomas Church himself volunteered to accompany me.

"But he doesn't know the area well enough to return by himself," I protested at our meeting at Millie's.

"Aren't you only staying a few days?" Georgia asked.

"Well, yes," I said. "But what if something should happen to me?"

"Reverend Church is going to prevent that," Doris said.

"I don't need a bodyguard! I've always taken care of myself."

"You're the one who has been ranting and raving about how dangerous Primer is," Georgia said.

"Out of town you can hear Primer coming a mile away. He's not much of an outdoorsman. Besides, Cosmo would eat him for breakfast."

"Nevertheless," Georgia said.

"Rev, don't you need to protect your flock from any heathen goings-on?" I asked.

"They're looking forward to any and all heathen goings-on."

I gave up. When the council meeting ended, Georgia came and put her hand on my arm. I felt dizzy and fractured until she dropped her hand.

"Are you all right?" she asked.

"Yes. I'm fine."

"Maybe you should wait."

"No. I want to get it over with."

Herb put his arm across my shoulders. I thought I would break into a million pieces again. I had to get away before anyone else touched me.

"I'll see you when I get back," I told them all.

I hurried out into the late afternoon. Someone touched my arm. Skin against skin. What a relief: no shattering. I stopped and turned.

Church.

His fingers lingered on my arm, and I did not mind. It had been days since I had been able to stand anyone's touch. Not since the last time Church had held my fingers in his bedroom.

"Do you want to stay down here tonight?" he asked.

I shook my head. "Let's leave from my place. I want to stop and see Stempler Jones on the way, and it's quicker from my place."

"All right. Millie is packing food for us. I'll bring it up with me in the morning."

"See you at daybreak."

Cosmo followed me up the mountain, yelping at me.

"No, I don't have time to play," I said. I was afraid to touch him, afraid I would fall apart. I veered at the stream and headed to Freedom. I had to see if Benjamin had gone to de Chelly. I had to know if this thing I had was temporary. Once he was in my arms, all would be well. I walked too fast and was exhausted halfway there. I sucked on berries I found along the way and hoped for the best.

It was past dark by the time I reached Freedom. The town was nearly deserted. No one at Kara's. Grandma Macha sat outside with Grandma Saisy.

"Good evening, daughter," Grandma Macha said, handing me a cup of squaw bush juice.

"Thank you, Grandma," I said. I drank the juice and then asked, "Is Benjamin here?"

"No. He's at the dances. We thought you were going, too," Macha said.

"We had an emergency in Coyote Creek."

"We heard." She reached for my empty cup and our fingers touched. Everything shifted. I moved quickly away; the cup fell from my fingers onto a rock and shattered. *Like me. Like me.*

"I'm so sorry," I said. I bent and picked up the pieces.

"The healer is not at ease," Grandma Macha said. I looked at her, barely visible in the night. None of us were anything more than shadows.

"You've got that right, Grandma."

I left them to the darkness and started back again, stumbling down the path, following Cosmo, who whined and growled at me. What I did was dangerous, we both knew: wandering in the desert on a night close to new moon was stupid. I could end up like Church's Jesus, lost for forty days. And nights. Only I would have no divine intervention.

My legs nearly gave out on me before I got home again, but I made it. I forced myself to eat my cold dinner even though it was the middle of the night and I was not hungry. Afterward, I curled up on my bed and slept. Once I felt Cosmo's nose in my face and a shattering began, until he moved away and howled outside in my dreams of sequences of numbers and letters.

I slept well past daybreak. When I awakened, I padded to the door and looked out. Church sat next to his pack and Cosmo, gazing into the morning.

Church turned when he heard me and then quickly looked at the ground. Apparently he could not get accustomed to seeing me in my underwear.

"Good morning," he said.

"Hello."

He looked up again, surprised. I turned away. No witty—or witless—banter from me today. I returned to my bedroom and stuffed clothes into my pack. Then I put on a shirt, slacks, jacket, and shoes. After I used the outhouse, I got my pack and joined Church. I knew I should eat, but the thought of food was nauseating.

"Are you ready?" I asked.

Church nodded.

Cosmo yelped and raced ahead of us. We walked in silence for a long while. The sun did not do much to warm the desert. Groups of deer walked by us, heading in the opposite direction to where we were going.

"Do they know something we don't?" Church asked.

I shrugged. I was still tired. I kept waiting for everything to click into place so I could be like I was just a week ago. I did not usually get sick. Until now. Maybe this was illness. Grandma Macha said I was not at ease. Ill at ease. Dis-eased.

No. It was temporary. The next time I touched a person, all would be well.

I was certain of it.

We reached Stempler Jones's place just as it began to snow.

I knocked on the door.

No one answered.

I went around back and then to the front again and opened the door.

"Stempler! It's Gloria!" The house was dark, but warm. The solar heating was working.

"Hello!" Someone called behind us.

I turned around. Barbara and Louis from down the mountain were coming up. The snow fell slowly, in huge fat flakes. When they got to us, they each hugged me, and I fractured a bit. I stepped back so no one could touch me. I introduced Church to Barbara and Louis.

"We saw you going up," Louis said, "and realized too late you were probably going to see Stempler."

"Where is he?"

Barbara shrugged. "He told us he'd be gone for a while. He had a new junkpile he wanted to explore."

"You're welcome to stick out the snow with us," Louis said.

"I think I'll drive Stempler nuts and stay in the house for the night," I said. "Thanks, though. You better get back before the whiteout."

We watched the couple go down the trail. The snow now stuck to the ground. Beauty Valley was covered in white. I wondered if it was snowing down in the desert around Coyote Creek: capping the cacti, trees, and bushes, and leaving the ground clear.

"We're going to spend the night?" Church asked.

I nodded. "Unless you want to go out in this."

Church looked around. The world had become a fog of white snow.

"Well, then, let's go inside," I said.

We stepped out of the quiet storm and into the silent house. Cosmo shook off snow and sniffed around. I turned on a light. I was always amazed to see a light come on by just pressing a button.

Church stood awkwardly at the door.

"Come on in, padre. Make a fire. Stempler left us a stack of wood."

Church cleared his throat, took off his jacket, and went to the fireplace. I looked around while he fiddled with the logs. Then I went up the stairs to the loft. It was nearly filled with a huge mattress on the floor. Above the bed was a skylight. I glanced downstairs at Church. This could all be too tempting even for the Reverend.

Cosmo hunted his dinner outside while we ate ours inside. My appetite was still dull, and I barely paid attention while Church heated up soup and bread.

"That is quite a stove," Church said as he carried a bowl to me. "This entire place is incredible."

"Yes. It's amazing to me they had this kind of technology available and instead used such destructive energy sources."

"Maybe the manufacture of the parts of this house was destructive," Church said. "We don't know."

"You're pretty magnanimous about the past," I said. "Is Church your real name?"

"Yes, why?"

"It's interesting. The word Church has its root in *'keu,'* which is a hollow or a cave."

"You just knew that off the top of your head?"

I nodded as I drank some soup. Then I said, "I must have memorized a dictionary in my youth. I like words. I enjoy pulling them apart and finding meaning."

"What about your names?" he asked.

"They pretty much mean what they are: glory and stone," I answered. "I picked them myself. I liked the look and sound of Gloria. And stone felt so solid and earthy. I like being close to the Earth. Sometimes I just stretch out on the ground. It's the only time I almost feel like I fit." I smiled and shrugged. "But enough about me, Rev. How'd a nice man like you become Christian?" I wanted to keep talking so I would not have to think about what kept happening to me every time I touched anyone except Church. What if I could never heal again? Never connect? I would be turned out of house and home.

"I had an experience when I was young, and I felt called," he answered.

"By Christianity?" I asked.

"By the divine. There was a traveling circus slash church in town, and I kind of ran away with them."

"A traveling circus slash church? What is that?"

"Just what it sounds like," Church said. "They have circus acts. Between acts, they preach."

I laughed. "I bet there was a woman involved." I heard Cosmo outside and got up and let him in. He shook off the snow and then lay in front of the fire.

"There was a woman," he said, "but it was more than that."

"Tell me about her."

Church blushed. "She was older than I was and very funny and intense and wise. She wasn't a Christian. She was along for the ride, I think. We would just talk for hours. She talked about the Earth the way you do. She said I thought about things too much. I needed to feel. She said God was in my heart not in heaven. On the rare occasions we actually touched, I felt struck by lightning. I just melted." He laughed quietly.

"Have you ever felt that way again?"

He looked at me. "Yes. Once."

When he touched me in the desert the night of the dance.

"Tell me more about your conversion to Christianity."

"I just felt excited by all they preached. It was all about love. I read the Bible and was fascinated. I suddenly felt free."

"Free? Why? Aren't there all kinds of rules and regulations?"

"It's more than that."

"The Bible is just a bunch of stories. Not that I don't like stories; I do. But to take those stories literally?"

"It is difficult to explain what's in my heart. Can you explain your religion?"

"I don't have a religion. I believe in the old adage: do what you will, but harm none. It seems to work."

"That doesn't say what's in your heart," he said, "or how you feel."

How did I feel? Like I never truly belonged. As if at any moment the rug that was my life could suddenly be yanked away from me. If it already hadn't been. I got up and went to the fire where Cosmo slept. Out of habit, I touched him. I started to shift, shatter, splatter. Cosmo whined, and I moved back.

Church got up and came and sat with us.

"Can you tell me what's wrong?" Church asked.

I looked at him. It was strange. I had been in life-and-death situations before, and I had not been frightened. Of course, it had not been *my* life or death. Now I was afraid. How long would it be before this shattering went away? Before everything was as it had been?

I glanced up and out the window.

"I think we're going to get snowed in," I said.

Church put his hand on my arm. His touch felt exquisite.

"I'm pretty tired," I said.

"I'll stay down here," he said, dropping his hand.

"We can both sleep upstairs. It's a big bed."

Church laughed. "You don't like me much, but you'll share a bed with me?"

"I like you fine. It's just your religion I find peculiar. Are you allowed to have sex?"

"Do you mean have I had sex? Yes. Before I ran off I was sexually active."

"And you just gave it up?"

He nodded. "I believe sex is a sacred act and should be treated as such."

"So you and Angel will have cosmic sex on your wedding night."

"I'm not in love with Angel," he said. "Do you love Benjamin?"

"Yes, I love him very much, but that does not mean he is the only person I will ever have sex with. Yes, sex is sacred and wonderful, *and* pleasure should not be hoarded." I sighed. Why were we having this conversation? Because I wanted the Reverend in my bed? I wanted to touch someone and not fall to pieces, and he was the only one I could touch.

"I guess before the epidemic I thought you were evil," I said. "I thought you were trying to trap me, to find out that I was a soothsayer, and have me burned at the stake."

"And now?" He reached over and took my hand. His skin felt warm next to mine. I wanted to cry. Cosmo whimpered.

"Now you just seem like a nice man."

"You know how I feel about you," he said. "I felt it the first moment I saw you."

"I know you're sexually attracted to me."

"I love you."

I stared at him. I had not expected that.

"Then let's go upstairs and make mad passionate love." I said, moving closer to him.

He shook his head. "Only if you are committed to me. It can't just be about sex."

I could not seem to open my mouth and tell him that at that

moment I did not care about sex: I only wanted to be held. I pulled away my hand.

"You go upstairs, padre. Cos and I will sleep down here."

Church leaned over and kissed my forehead. "Good night," he said, and then went up to the loft.

I pulled down one of the sleeping bags Benjamin and I had used during my last visit and curled up inside it.

I closed my eyes and dreamed Benjamin and I were making love. Suddenly my arm fell off. Then my legs. Lines fractured through the rest of me, like crevices on the hills of Beauty Valley, except when the lines stopped I shattered.

I opened my eyes. My heart raced. Cosmo slept near the dying fire. I started to reach for him but stopped. What if I shattered again? I got up and went upstairs. I watched Church sleep for a time. Then I lifted the covers and got into bed with him. I laid my head on his bare chest. He put his arm around my shoulder and breathed deeply with sleep.

I closed my eyes. I felt grounded. My heartbeat started to go back to normal. I felt completely connected. At home.

Church stirred. "Gloria?" he whispered.

"It's me."

He pulled me closer. I kissed his mouth and put my arms around his neck. He pushed himself gently against me. "Gloria."

I sat up and pulled off my shirt. Then I leaned down and kissed his chest.

He held my face between his hands. "You are beautiful," he said.

"I just want to feel—"

"What? What do you want to feel?"

"Like myself again," I whispered.

I lay down on him, and we held each other tightly.

Then we turned over, and he moved inside of me. Yes. This was what I needed. Wanted. No shattering. I was connected again.

"I love you," he whispered.

I wrapped my legs around him. Giggling, we rolled over. I

sank down onto his chest, felt him inside, and sat up again, with his hands on my thighs. I got lost in the ecstasy of it, of him and me. After we climaxed, we lay against one another, sweaty and hot, breathing in sync.

I fell to sleep.

When I awakened, it was still dark and Church was spooned up behind me.

I turned to him. His eyes were open. "How long have you been awake?" I asked. I held out my arm, and he laid his head on my breast.

"I never went to sleep," he said. "I don't know how you could sleep. The whole world seems to be pulsing with divinity."

I laughed softly. "I could make a crude joke about pulsing, but I'll refrain."

He kissed my breasts, and I kissed the top of his head. He glanced up at me. He looked so young, vulnerable, and beautiful.

He smiled, kissed my mouth, and we made love again. Later when the sun came up, we made love again, faster than the first time, eager to feel the release, to feel each other. He took my breath away and then gave it back.

"Wow. I should have found me a religious man a long time ago." I laughed.

Finally, we slept again. When we awakened, it was midday and Cosmo yelped to be let out. I wrapped a blanket around me and stepped outside. Cosmo nearly knocked me over as he raced to get out. The sky was clear light blue. The mountain and Beauty Valley were bright white, becoming giant reflectors of the sun.

I went back inside, and we heated up bean and rice burritos and ate them with tea. Then we sat by the fire with one blanket across our naked bodies. Stempler would get an eyeful if he suddenly came home.

"This will be difficult for Angel," Church said as he ate.

"Church—"

"We've made love several times now," he said. "I think we should be on a first-name basis."

"What is your first name?"

He raised an eyebrow.

"All right, *Thomas*. What will be difficult for Angel?"

"I'll have to tell her there's no chance of us getting married."

"Not because of me. If you don't love her, that's up to you. But what happened here doesn't change anything. I mean, it was wonderful. Actually, it was great, but our lives haven't changed."

He moved so he was sitting across from me. "Your life hasn't changed? We created love together."

"I know." I sighed. "I'm not saying this right." I never said it well. I did not connect unless I was healing or making love. Afterward, I was at a loss.

"I shouldn't have come up last night," I said. "I was—I was frightened. And you're the only one I've been able to touch since the healings."

"What do you mean?"

I got up, went to my pack, and pulled out some clothes and put them on. Church drew the blanket closer around him.

"I had never done that many healings all at once. Something happened to me. Now every time I touch anyone I feel strange. Like I'm going to fly apart."

"I noticed you kept pulling away from everyone but me. Usually it was the other way around."

I nodded. "When I touch you, everything is fine."

"That's why you wanted to make love with me?"

"Church, that's what I do! That's what most people do to connect with one another."

"But you knew how I felt about you! You took advantage of that."

"Thomas, do you really feel taken advantage of? I feel pretty good myself."

"What about Benjamin?"

"What about him?" I asked.

"You mean you could have an intimate ongoing relationship with both of us?"

"Ongoing? I don't know!"

We were silent for a few minutes.

"Why did you want to come here, anyway?" Church asked.

"When Benjamin and I were here before, Stempler mentioned something about G-men hanging around. He said they were asking questions about Coyote Creek. I thought maybe one of them was Primer. Maybe Stempler saw something that could prove what Primer did."

Cosmo yelped. I went to the door and let him in. He pushed himself against my legs, and I bent to rub his head. Nothing shifted or shattered.

I laughed, dropped to the floor, and embraced the wet coyote.

"Church! It's gone!" I jumped up, grabbed Church's hands, and pulled him up. I hugged his naked body. "You cured me. The shattering is gone."

He put his hands on my clothed waist where it curved to my hips. "You make me feel out of control."

"And you are my good luck charm."

He smiled. "I feel stupid standing here stark naked."

"Why? Your momma and daddy gave you a gorgeous body. Be proud. You want to play in the snow?"

His hands dropped to his side. "I think I'll get dressed first."

"Chicken!"

Later the three of us ran around in the snow as it slowly melted. Church and I made a snowman and snowwoman, and Cosmo knocked them both over.

The day before had been silent with snow; this day, the sound of running water came from all around. It felt more like spring than near winter. The melting snow created dangerous climbing conditions, so I decided to stay at Stempler's for another night—at least that was my excuse.

Cosmo ran with the other creatures of the dark. Church lit candles downstairs and spread the sleeping bag open near the fire. He took off my clothes and massaged me head to foot and then he massaged me again. His fingers discovered places on my body that had not been found before. When he took off his clothes, he sank into me, like a root into the Earth, and we moved so slowly together, until I came almost unexpectedly, and still he stayed inside of me, my orgasm massaging him. We held each other, and I breathed into his sweaty chest, kissed it, and after a time, we climaxed together, the orgasm spreading through my body gradually at first and then spinning out of the top of my head.

"I will love you forever," he whispered. "You are my beloved."

I could not move from his arms. Did not ever want to leave this place.

We slept and then made love again. Every position we lay in was comfortable; every place we touched on each other's bodies felt familiar.

Something in my chest hurt.

Church pressed his ear against my breasts. "I hear your heart."

"Good thing," I said.

"I want to live with you forever. Have a million babies. Help you in your work."

"I can't have children," I said.

He looked up at me. "I'm sorry."

"I'm not." I turned away from him. He hugged me from behind. I entwined my leg with his.

"Actually, I may have had children."

"What do you mean?" he asked.

"I don't remember anything past ten years ago. I woke up in a cave with no memory about myself. That's why I named myself. I couldn't remember my real name."

I turned to face him.

"Maybe that's why you have trouble getting close to people," he said. "Our past influences us, but you don't remember yours, so you don't know what is influencing you."

"So it has been observed," I said.

Church laughed. "My observations about you aren't very original then?"

"Every lover has cataloged my faults to me. Well, almost every lover."

He pulled me closer. "I was not cataloging your faults."

"I wish I did remember my past. But I can't worry about it. Besides, maybe I'm lucky. Instead of being held back by the past, I'm free of it and formed only by the present."

"Or," he said, kissing my chin, "those who don't remember the past are doomed to repeat it. Like The Fall. We should know more about it so it can't happen again."

"It won't happen again. We won't let the technology in."

"Wouldn't you like to know exactly what happened?" he asked.

"It was a long time ago," I said, "and most of the information about that time was destroyed so we won't ever know. As far as I can tell, life is better now."

"I have no complaints."

"At this moment," I said, "neither do I."

Five

The snow was gone the next day. I waited a few hours, hoping Stempler would turn up. When he did not, I straightened up the house and left him a note and a couple jars of a salve I knew he liked for his feet. When we were ready to go, Church stood in the doorway and looked around.

"I don't want to leave," he said, grasping my hand.

"You are so sentimental." I reached in front of him and closed the door. I kissed his lips. "We'll be back."

The day was cool and perfect for travel. Cosmo ran ahead of us, spooking small creatures into mad dashes for safety. Church and I walked mostly hand in hand: we had to touch. It was weird and wonderful. We headed in the general direction of Mount Humphries, which was covered in snow. Eventually, we came out on Old Highway 17.

That night, Cosmo found us a small empty cave off the trail. Church and I lay in each other's arms.

"Do you remember at Freedom when I told you I had a strange dream?" I asked.

"Yes. I heard you scream and came to see if you were all right."

"I've had the dream several times since then."

"What's the dream about?" he asked.

"It's just a sequence of numbers and letters."

"Are they always the same numbers and letters?" Church asked.

I laughed. "What a smart man. I never noticed. I wake up so afraid that I forget everything else."

Church squeezed me. "You don't seem to scare very easily. But then I guess we all have things which terrify us."

"What scares you?" I asked.

"Being without you," he said.

I laughed. "What a child you are!"

"Why? Because I'm in love and express it? Just because something sounds sweet and loving doesn't make it childish or clichéd. I love you."

"Okay. Okay. Go to sleep. I love you, too."

As we traveled the next day, we talked. I only had ten years of stories, but he wanted to hear them.

"It must be an incredible feeling to affect so many lives," he said.

I stared off ahead of us. "I don't know if I affect anyone, really, deeply. Sometimes I just feel . . . lost, disconnected. Do you know what I mean?"

He nodded. "I've been searching my entire life to fill some kind of unexplainable void. When I was in the traveling circus and I met Sarah, I thought she would fill that void." He smiled. "Or at least teach me to fill it myself. She was something. She did not take any garbage from anyone. But she saw me as a kid. One morning out of the blue she came into my tent, kissed me good-bye, and left the circus. I never saw her again. Since then, I have always felt alone. It's silly, isn't it? A man of God feeling alone."

"I'm a woman of the Earth, and I feel the same way sometimes. And human beings have been feeling this way forever, I guess. Human nature?"

"Do you think animals or trees or rocks get lonely?" he asked.

I laughed. "I don't know about rocks, but I would guess animals do, trees, too." I laughed. "You and I talk about things that I have never talked about, or haven't for a very long time."

"And what do you think of that?"

"It's nice. You're learning all my deep dark secrets, and you're still here."

"Deep dark secrets? I must have missed something."

"I'm the witch, and you're the preacher. I'm supposed to turn you into a frog, or you're supposed to burn me at the stake."

"Sounds like you get the worse deal in that," he said. "It wouldn't be so bad to be a frog." He grabbed my hand and pulled me toward him. "I wouldn't burn you at the stake. I wouldn't hurt you, ever."

Cosmo stayed with us part of the day, then took off howling.

The vegetation got greener, the earth redder, and the line of snow on the mountain lower. We slept in a run-down shack along the highway. The next day we caught a ride to the park entrance from a solar buggy on the way to Las Vegas. The driver did not say much more than hello and good-bye. After he dropped us off, we had not walked too far down the park road before someone pedaled up to us in a peculiar contraption that was part cart, part wheels, with foot pedals to make it go.

"Hello. I'm Caroline," the driver said. "You are Healer Gloria and Council Church. Welcome. Governor Duncan is expecting you."

I looked at Church. He shrugged, and I climbed into the vehicle. Church got in behind me.

"If you'll pedal with me, we'll get there sooner," she said. She smiled and I put my feet on the pedals and pushed. "It's not much use except on flat paths or highways, but it's something."

We pedaled by ponderosa pine and gambel oak. A herd of deer watched us. We passed a few people walking, and they waved. Soon we saw log-and-stone buildings, and then Caroline stopped the vehicle.

"The governor wanted to make certain you got a view," she said.

We got out and walked along the stone walkway, through piñon and twisted juniper, to a view that made me gasp. I leaned against Church. Suddenly the world was completely silent as we gazed into the beautiful zigzag opening in the Earth. The Grand Canyon. Layers of red, white, green, turquoise. At the bottom of the canyon the river looked solid and immobile like a green vein on a young girl's arm. No, an old lady's arm: this place had been here forever. Just below the rim, a condor rode the thermals—the breath of the canyon. I moved closer to the edge. Inside, the rocks twisted and turned and had stood just the same since before The Fall, before anything people remembered, no doubt.

After a few minutes, Caroline said, "Shall we go see the governor now?"

My heart started to race. I had dreaded this moment and avoided it for some unknown reason for all of my remembered existence. Following Caroline, we walked the rest of the way down a tree-lined path to a huge building made of stone and logs. Caroline opened a heavy wooden door, and we stepped inside.

The floor was parquet, the tiles in the center shaped into an eagle. On the wooden walls were carved animals—a deer, badger, mountain lion, coyote. Across the foyer were floor-to-ceiling glass windows looking out over the canyon. In the center of the room was a round fireplace where a fire burned. Hallways extended to the left and right of the circular room. I stepped out of the foyer, closer to the fireplace and the sofas and chairs surrounding it. The ceiling vaulted upward. The second floor balcony went around the entire room.

A man stood with his hands on the railing looking down at us. His hair was brown and shoulder-length, his eyes light-colored. He smiled. "Jules Duncan. Welcome," he said.

I glanced at Church. He squinted as he looked up at the governor, his face tense.

Duncan turned around and disappeared from view. A

moment later, he came down the hallway on our left. Caroline stepped back. Duncan held out his hand, and I shook it.

"You must be Gloria Stone." He gripped my hand firmly and did not seem to want to let go. Finally, he did. He grasped Church's hand momentarily. "Reverend Church. Thank you for keeping Healer Stone company on her long trip here. We have waited a long time for this visit. Caroline will show you to your rooms. We're about ready for lunch. We'll meet you?" He inclined his head, then turned and walked away again.

Caroline took us down the opposite hallway from where Duncan had gone. Although the way was wide, it was dark, the only light coming from the picture window at the end of the hallway. Caroline stopped and opened one of the doors.

"This is your room, Healer," Caroline said.

I stepped inside a large room. The walls were made of dark wood. A huge window took up most of one wall and looked out over the canyon. A king-sized bed was against another wall, with a nightstand next to it. A table and chairs were the only other furniture.

"You have your own bathroom," Caroline said. "And a shower. The water is from a natural hot spring, so you can take as long a shower as you want. Reverend Church? Shall I show you your room?"

Church and I glanced at each other.

"We'd like to stay together," I said.

Caroline frowned, started to say something, then stopped. "If you'd prefer. But we have lots of room."

"This is fine," I said.

"Well, when you're ready," Caroline said, "go back to the main room. Take the hall on the left until you come to the dining room."

She stepped out and closed the door behind her.

Church laughed. "This feels very peculiar."

I nodded. "And claustrophobic." I went to the window and slid it open. A cool breeze came in. The spires of the canyon looked so close, as if I could take a few steps and fly into it. A jay squawked from one of the piñons. Church came up behind me and put his arms through mine and folded his hands over the round of my belly.

"Are you still nervous?" he whispered, his breath in my ear. My knees nearly buckled. I had never felt the kind of desire I felt with him, passionate and comfortable at the same time.

"Who said I was nervous? We'll tell the governor what Primer did—or what we think he did—and then we'll be on our way."

"Uh-huh." He kissed my neck. "I can't believe I haven't known you always."

I turned to face him and slid off my pants. I stood half-naked before him.

"You are so beautiful," he said.

"You, too."

We kissed, and when I opened my legs, he slid easily into me. He held my legs, and I put my arms around him as he gently pushed me against the wall.

"You're pretty good for a beginner," I whispered.

And then we lost our balance and tumbled to the floor.

"So much for grand passion." I laughed as we lay sprawled on the floor. Church pulled up my shirt and kissed my breasts loudly.

I pushed him over onto his back and straddled him. "Enough laughter, Reverend. You've got some unfinished business here."

"No, wait," Church said. "Let's take a shower."

"I forgot!" I jumped up and went to the shower room. Church came in as I was fiddling with the knobs.

"How does this work?" I asked.

"Try this." He pulled one knob out and turned another. Water shot down. Church turned the knob until the water temperature was right. Then we took off our clothes and got into the shower, closed the door, and stood side by side, letting the water run all over us. I had preserved and conserved all my life; it was a peculiar feeling to stand and just let hot water flow all over me. After a few minutes, Church and I began washing each other and one thing led to another, which meant we almost broke our necks slip-sliding into the shower. We eventually spilled out onto the bed; with our bodies squeaking like creatures from the sea, we came together. And then fell apart, laughing.

After we dressed, we left our room. The lodge was quiet. Past the main room, we went down the darkened hallway until it turned into a dining area with a glass ceiling and three glass walls. The Grand Canyon opened and curved away from us. For a moment, the canyon was all I saw; then Church touched the small of my back lightly and the rest of the room resolved into itself. A long oval wooden table stood near the three windows, surrounded by chairs with people sitting in them. On the other side of the room was a buffet table nearly overflowing with food.

Governor Duncan sat at one end of the table but stood when I looked at him, his chair scraping across the stone floor. The conversation stopped.

The governor came toward me, his hand out. He took my hand, put his arm lightly across my back, and said, "Everyone, this is Gloria Stone. I'll let you all get to know one another." He glanced behind him, "And this is Reverend Thomas Church."

"Hello," they said, almost in unison, and then laughed at themselves.

"Here," Duncan said, turning me toward the buffet table. "Eat all you want."

I took steamed squash, beans, corn, various winter greens, bread, seeds, currants, and hot chocolate. I tried some dishes I did not recognize and then let Duncan lead me back to an empty chair next to his. I glanced at Church, but he was busy filling his plate. Duncan and I sat next to one another. A few moments later, Church took a place next to Caroline.

"This looks great," I said, poking the food with my fork.

Duncan laughed. "How awkward for you to have us watching while you eat. Shall we talk around you?"

"Please."

"I'm going to get some of that carrot cake." A blonde stood and went to the buffet.

"I think Terry's got a tapeworm," a red-haired man said, following the woman.

"That's a lovely image, Edward," Terry said.

I began eating. Duncan leaned back in his chair, his hands behind his head. He was not what I imagined. I glanced around the table: no Primer.

"This is very good food," Church said. "Do you have one cook, or do you share?"

"We were very cooperative for a couple of years," Duncan said, "after my mother Governor Elizabeth Duncan died. She had always had a cook, servants. Anyway, we all shared the chores after she died."

"We?" another woman said. She was darker than Benjamin, her eyes black.

Duncan laughed. "The royal we, then. *I* did not cook. But China came, and she was so much better than anyone. We elected her full-time cook. She lets Lester help sometimes."

One of the men hooted, "Yes, I follow direction well."

"I couldn't do it without you," China said.

The backslapping was a bit cloying.

"Do many people live here?" I asked.

"Off and on," Duncan said. "We need enough to manage the farms, along with the border patrol."

"Farms?" That was odd. "I didn't know the governor was obligated to be a farmer."

Duncan leaned forward. "I'm not. I like farming. We trade with nearby towns."

I put down my fork. "What about the argument that mass farming depletes the ecosystem and causes overpopulation?"

Several people laughed. Church frowned.

"You follow the laws rather strictly," Duncan said.

"I adhere to the sound judgment of our ancestors. Yes."

A short uncomfortable silence followed. Then Duncan sighed. "You're absolutely correct." The room sighed, too. "I agree with you. We don't mass produce. Some years we just have more than we can use. So we trade. I'll show you around and you can see your tax dollars at work."

"Tax dollars?" I said.

Duncan smiled. "Old bureaucratic humor. We hope you'll be so impressed, you'll stay with us."

Church looked at me.

"Yes, it's true, Reverend Church," Duncan said. "I do hope to steal her."

"I'm afraid Coyote Creek has already stolen my heart," I said.

I heard several groans, including my own. The banal sweetness was apparently catching. Church laughed quietly.

"Actually," I said quickly, "I came to talk with you about something illegal that happened in Coyote Creek."

"Food first," Duncan said. "Then business."

Terry brought Duncan a piece of carrot cake. They talked about the weather and a sick deer Edward was tending. I looked out the window at the tops of the rock formations. From the west, dark clouds moved. I unexpectedly relaxed as I looked across the gap in the Earth. I felt as though I could just sit and stare forever. Mesmerized, I ate slowly. People got up and left, one by one. The light changed. Clouds moved in and slowly dropped into the canyon, like mist over falls.

My plate was finally empty, and I looked back at the table. Only Caroline, Duncan, Church, and I remained.

Caroline stood. "I'll show the Reverend our spiritual center." She looked at Church. "If that would be all right with you?"

Church nodded and got up. He squeezed my shoulder as he went by. I smiled. Duncan and I were alone in the quiet. Outside, the trees began to bend to the will of nature. The table was clear except for my plate.

"I seem to have drifted," I said. "I guess I must be a little tired."

"What is it you wished to discuss with me?" He had an easy voice, one with soft inflections. Listening to him made me feel sated and sleepy, the way I did at the end of our celebrations in Coyote Creek or Freedom.

I sat up and shook myself. "I was under the distinct impression you wanted to see me."

He laughed. "Yes, I have heard of your healing, and I wanted to meet with you."

"Is that all? Primer came to my home and demanded I return with him," I said. "When I didn't, people in Coyote Creek started getting sick. We traced the illness to our water supply. Primer pretty much told me he had caused it and threatened to do worse if I didn't come here.

"The Coyote Creek council agreed Primer was probably the culprit. We wanted you to know what your agent had done and ask you to take the appropriate action."

Duncan was silent for a few minutes. Then he said, "Primer does overreact in some situations, but I find it difficult to believe he would poison your water. Where would he get poison? Couldn't it just have been caused by bacteria from animal feces?"

"Yes, it could have been, but we don't think so." I told him everything that had happened from the time I first met Primer on the mountain to our last encounter by the clinic.

When I finished, Duncan shook his head. "I will certainly investigate this. Primer is not a friendly man. I was hoping that he'd pick up some people skills."

I laughed. "I've seen no evidence of that. But you are well liked and respected. We thought you should know what happened. Also, Stempler Jones said two government men were snooping around his place about tech violations. I suspect one of those men was Primer. As governor, you know, of course, that you have no jurisdiction over tech violations. That is under local control."

I thought he stiffened a bit. But he said, "Of course."

We sat in silence for a few moments, and then Duncan glanced outside. "I was going to take you out to the farms, but it wouldn't be wise in this weather."

"I've seen farms." My drowsiness was receding.

Duncan smiled. "What would you like to see?"

"The inside of the canyon."

Duncan nodded. "If the weather's good, we'll go tomorrow."

The clouds had a purple hue to them. Lightning sliced. Rain poured from the clouds, looking—from this distance—like shafts of light streaming to the Earth.

"Would you like to see the rest of our humble home?" Duncan asked.

"Sure."

Duncan took me to the library on the second floor. Once again, we had a panoramic view of the storm. The clouds were gray now, almost white. The room was two stories high and filled with books. The selection was vast, considering many books were lost before and after The Fall. Before because so much was put on computer; after because of the furious destruction of everything.

"It's beautiful," I said. "Are you a reader?"

"I try when I can. You?"

"I used to read more, but at Coyote Creek I have so many responsibilities. When I'm finally alone, reading does not usually have priority." I thought of Cosmo and me sitting on the desert floor behind our house watching the sun go down. He would like this storm and enjoy chasing all the little creatures scurrying for cover.

Duncan took me to the kitchen, which was bigger and shinier than any I had ever seen. China sat at a table against the window, thumbing through a cookbook. Lester stood at the chopping block on the cooking island, slicing multicolored corn from their cobs. He smiled and nodded to us.

"We cook by a variety of methods," Duncan said. "We have earthen ovens outside. Inside we have efficient woodstoves and solar power for refrigeration and other appliances."

"Any trouble getting parts?"

Duncan shook his head. "We're fortunate. Much of this was made to last forever. Plus Lester is good mechanically."

"Isn't most of this computerized?" I asked, trying to recall what Stempler had said about his house.

"Unlike some of my cohorts," Lester said, "I don't believe computers are evil or haunted by demons. I'll work on anything."

"I didn't say I thought they were evil," I said. "I just know they don't lend themselves easily to tinkering."

Duncan put his hand on my elbow. "Not much goes wrong here," he said, leading me away.

He took me to a large playroom; no children were inside.

"We don't have any children at the lodge permanently at this time," Duncan said. "But some of us adults come here to play with the toys."

"Good," I said. "That'll keep you healthy."

We walked to the main room I had first seen on entering the lodge. Duncan sat on the couch in front of a fire that filled the stone fireplace. I sat in a nearby chair.

"You could have a good life here," Duncan said.

"I already have a great life."

"Here you would be more involved in the bigger issues. We turn away a lot of sick people at the borders. You could help them."

"Governor Duncan," I said, "I am not really much of a humanitarian. Indiscriminate healing doesn't interest me. I like being a part of a community, knowing people, having my needs met: food, clothing, housing. I have a great deal of freedom at Coyote Creek."

"How do you heal?" he asked.

"I listen, prescribe herbs, diet, things like that."

"What about hands-on healing?"

I glanced over at him. The last crisis at Coyote Creek had forced my healing abilities out in the open. Or had forced me out of secrecy. No one had seemed surprised.

"I suppose I do some hands-on. I think the human touch is very important."

Duncan nodded. "They have said you are a very good healer."

I stretched my legs out in front of me. The heat of the fire reached my toes and spread up to my thighs.

"But you deny being a soothsayer."

I was feeling sleepy again. I wondered where Cosmo was. And Church.

"I have never met a soothsayer," I said. "Maybe they are a fabrication. I do know it is not safe to be a soothsayer. Sometimes they are welcomed in a community, sometimes they are run out of town."

"Do you know why?"

I locked my fingers behind my head. "Obviously people fear them. I don't wish to be feared. It would be dangerous to my health."

"You would be safe here. Soothsayers are welcomed, even cherished. No one would turn against you."

"No one would turn against me at Coyote Creek, either." This was a peculiar conversation.

"You like Coyote Creek because you are the most important person in town. Here you fear you'd be eclipsed. I assure you that wouldn't happen. You would hold sway over death-and-life decisions."

What a voice he had. I was ready to fall to sleep again. I closed my eyes. Suddenly the sequence of numbers and letters flashed across the back of my eyelids. I heard a scream.

I opened my eyes. The fire was much lower. The candelabra above us had been lit. Someone touched my arm. I looked up. Duncan smiled.

"You fell asleep."

I sat up. "I guess I was tired."

Duncan laughed softly. "I guess. Supper is ready."

I stood and stretched. "I want to wash up. I'll be there in a minute."

Duncan took a lit candle from the mantel and handed it to me.

I walked down the dark hallway until I reached my room and opened the door. Blackness. Church was not here. I put the candle on the table, then went into the bathroom and splashed my face. What was wrong with me? I felt half-drunk or three-quarters asleep. Maybe it was this building. I was accustomed to being outside, or at least being in a small building with lots of ventilation.

I patted my face dry, went into the hall again, and walked to the dining room. Inside the dimly lit room, people were lined up at the buffet table. Church stood off to one side, looking bereft, plate in hand. He smiled when he saw me. I went to him. He took my hand and kissed me.

"I wondered where you were," he said.

"I was in the main room sleeping. You couldn't have missed me."

He frowned.

"Are you all right?" I asked.

"Something about this place is kind of strange."

"Yeah, it makes me sleepy," I said. "We're going inside the canyon tomorrow."

"I thought we were leaving tomorrow."

"I still haven't seen Primer," I said.

"I didn't know you wanted to see Primer. I thought we just wanted to tell the governor about him."

I felt a little irritated. "Church, relax. I've told the governor. He'll take care of it."

"I am here as a representative of the council. I'd like to speak with him, too."

"Then do it!"

I picked up a plate and eating utensils. Why was Church suddenly being such a nag?

Edward stood on the other side of the table. I dished up fried squash blossoms, along with corn bread, carrot hash, and a stuffed pepper.

"Would you come look at the sick deer after dinner?" Edward asked as he ladled soup into a half of a small pumpkin and set it on my tray.

"I normally try not to interfere with the process of nature and wild animals," I said.

"She got caught up in some old barbed wire we didn't know about. She struggled long and hard."

I nodded, remembering Cosmo's scars after his encounter

with that macabre creation of our ancestors. "Yeah, I wouldn't call barbed wire Mother Nature either. I'll be glad to look at her."

I followed the person in front of me out to the main room. Duncan seemed to be the center of the activity although he sat off to the side, near the fire. He laughed and talked and ate. I sat near Terry on the floor. Caroline moved over on one of the couches to make room for Church. He sat next to her and ate slowly, glancing around the room uneasily.

I ate the pumpkin soup, spooning bits of the pumpkin into my mouth as I got near the end of the liquid. Then the hash. Corn bread. Red peppers. The food was exquisite.

China brought in a platter of fry bread sprinkled with powdered sugar and took jars of cactus jelly out of her pockets and handed them around. Lester followed her with cups of some kind of hot liquid.

Later Lester and Edward collected empty plates. Then Duncan storytold while Terry accompanied him on a small drum. Church sat behind me, and I leaned against him. He wrapped me in his arms. My irritation had disappeared with the food. Church relaxed, too.

After a time, Edward knelt next to me and asked me to come outside. Church and I followed him. The storm had ended. The air was clean and crisp. He led us to a barn. Once inside, he lit a lamp and carried it to one of the stalls. Horses or mules snorted and chewed. I had heard people kept some animals this way, but I was surprised the governor did.

Edward opened the stall door. A doe lay on the straw. She bleated at me. Her body was ragged where the barbs had torn her.

"How long has she been down?" I asked.

"A couple of days.'

I shook my head. "Then her lungs are probably congested by now. What about the wounds? Did you put self-heal on them at first?"

Edward shook his head.

"All right. Do you know what plantain is?"

Edward frowned, "No."

"I do," Church said. "I'll show him."

Church knew I was trying to get rid of Edward. He grabbed the lantern and gently turned Edward around. As they walked away, Edward muttered, "How are we going to find anything in the dark?"

I turned to the deer.

"Hi, sweetheart." I put my hand on her chest to calm her. Then I laid my other hand just above her ribs. My palms tickled. The doe sighed. I could feel her body's defenses surge. The cuts created scars. I heard a whisper or a flurry of wings. I looked up but could see nothing. The doe whimpered. Her breathing became shallow.

She was dying.

Quickly I moved away my hands. I turned my palms toward me and looked at them. They were ghostly body parts. I rubbed them together. Then I pressed them against the doe. Her breathing returned to normal. As soon as I sensed she was out of danger, I stepped back from her. She shook herself and stood. I opened the stall door, and she leaped into the darkness.

I let out a breath and leaned against the stall. My breath came in gasps, as if I had run a long distance. Fear shot my heart with adrenaline.

What had happened? Why had the doe started to die? This was my first healing since Coyote Creek. Had I changed in some permanent way after the epidemic? Had I lost control? That bastard Primer.

I pushed myself outside and breathed deeply. Edward and Church soon came out of the night to stand next to me.

"Edward was right," Church said. "It's too dark."

"I had some salve in my pocket," I lied. I put my hand on Church's arm to steady myself. "The deer felt better and left."

"Left?" Edward said. "You mean you let her go?"

"Were you going to keep her? She is a wild animal."

"No-no. I just thought she'd be better off. I mean, don't you have a coyote as a pet?"

"No. Cosmo is a companion. He comes and goes as he wishes," I said. "Church, I'm tired. I'm going in."

Church handed the light to Edward, and we walked toward the lodge.

"Thank you," Edward called.

"What's wrong?" Church asked quietly as we stepped inside the kitchen, where a single candle burned.

"I'll tell you later." I picked up the candle holder, and we walked back to our room.

I did not tell him what had happened with the doe. We went to bed, and I lay on Church's shoulder until he fell asleep. Then I moved away, and he turned on his side. I curved my body around his back.

Something had happened to me, or was happening to me. And I did not know what it was. I had hurt that deer in the middle of my healing. But how? I had not been aware of any changes in myself. Just that stupid whispering. Or whatever it was.

First the shattering after the epidemic. Now this. I had pushed myself relentlessly when Coyote Creek needed me. Perhaps I had overstressed my body, and now it would just take a while to balance out again.

Yes, that was it. I kissed Church's back and fell to sleep.

I dreamed about Cosmo. He sat on the edge of a butte howling at the moon. As I got nearer to him, I saw that the sequence of letters and numbers had been carved onto his chest. The blood dripped down onto his feet, forming a stream that opened into the Colorado River pouring through the Grand Canyon. Above it all, Primer laughed.

Church kissed me awake. He was already dressed. I sat up.

"What's going on?"

"Caroline said there's a small Christian community not far from here. I thought I'd go see them."

"Aren't you coming with me today?"

"If I go with her now, we'll be able to leave sooner," Church said, gently moving my hair out of my eyes. "We'll be freeing two birds at one time."

I wanted to tell him about my dream. I wanted to ask him to stay with me. But I kissed his lips, smiled, and said good-bye.

"I'll see you tonight," he said.

Then he was gone.

I got out of bed, put on my clothes, grabbed my pack, and went out into the hall and down to the dining room. Duncan and Edward were the only ones at the table. I yawned and gazed out the window. The gray was dawning into gold, turning the few remaining thunderclouds into black gold.

I turned from the view and sat at the table with the two men. We ate silently as the sky changed colors. I did not feel very hungry and was barely able to eat the blue corn pancakes spread with jelly. I kept having flashes of the dream—a bloody Cosmo and laughing Primer.

When we finished, we went to the kitchen where China and Lester filled our packs with water and food. Then I followed Duncan and Edward out into the morning.

They led me to the rim of the canyon. Edward stepped over the edge. I grinned. I was going to like this. I followed him.

At first, it was like walking back into dawn; the sun had not reached all the way inside yet. We quietly walked through a small stand of Douglas fir growing on the hard sloping ground. Several crows sat in one of the trees and took turns calling out to us.

We continued down through mountain scrub and some piñon-juniper. Across the canyon, the sun lit the green mountain scrub and red walls. The layers of rock were distinct, reminding me of stacks of thick, multicolored pancakes.

As we moved downward, I began to awaken. The heat of the sun drew small clouds of mist out of the canyon. Jays cried out noisily. I was descending into a world I had never experienced before. The canyon seemed to sigh, and I breathed deeply, filling my lungs with the breath of the Earth. I wished Church were here. I wanted him to feel surrounded by the Earth, cradled, to know that God was not in heaven; she was beneath my feet. My body and his had been nourished for a lifetime with food grown from her, the air we breathed, the water we drank, all from the Earth and her processes. I felt giddy. I was going deeper into the Earth than I had ever been. When I waded into the Colorado River, would I be touching the heart of the Earth?

We suddenly came out on a shelf of rock, a red rock terrace. The canyon opened before us, massive and profoundly majestic, close and far away. I wanted to cry.

Someone screamed. I looked down. On a terrace below us, a man stood over a mangled coyote bashing the animal's head in with a piece of wood. The animal did not move. The man kept hitting, grunting each time he brought the wood down.

My dream!

I pushed Edward and Duncan out of the way and ran down the path.

"Gloria!" Duncan called.

For a moment the man was out of view, and I heard another grunt. Then I turned the corner and was on the bloody terrace. The man was on his knees, his head bent. His body was covered in blood. I knelt by the coyote. His head was crushed beyond anything I could do. I stroked the bloody fur. My fingers met a scar. I brushed the hair back. Barbed-wire scars. My heart started to race. I gently pulled his front paws toward me. An extra toe on each.

"No!" I screamed. "You motherfucker, why did you do this?"

"He attacked me."

The man slowly raised his head.

Primer.

A fog descended over me. Everything felt unreal. The world slowed until I thought I might fall off. I could not bear the sight of my battered friend or the evil man who had killed him. I screamed and leaped across Cosmo. The scream echoed in my brain, a whisper and flutter of wings. I pushed Primer as hard as I could. He fell backward, soundlessly disappearing into the canyon.

I heard a thud as he hit ground.

The fog lifted.

What had I done? I jumped up and ran down the path until I found Primer crumpled below the terrace.

I laid my hands on him.

Felt the connection. Had seen into this being before. Something. Some *thing* peculiar. Felt his bones crack back into wholeness. Wounds knit.

Primer sighed and looked up at me.

"Is he all right?" Duncan squatted next to me.

"He'll live," I said, my own breathing ragged, "which is more than I can say for Cosmo."

"I'm having trouble breathing," Primer said.

"You've got bruised ribs. They'll be sore for a while. They can bind you up at the lodge."

"No. Fix it now. I know you can do it. You did it with my ankle."

"Gloria?" Duncan said.

I stood. My relief that Primer was not dead faded as my anger returned. "I told you I am not a humanitarian."

Edward knelt next to Primer and opened his shirt. "He's bleeding."

"Please help him," Duncan said.

Disgusted, I leaned over and put my hand on Primer's head. We connected.

"You killed Cosmo," I said.

"He attacked me."

Some *thing*. I heard a whisper. Duncan? Said something. Gibberish? I glanced at him. He stared at Primer.

"Cosmo never attacked anyone in his life," I murmured.

"Maybe he remembered I'd poisoned him."

I looked down at Primer. "You admit it."

"Of course. I'm proud of it. It got you here."

Some thing.

Wrong. Fog. Clarity.

Primer gasped. Whimpered like the doe.

Someone whispered.

Primer collapsed, his head falling away from my hand.

I dropped down and put both hands on his body again.

No connection. I pulled away.

Edward felt for his pulse. "He's dead."

Edward and Duncan looked at me.

"I-I don't know what happened," I said, holding up my hands. "He was all right one moment and then . . . he was gone."

Duncan patted my arm. "You did what you could."

Edward picked up Primer and put him gently over his shoulder.

"But I pushed him over the cliff!" I could not believe what had happened. I had never touched anyone in anger before. At least not in the ten years of my recollection.

Duncan looked up at the terrace. "He only fell about fifteen feet. That fall did not kill him."

"Where are you taking him?" I asked.

"Back up," Duncan said. "To our cemetery."

Why were they both so calm? Everything seemed skewed. Off-kilter.

"Don't worry," Duncan said. "The coyote did it. You are not at fault."

He squeezed my arm and turned to follow Edward up the trail again.

I was stupefied. My feet felt huge and heavy, and it took all my energy to pick up one foot and then the other and push my body up the trail. I had had clients die before, but not by my own hand.

No. That was not what happened.

No.

We reached Cosmo. I stopped. They continued on. Primer's body bounced rhythmically against Edward's back. Duncan followed. They made a peculiar, solemn procession. After a few moments, they disappeared around a corner. I listened until I could not hear their feet over dirt.

I breathed deeply. The sky was clear, milky blue. I smelled dry leaves and piñon pitch. Two turkey vultures circled. A chickadee alighted on a nearby cliffrose. As the tiny bird picked at the leaves, I thought I smelled spiced honey, the fragrance of the scrub's now nonexistent flowers. I glanced up again. More vultures. Good. Cosmo's death would at least provide nourishment for other living creatures.

"I'm sorry I ever came here," I whispered. "May the Earth receive your spirit, my friend."

Six

I stood for a long while, frozen between the bottom and top of the canyon. *In medias res.* When the vultures began to descend, I walked up the path slowly.

At the rim, I stopped and looked around. I saw no people, only a herd of elk. One of them looked up at me and snorted. A jay screeched as it flew by.

Church. I had to find him. I went to the lodge. China and Lester worked on lunch together. Both looked up and smiled as I walked through the kitchen. Clearly Duncan and Edward had not told them about the accident.

About me.

I hurried to our room. Empty. What had I expected? Church had only left a couple of hours ago; he would not be back yet. I sat on the edge of the bed and stared at my hands. What had happened?

The power to heal and the power to kill?

No.

Primer was dead.

And Cosmo.

Life changes on a breath.

I sat for a long while, it seemed, before someone knocked on the closed door.

"Gloria?" The door opened and Caroline stepped inside. "Are you all right?"

"Does everyone know?"

Caroline nodded. "We're going to have a ceremony after lunch."

Nothing stops the food at Rancho Duncan.

"You're welcome to come to the ceremony. And lunch, of course."

I looked at my hands again. Caroline sat next to me on the bed. "Duncan told me what happened. It's not your fault. Just a series of unfortunate mishaps."

"I thought you were with Church," I suddenly realized. "Is he back?" I quickly got up and started to leave.

"He's gone," she said.

I stopped and turned to her. "What?"

She reached into her back pocket and pulled out a piece of paper. "He left this for you."

I took the proffered note. "I don't understand."

She shrugged. "We started out this morning and then he decided he'd rather go with you. We came back here and I showed him which trail you probably took. Not long after, he returned very shaken. He wrote this note and asked Terry to take him as far as she could with our solar buggy."

I opened the note and stepped close to the window:

"Gloria—I saw what happened. I would never have believed you capable of such barbarism. I'm going home. Thomas."

No.

Church believed I had murdered Primer.

He was right.

I looked over at Caroline, who stood waiting in the doorway.

"Thank you," I said. "I won't be coming to the ceremony. I'm returning to Coyote Creek."

"Now?"

I picked up my pack and put it on. "Tell Duncan thanks for the hospitality."

"But he'll want to see you."

I walked quickly past her and out into the hall. When I got to the main room, I glanced around, but no one was about. I pushed open the heavy front door and went into the sunshine. My life had totally changed, I felt in a peculiar panic, yet the sun was out, and it was a beautiful autumn day.

I was half a mile down the road when Duncan tapped me on the shoulder. I had no idea where he had come from, but I did not really care.

"Please don't go," he said.

"I can't stay."

"You didn't do anything wrong."

"How do you know?" I said, continuing to walk. "I had my hands on him, and he died."

"We don't know how injured he was from the fall—"

"I pushed him!"

"Or from the coyote attack."

I knew. I knew.

"I have to find Church," I said. "I need to go home."

"All right, but remember you always have a place here." I thought I heard the whir of wings again, the murmur of voices.

I nodded. "Thank you." And I walked away from him.

It was the loneliest journey I had ever taken. Vultures followed me partway, a mountain lion partway. I kept looking over my shoulder for Cosmo. At night, I dreamed the scene on the trail again, only this time Primer and I were locked together in some kind of obscene embrace, and I did not know who healed whom or who was killing whom. At our feet, Cosmo whimpered, and I struggled to release Primer so I could help Cosmo, but I could not let go. Primer grinned and blood flowed between his teeth.

During the days, I walked, passing no one, or if I did, I did not see them. I just wanted to get home. I would explain it all to Church. He loved me. He should have waited for my explanation. He had promised he would never hurt me. Had promised to love me always. And I had been silly to believe him. In his heart, he must have always thought there was something evil about me or else he would not have jumped at the chance to run away. His religion had gotten in the way, after all. Except when it came to murder, our beliefs were the same: it was wrong. My philosophy to harm none had gone out the window—or into the canyon, as it were—the moment I pushed Primer. How could I have gotten so out of control?

Finally, Sugar Mesa came into view in the distance. And then Black Mountain. Coyote Creek. A chilly autumnal night enveloped me. Coyotes howled at the rising moon.

Home. My heart raced in anticipation. Soon I would be in my own bed. Maybe Benjamin would cross the silvered desert to make love with me. I would tell all to Georgia, and she would have a reasonable explanation for what happened. I would open the clinic, and my life would return to normal.

I stepped down into the main throughway of our little burg. The moon lit the front of Millie's Cafe.

"Hello?" I called.

No one answered.

I turned and looked in the direction of the church and refectory. All was in shadow. I could go wake Church now or wait until morning.

I squatted to the ground and fingered the Earth. It was good to be home.

"Gloria?"

I looked up.

"Millie!" I stood and embraced her. She returned the hug.

"We heard what happened to Cosmo," she said. "I'm so sorry."

"And Primer?"

"And Primer," she said. We walked to her front porch and sat on the bench. I leaned back against the café wall. The coyotes continued to howl.

"You can stay here tonight," Millie offered.

"I can make it home. It's light enough with the moon."

Millie glanced at me and then away. "Someone is staying in the house."

"Oh? The council had visitors? Well, that's a pain in the butt, but I can sleep on the floor until they leave."

Millie was quiet.

"What's going on?" I asked.

"Another soothsayer is living there."

Living there? I was so stunned I did not even protest her saying "another soothsayer."

"A lot has happened," Millie said. "We didn't know you'd be returning so soon."

"I don't understand."

"It's late," Millie said. "I'll make arrangements for the council to talk with you in the morning. Come stay with us. I'll make you something to eat."

My stomach hurt; my heart thudded in my ears. "No. Thanks. I'll go to the clinic. There's no one there, is there?"

"No. No, of course not."

I got up and left Millie on the porch. I wanted something familiar. I wanted to walk the moonlit path to the clinic and find Cosmo on the porch. But the porch was dark and empty. I opened the clinic door and stepped inside. I breathed deeply the familiar aromas of mingling herbs. As I walked toward the center of the room, I ran into the examining table.

Someone had moved the table.

I dropped my pack on the floor and lay down next to it. I just wanted to sleep. I closed my eyes and listened to my heart beat.

I spent most of the rest of the night out on the cold porch, unable to sleep. I dozed a few times. Just before dawn I forced myself to eat something from my pack. Then I walked around town until it was light.

When I knocked on Millie's door, she opened it and invited me inside.

"I'll make breakfast," she offered.

Why was everyone always trying to feed me?

"No, thanks. I'm not hungry. When can I speak with the council?"

Herb came out of the back room. "Hello, Gloria. The council will meet after breakfast at the oaks."

I nodded and turned away. I could not remember ever feeling this tense. Everything seemed blurred, pulsing. I walked to the refectory and knocked on the door.

Angel answered. Her eyes were red and puffy. When she saw me, she put her arms around my neck and sobbed. I held her tightly for a moment, relishing the human contact, and then I gently pulled away.

"What's wrong?" I asked. Had Church told her about us?

She took my hand and pulled me inside.

"Reverend Church has gone," she said.

"But I thought he came back?"

We sat on the hard-backed sofa. How dark the room was; how unlike Church it now seemed. And Angel. She was suffused in a soft blond light. Her cheeks were red.

"He did come back," she said, "but he didn't want to see me, I guess. He got his things, left a note, and was gone before I got up."

"When was this?"

She shook her head. "Several days ago. I don't know what to do."

I put my arm around her shoulders, and she leaned against me for a moment. Then she went to the desk, picked up a piece of paper, and came back to sit next to me again.

She opened the letter and handed it to me. I took it and read: "Dear People: I am resigning from the council and my post here at the church for personal reasons. Effective immediately. I'm returning home. Sincerely, Reverend Thomas Church."

"Something must be terribly wrong," she said. "This isn't like him."

"No, it isn't." I heard that fluttering again. Whispering. Something was wrong. I wanted to look at the note, ask questions, but I did not. I was exhausted by sorrow.

"He didn't even leave me a note," Angel said.

"What are you going to do?" I asked.

"Find him," she said.

And then Church and Angel would live happily ever after? That was how it should be. I should never have seduced him.

"I have a council meeting," I said, standing. "I'll talk to you later."

Angel smiled weakly, tears shining in her beautiful eyes. She was who Church should have been with always. She was unselfish and uncomplicated. She loved him wholly. Holy love.

I left her and went to the oak where the council members were gathered along with some of the townsfolk. I stood in front of the council.

"What's going on?" I asked. "I'm gone a few weeks, and you replace me?"

"That's not what we've done," Georgia said. "Church returned and resigned. The woman with him told us something had gone wrong with a healing and a patient of yours died."

"I've had patients die before."

Herb and Georgia glanced at each other.

"The next day, a healer came to town," Herb said. "The woman who brought Church said you weren't coming back to Coyote Creek."

Why would she say that?

"Gloria," Georgia said gently, "a man was under your care. You were angry with him, and he died."

"We know the epidemic here caused you to strain yourself," Herb said. "You're only human. We forget that your energy is not inexhaustible."

"That's true. I saved this community, and I got a little burned-out. That's all."

"We're very appreciative of what you've done for us," Doris Canyon said.

"But how do we know you won't kill one of us?"

I turned around. The man who had spoken was someone I had cared for since he was a gawky teenager troubled with mood swings. Hadn't I held his hand and reassured him all was normal? Now he looked at me as if I were a stranger.

"Dexter!" Georgia said. "Gloria didn't kill anyone."

"Didn't she?" he asked. "Primer poisoned us, everyone knows that. Then he killed Cosmo. She loved that wild animal more than anything. How do we know she didn't kill Primer in retaliation?"

Everyone looked at me and waited. What could I say?

"I don't know what happened," I said. "I was angry. I pushed him down." The group gasped, one loud single sound as if uttered by the mountain or some unseen giant. I hurried on, "And then I went to help him. He was almost better, and then he just died." No, first he had whimpered like the doe had. She had gasped for life just as Primer had, only in her case, I had allowed her to live. What hubris! I did not have that power.

"That's our point," Herb said. "You don't really know what happened. You don't have control over your own abilities. Until you get control, we can't let you treat us."

I looked down at them and around at the others gathered. "I have been a healer here for a long while. You all know me. I have never hurt any of you. Now suddenly, because of Primer, you don't trust me?"

Dexter looked at his feet. Georgia came over and put her hand on my arm. "We know you wouldn't hurt any of us on purpose."

I shook off her touch and stared at her. "Well, you certainly didn't waste any time replacing me and moving someone into my house. Thank you for making me homeless during this time of need."

I hurried away. I did not want any of them to see my tears or hear the tremor in my voice. I did not want any of them to know how close to out of control I was.

"We didn't replace you!" Georgia called. "Think of it as a leave of absence."

Absence. The key word. They wanted me absent. I grabbed my pack from Millie's porch. Kicking up dust as I went, I climbed the mountain. I did not look down at the town again until I was far enough away that I could not see the faces of those still sitting under the oak. They had meted out their punishment; they had banished me without thought or consideration for me. Just as Church had.

I hurried up the path, listening all the while to my heart beat, trying not to feel anything. I had moved before. I could do it again. I glanced down at the stream where I regularly bathed, where Church had first seen me naked. Then up farther, I could almost see Cosmo running to meet me. Up past the juniper. To my little house.

What could I take from here? It was all me. Even the piñon and saguaro and prickly pear and cholla which had lived here longer than I were a part of me. I hesitated at the door to the house and wondered if I should knock.

"Fuck it," I said and opened the door and stepped inside.

The new healer was not here, I knew immediately. The place looked almost the same. My place. My cupboards. My table and chairs. I went into the bedroom. This was different: the bed was neatly made. I opened the dresser drawers, but my clothes were not inside. I slammed the drawer shut and looked around the small room. I found my clothes in a wooden box at the end of the bed.

"Gee, thanks for not throwing them out into the desert. Taking a leave, my ass." I rummaged through the clothes and put what I wanted into the pack. I also took the blanket from the top of the bed. Benjamin had given it to me, not the council. Then I went to the kitchen and took what food would keep and I could carry. When I hoisted the pack onto my back again, it weighed a great deal more than it had when I entered the house.

I breathed deeply and took one last look around. I did not know where I was going or what I was going to do about anything, including Church. I shook my head. It hurt too much to think about him. He should have stayed and talked to me.

He would have.

I heard the flutter again, the whisper of words I did not comprehend.

Freedom. Maybe Benjamin would know what I should do.

Maybe Benjamin would hold me in his arms, let me touch him and know my touch would not hurt him.

I left the house. Without looking back, I headed for Freedom.

The village was noisy with children and barking dogs. I went to Kara's house. She sat outside with Grandmother Saisy. I greeted both with a kiss on their respective cheeks, and then I put my pack on the dusty ground. Kara offered me squaw bush juice. I accepted out of politeness, but I still had no appetite. The three of us stared out across the desert bathed purple by the slanting light of an afternoon sun. Long saguaro shadows draped the prickly pear bushes near them and stretched out across the desert, away from the light, toward the darkness.

"Has Benjamin returned?" I asked.

Kara shook her head. "But I've been told he left the pueblo a while ago. My guess is that he's looking for you."

I shook my head. "I don't think so."

"How was the Grand Canyon?" Saisy asked.

I sighed. I could not tell the story. Not again. Not yet. I felt too close to tears. "A lot has happened. I can't talk about it. If you see Benjamin, tell him I've been fired." Both women looked at me, eyes wide. "I don't know where I'm going." Duncan said I could return to the Grand Canyon. "Maybe back to the canyon." I shook my head. "I don't know."

Kara said, "Stay here until Benjamin comes back."

I remembered Benjamin and my joke about never seeing him and Cosmo at the same time. My stomach butterflied. That was nonsense. They were not the same. Benjamin was safe.

"I can't stay." I couldn't explain why. I did not really understand it myself. What if Benjamin came back and spurned me, too? I could not sit and wait for that.

"I may go up to Stempler Jones's," I said. "Let Benjamin know." I picked up my pack. "I'll see you!" I hoped.

I nodded to the women, then walked through the running group of children out into the shadows of the saguaros.

I slept in the desert, chilly, hungry, and lonely. I got up in the middle of the night and ate a little something, which I promptly threw up. Midmorning, I made it to Stempler's. I knocked and went inside. The place was exactly as Church and I had left it. That was strange. Stempler was a wanderer of sorts, but I understood he did not like to be away from home for too long.

Then I heard a moan. I ran up to the stairs to the loft. Stempler lay on the bed.

"Stempler?" I leaned over him, but he was not responsive.

I held up my hands, hesitated for a moment, and then laid them on him. We connected. For a moment, I was nauseated and then a blinding flash seared through my brain, just like it had with the Booths and their children in Eden, only this was more intense. I wanted to pull away, but I did not. The light got dimmer, and I sensed a hole in Stempler's being. I tried to fill it, as I had tried with the others, but the hole was an abyss. I concentrated on his body. His systems kicked in. My strength poured through him; no one would die tonight.

He opened his eyes. "What the hell are you doing here?"

I laughed. "Saving your ass, you old coot."

Stempler slept after the healing. I made a fire downstairs and sat in front of it. How different this visit was from my last. No Church or Cosmo. No snow. But I had facilitated Stempler's healing. I could still do it. That was something.

Early the next morning, I made soup from root vegetables I found in Stempler's cellar. When I brought a bowl up to Stempler, he took it and watched me while he sipped from it.

When he finished the soup, he handed the bowl back to me. "You seem mighty comfortable on this bed."

I smiled. I had not even realized I was sitting on it.

"I came to see you and got snowed in," I said, "so I slept on your bed. Do you mind?"

"Yeah."

"Too late." I stood. "How are you feeling?"

"Better."

"When you're ready," I said, "I'd like to talk to you."

He grunted. I went downstairs and Stempler soon followed,

heading straight for the stove and the soup pot, where he shook some herbs into the brew and stirred it. Then he ladled some into a bowl.

"What are you doing here?" he asked as he sat at the table.

"I'll tell you later." I sat in a chair next to him. "You first."

"What's to tell? I went on a junk run and got sick."

"That's all you remember?"

"That's all. I guess I had a fever or something. I passed out. I came to really sick, and I guess I dragged myself back here."

"Where were you?" I asked.

"Why all these questions? Worried about a tech violation?"

I turned away from his sneer. "Your symptoms are similar to those of four other people I treated recently."

"The junk was near Area 27. But I never go inside those places." He squinted, looking ahead but trying to remember the past, I knew. "I was going through some garbage and thought I saw a transistor radio."

"A what?"

"You Luddites kill me. You don't know anything about history."

"Stempler, what on Earth would you do with a transistor radio? The transistors would be broken, and even if you had an energy source, what would you listen to? No one else is out there."

Stempler raised an eyebrow and glanced at me. "You feign ignorance about technology."

"I *feign* nothing."

"Sure," he said, with more than a hint of sarcasm. "So I was looking through the junk. I thought I saw this radio, and then I can't remember anything else. Must have been quite a bug."

"I'm concerned there might be a toxic leak or something. Restricted areas are not supposed to be easily accessible."

"There were fences and signs. And I stayed away!"

"All right. Don't get your knickers in a knot. I was just asking."

Stempler finished the soup, banged the bowl on the table, and looked at me.

"So why are you here? Why aren't you with your fellow Luddites banishing all technology from the planet Earth?"

I looked away from him. I wondered if he would notice if I just got up and left. I could stand outside and stare down at Beauty Valley and try to imagine the many-breasted priestess. Find the giant fingers. Pray for them to reach up and take me down into the deep, warm, cozy, nullifying Earth.

"I am no longer working in Coyote Creek."

"They fired your ass?"

I looked at him again. "Yes, they fired my ass."

"Caught you using?"

I shook my head. "Good grief, Stempler, I'm more antitech than anyone I know."

"Got that right. So why? You're the best they've had, so I hear."

"I was doing a healing and the patient died. A government man. Primer."

"I remember you asking me about him. He a prick?"

I could not help but smile. "He *was* a prick."

"You can't stay here."

"Yeah, that's why I'm here, Stempler. Begging." I pushed away from the table. "Fuck you, old man."

I picked up my pack and headed for the door.

"Wait, Stone. I'll take you to Area 27 tomorrow."

"Fuck you," I said again, and was out the door into the cold afternoon.

I walked up along the ridge and then down a bit. I went quickly, wanting to put all of them behind me. Soon I felt the stony desert floor beneath my shoes. Went through a stand of saguaro, some of them mutated so their tops fanned out like the tops of marble Roman colonnades. I skirted scrub brush decorated in burnished red leaves. Went around huge patches of prickly pears. Birds dived around me, at me, fluttering away at my approach and then back again. I had saved Stempler's life. I had saved many lives in Coyote Creek. Or at least had made their lives less uncomfortable. Now, every one of them had deserted me. Georgia. Millie. Herb. Church. How could he have done it? He just left me. As if it had all meant nothing.

I stumbled and almost fell into a spiky agave. Its spears would have bruised me into pretty shades of green and purple. Wandering the wilderness while my mind was elsewhere was dangerous. The sun was setting, and I needed to find a place to sleep. I headed for a ponderosa forest that spilled between two hills like a beautiful dark green glacier slowly rolling down between the breasts of some giant goddess.

When I got closer, I saw a stone cottage just outside the forest. I knocked. No one answered. I peered inside a window. It did not look half-bad. I tried the door handle and it turned easily.

I went inside. Stuffy. Dust covered the table, chairs, and daybed. Spiders had made webs in every corner. I left the door open and slid a window up to let in fresh air. Then I looked around the small one-room house to make certain no wild animals had taken up residence.

When I was satisfied I was relatively alone, I shook off my pack. I took several logs from the basket and threw them into the fireplace along with some wood chips. I found the flint on the mantel and struck it; a spark flew, and the fire caught.

I grabbed an empty bucket and went outside, following a trail up into the woods. As soon as I stepped onto the floor of needles, all seemed hushed and different. The trees swayed slightly in the breeze, soft needles brushing against one another, creating an evergreen lullaby. I stood for a moment and let the sound sink down into the soles of my feet. Still. Solid. *I was all right.*

The path took me to a stream pouring over smooth round rocks and several nurse logs to form a little waterfall with a blue-green pool beneath it. I knelt at the water's edge. "I thank you for this gift of water," I said. I dipped the bucket in the water until it was full and then went back to the cottage.

I cleaned up the place and cooked a dinner of rice and beans. I had no imagination or appetite for anything else. I fell to sleep in the cottage situated on the edge of a desert and woodland, to the sound of a coyote baying. I dreamed Church and I made love in this cottage and then slept in each other's arms. He whispered in my ear, "Help."

When I awakened, tears wet my face. I sat in the gray morning for several long minutes. What was I doing? Where was I going? Was I just going to go and go and go? Never stop and think about what happened? Never try to find Church? Or Benjamin.

In the silence, I felt the knot in my stomach rising to my throat. My body tingled with panic. I was all alone. Alone. All one. One was all.

What I had secretly feared all these years had finally come to pass: if I did not perform exactly up to expectations, terrible things would happen. I'd lose hearth and home, love and a living. *Because I was not like other people.* Because I did not understand how they connected with one another. Except when I healed or made love.

Only then.

Now I had neither of those ways of connecting.

No. That was wrong.

I swallowed the knot in my stomach, got up quickly, and made breakfast. I might not be healer for Coyote Creek, but I was still a healer. And Eden had always welcomed me.

I closed up the little cottage and headed southwest. In order to stay on the desert floor, I would have to head back a little, then north again. But I was not in the mood for mountain climbing or bears. My mind was too scattered. I was more fit to tangle with rattlesnakes, ticks, and cacti spears. I laughed at myself. I was not really fit to tangle with anything or anyone.

I traveled all day toward Eden. I thought I was being followed, yet every time I turned, I saw nothing except the occasional deer, jackrabbit, or fox. I tried to hurry across the plain to Bear Butte. Haste in the desert was a waste of energy—unless you were in a wash about to be flash-flooded or on scree in the path of an avalanche. Trying to get quickly to a point in the distance usually left the traveler frustrated and exhausted.

I was too tired to be frustrated. Near Eden, a group of children ran out to meet me. Lizbeth Booth was one of the group. She looked much healthier than the last time we had met. Her smile seemed to light up the entire dusk-covered plain. She hugged my waist, pressing her cheek against my belly.

"Hi, Lizbeth."

"Hello, healer lady."

Another child tugged on my hand, and I nearly tripped as Lizbeth held on tightly. Then she let go suddenly and hopped in front of me as we walked.

"Have you come to stay?" she asked.

"For a little while, at least," I said. I hoped. Unless they had heard about Primer.

If they had not, of course, I would tell them.

When we reached the village, Paula greeted me.

"Welcome," she said. "We didn't expect to see you so soon."

The children giggled and scurried away. Lizbeth was the last to leave. "Bye, Glo-ria!"

"I'm afraid I'm now a wandering soul," I said. "May I stay a little while?"

"I told you you are always welcome. You can stay with Daniel and me."

"Thank you," I said.

Eden was not home, but I could get my bearings here and figure out what to do next.

Seven

After a couple of weeks in Eden, I stopped scanning the horizon for signs of Church or Benjamin or anyone I had known in Coyote Creek. I stopped wondering when they would come and tell me it had all been a mistake. It stunned me that I could drop out of their lives so quickly and completely and no one minded.

Still, I watched the mesa tops and desert for Cosmo, even though I knew he was dead. I vacated Paula and Daniel's place for the quarantine house, converting it into a clinic and my home. During the day, I gathered herbs, nuts, berries, and roots for the winter. Or else I took some of the children on weed walks. They moved more carefully in the wilderness than I. They seemed to know intuitively whether other creatures were about, ably sidestepping the ones who might cause harm.

After gathering herbs, I would return to the house and make tinctures and remedies. Lizbeth and Amy visited often and were particularly enthusiastic about my herb work. They gleefully stuffed whatever herb matter I was working on into jars, then awaited me. Invariably, I loosened the packed herbs a bit and guided the girls' hands as they topped each jar with vinegar or alcohol. Sometimes I found them just gazing at the jars, watching as some of them oozed liquid onto the countertops. For me, this was ordinary work I had done for years, yet I was amused to see it become extraordinary through the eyes of the children.

I missed the view from my old home, but I enjoyed climbing the butte or traveling up the nearby Two Sisters. Meanwhile, the community and I did not formally, or informally, discuss my status. I was left to feed and clothe myself. Thankfully, the village nearly always had at least one common meal together a day. In the future, I knew, I would have to barter clothes and other sundries. If I stayed.

One evening, Paula and I sat under the new moon sky watching the stars.

"Have you seen Lizbeth and Amy's parents lately?" she asked. She popped roasted piñon nuts into her mouth.

"No. I see the kids a lot."

"I wish you would check on the parents. They seem depressed."

I glanced at her. "Sure, I'd be glad to."

"The council met today. In the past, you know, we had a trade agreement with Coyote Creek. We used their healer and traded them certain items each year for her services."

Of course I knew all this, but I did not interrupt.

"We didn't think we could support a healer full-time. Since you have been here, however, you have participated fully in the community. You have been helpful in preparing for winter. You seem to have endless knowledge."

I laughed. I knew my knowledge definitely had an end.

"We would like to offer you a post here on a trial basis. We'll provide for your basic needs: food, housing, clothing. In return, you would remain here as our healer. You would agree to provide medical care and teaching."

I sighed. I felt as though I had been holding my breath for weeks. Now that I had an offer of work and home, I could relax.

"This is wonderful," I said. "I'm very grateful. Give me a

couple of days to think about it. And I'll look in on the Booths in the morning."

Paula pointed. "Look, a falling star. Make a wish."

"Don't need to. My wish just came true."

That night I dreamed the series of numbers and letters again. I awakened just after dawn. The horizon was a line of purple, then white, peculiarly bright although we were still in darkness. I piled on clothes to get rid of the chill.

I did not eat; my appetite had not yet returned. Instead, I walked through the village to Tricia and Timothy's abode. When I knocked on the door, Amy opened it. She smiled shyly. I leaned down and kissed the top of her head. Then she stepped aside. Timothy and Tricia sat at the table while Lizbeth poured steaming meal into their bowls.

"Dad, Mom, pick up your spoons. Time to eat."

The parents dutifully did as they were told and began slowly eating.

Lizbeth started when she saw me, almost dropping the pot. Amy ran to the table and held out her bowl unsteadily as her sister spooned breakfast into it.

"They'll be all right after they eat," Lizbeth said, putting down the pot.

I felt stupid and inept. Although I had been with the girls nearly every day, I never asked them about their parents or even noticed any depression or anxiety in the children.

I went and stood next to the couple. They did not look at me.

"May I treat you?"

They did not answer. I put a hand on Timothy's right shoulder and on the back of his head. We connected. The bright light was blinding, sickening, caving in on itself and getting bigger, cascading into an abyss. I wanted to scream. I tried to heal. Tried to fill the hole. Rebuild. But I had no idea how to do it. I let instinct guide, as always. The light dimmed a bit.

I moved my hands away and stood momentarily blinded in the semidarkness.

Timothy turned and looked at me. "Healer, it is good to see

you again." His chair scraped the floor as he stood and held his hand out to me. I shook it.

"I told you," Lizbeth said.

Was it the food or my touch? Tricia showed no signs of change. I went to her and touched her. Connected. Was hit by the light. Tried to help. Move. Make whole.

I stepped away.

Tricia smiled wanly and shook my hand.

"I don't remember," she said.

"You don't remember what?" I asked.

"Anything," she murmured. "My childhood."

Join the club, I thought.

She looked at me. Even in the subdued light of dawn, I saw her terror.

"It's more," she said. "It's as if I were made of stone, and the stones are dissolving. One by one. A million by a million." She gripped my hand. "Can you help?"

"I tried," I said. "I'll try again."

She nodded and released my hand, looking unconvinced. Then she leaned over and gathered her children into her arms, for a moment reminding me of a duck shielding her ducklings with her wings.

She kissed each daughter. "Do you want to come with us today?" she asked them.

The girls nodded eagerly.

"Come see me when you get back," I said. "Good-bye, girls. Have a good day, all."

Feeling uneasy, I left them. Whatever ailed them, I seemed unable to fix, and it appeared to be getting worse. What about the girls? They had the same ailment. And Stempler.

I rummaged around my cottage in the hope of discovering notes or old medical texts which might explain what was happening to these people. I found nothing. I made myself something to eat. Afterward, I searched Eden for Paula, but she was out. I offered my services at the mill and helped grind corn into meal. By midday, I knew something bad was going to happen, and I couldn't wait around any longer to see what it was.

I put food and water into my pack and went looking for the Booths. I wished Cosmo was with me; he could find them in an instant, or close to it. I traveled south into the desert for a while. Then I glanced back at Eden and the mesa and thought I saw a coyote on the ridge. I blinked, and it was gone. I was not one to ignore omens, so I turned and went north, skirting the village and hurrying up the path to the mesa top. The sun would drop soon, and I did not want to get caught up top at night.

The wind whipped around me when I got to the top, cooling my sweat and sending shivers through my body until my teeth chattered. I glimpsed the coyote again and followed it. I came to a lone twisted juniper, which clung to the edge of a split in the mesa top which created a chasm. As I stared into the abyss, I wondered what it was like to be that juniper tree, always on the brink of extinction. My gaze settled on a bright patch of green amongst the giant red boulders which failed to fill the chasm. I tried to identify what vegetation wore that shade of green—until I saw the green was attached to blue.

I groaned. Legs, arms, head. I squinted. Timothy. Near him. A splatter of color. Tricia.

"Timothy! Tricia!" No movement. "Lizbeth. Amy." I dropped to the ground, lay flat, and hung my head over the edge. "Hello!" I strained my eyes, hoping not to find the girls next to their dead parents.

I got up and turned around. "Lizbeth! Amy! It's Gloria." The wind snatched away the sound. I glanced about. No place to hide in the near vicinity. Ahead were the tops of several piñon-juniper. I hurried toward them, calling to the girls. I followed the path down. The wind lessened.

"Lizbeth, Amy!"

This time, I heard my voice spread out, echoing, reverberating back to me. Two bodies suddenly moved away from a tree I had just looked at. They had been a part of it, so still, and now, they were two children, crying as they ran to me.

I knelt on the ground and gathered them into my arms, just

like their mother had earlier, and held them tightly. I was so relieved to feel their warm living selves.

Eventually, all our breathing seemed to return to normal, and I looked at their dirty tear-streaked faces.

"They died," Lizbeth said.

Amy put her fingers in her mouth and stared at me.

"I know. Can you tell me what happened?"

"They said we were all going to fly away from this place," Lizbeth said. "But when they said 'three,' they jumped, and we stayed." The children stared off past my head.

"You did the right thing," I said.

"They said it would only work if all four of us did it," Lizbeth said, "but we didn't jump."

"Listen to me. Even if you had all stepped off that cliff, none of you would have flown! All of you would be dead."

Lizbeth looked back at my face. "Really?"

"Really."

I pulled off my pack and took a jug of water out of it. I handed it to Lizbeth.

"Go slow, sweetie." When she finished, she gave the water to her sister, who stared at it for a moment before drinking a bit. I gave them each two pumpkin cookies and insisted they eat them.

"Lizbeth, can you carry my pack?"

She lifted it easily. Good thing I had packed light.

"If you get tired, let me know. Amy, hop on my back." I turned around and the tiny girl put her arms around my neck; I took ahold of her legs and stood.

"We'll get down together. Don't worry."

I steered as far away from the chasm as I could without wasting time or getting too far off the path. By the time we got off the mesa and on level ground again, it was new moon dark. I could barely see my hand when I put it in front of my face. I stopped, squatted, and let Amy down. Then we all sat on the ground next to each other.

"Drink and eat whatever's in my pack," I said. "When the

stars come out, they'll give us some light to travel by." The girls huddled close to me and ate. I took a swig of water.

What had happened to Tricia and Timothy, and would the same thing happen to the girls? Stempler? They had all been near restricted areas. Something must be leaking. A chemical? Radiation?

"Look," Lizbeth said. "A light."

To the south, a light bobbed up and down in the distance. As I watched it, I wondered if this was a desert equivalent to ignis fatuus. Desert gas instead of swamp gas? More likely someone looking for us.

I stood and called, "Hello! Hello!" I waited. A moment later, I barely heard, "Hello."

"We're here!" I shouted. "Here!"

The girls clung to me. We watched the light come closer.

"Is it Mommy and Daddy's ghosts?" Lizbeth asked.

"No. It's probably Paula."

"Hello! Gloria!" Paula's voice.

"Paula!"

Soon, a group of villagers came out of the darkness and gathered around us.

"See, flesh-and-blood people," I told the girls.

"Are you all right?" Paula asked.

"Timothy and Tricia are dead," I said.

"What?" Paula said.

"They jumped. I'll give you details later. Right now we need to get the kids home."

Lizbeth caught hold of my hand and would not let go. Amy climbed onto my back again. When we reached Eden, the girls said they wanted to stay with me. I took them to my home, had them get into the pajamas Paula brought from their house, and tucked them into my bed.

When I was certain they were asleep, I stepped outside, where Paula and Daniel waited.

"So what happened?" Paula asked.

"I went to see them this morning," I said, "after our talk last night. I did a healing, but something was wrong with them that I knew I couldn't fix even though they seemed better when I finished the healing. They even wanted the kids to go out with them. As the day went on, I had a feeling something was wrong. I went looking for them, but I was too late. Timothy and Tricia were already dead. They had jumped into a ravine."

"The cleft on top, just off the path?" Daniel asked.

"Yes. Lizbeth said they wanted to fly. When they jumped, the girls remained mesa-bound. They're feeling a little guilty about that."

"You'll take care of the girls until we figure out what to do?" Paula asked.

"Sure."

"We'll retrieve the bodies in the morning," Daniel said. "What do you think was wrong with them? Why would they do it?"

I shrugged. "Unfortunately, I know three other people who have the same condition. Two of them are sleeping in my bed."

I said good night and went back inside. I listened to the girls' deep breathing for a while, then made a bed on the floor next to them and went to sleep.

In the morning, I was awakened by a knock on the door. Several people came in bearing gifts. Genevieve, one of the village elders, showed me precious eggs and whispered that the chicken had laid them especially for the girls. It was somewhat of a miracle given the time of the year. She fired up my woodstove; I used it only occasionally and reluctantly because I hated putting out any air pollution.

"We have lots of filters on our stoves," she reassured me. "Don't worry." She fried the eggs. Roberto cooked pancakes. Another woman put out pies and a loaf of bread.

The girls awakened slowly and seemed reassured rather than frightened by the intrusion. They dressed themselves, made the bed, then came and stood by me.

"Momma and Daddy died," Amy said. These were the first words she had spoken since I found them yesterday on the mesa top.

"Yes," I agreed.

"And we'll have a ceremony for them today," Genevieve said. "We're sorry for not knowing how ill your parents were." She gently guided the girls to the chairs. "You need to eat."

I sat with the girls while Genevieve and Roberto served us. Although I still lacked any will or desire to eat, I forced myself so the girls would follow my example. The girls watched me for a moment and then began eating with enthusiasm.

Afterward the good neighbors cleaned up, put casseroles in the oven to heat slowly, and left us alone.

"How are you feeling today?" I asked the girls.

"Do you remember your mother and father?" Lizbeth asked, not answering my question.

I shook my head.

"I remember my mom used to laugh," Lizbeth said.

"Do you remember when she stopped?" I asked.

"When she fell into the hole," Amy said.

"I mean before yesterday, sweetheart."

"No, Gloria," Lizbeth said. She rolled her eyes. "Before, when we all fell in the hole. Or it fell on us." She frowned.

I had no idea what she was talking about.

Lizbeth sighed, sounding slightly exasperated with my ignorance. "When we got sick. Before you came."

I nodded. I was a little slow this morning. "When you were at the restricted area."

"Yes. There were other people there, too," Lizbeth said.

"You remember that?"

Both girls nodded.

"Did they go to the mesa top to get Mom and Dad yet?" Lizbeth asked.

"I'm sure they're doing that." I squeezed her arm. "Don't worry." What a stupid thing to say to two children who had just become orphans.

"We better get clothes to wear to the ceremony." Lizbeth pushed away from the table and took her sister's hand. She looked up at me. "Will you come, too?"

"Of course." She grasped my hand, too, and solemnly led us outside and to her empty house.

Lizbeth hesitated on the threshold, then went inside. Together, the girls neatly folded clothes and put them into their packs, along with a few other personal possessions. Then Lizbeth opened cupboards and took out jars of jelly, jams, fruits, and vegetables and carefully placed them in a box. *Waste not, want not.*

"Can you carry this?" Lizbeth asked me, indicating the box.

"Yes."

"We're ready to leave then," she said.

Amy grabbed a doll from her bed and nodded in agreement.

I glanced around. "Would you rather stay here?" I asked. "I could stay with you."

Lizbeth looked at her sister, then at me. "No, we want to live with you."

"All right," I said. "Let's go home."

The girls put on their best clothes and waited for the ceremony. When the preparer came, Amy gave her the doll; Lizbeth gave her a piece of her mother's jewelry. Before we left my house, Lizbeth cut off a lock of her white blond hair and kept it firmly in her hand. Then we went outside where the others waited. Chanting, we all walked to the burial grounds. We sang thanks to the Earth as the hole was dug. The girls kissed the bruised faces of their parents before their wrapped bodies were lowered into the ground together.

"May the Earth accept Tricia and Timothy back into herself. Dust to dust. Ashes to ashes."

Just before we poured the dirt over the bodies, Lizbeth held her tightly closed hand over the grave. Her hand opened. The lock of hair slowly fell toward her parents' bodies. I wanted to snatch the hair away. Lizbeth should not bury any of herself with them. She should be free of this tragedy. But she was not, and I did nothing. It was her wish. The hair landed on Tricia's breast where her heart no longer beat. Then dirt covered the hair and the bodies, and we all turned away.

The community gathered together at the center to eat and mourn. The girls played quietly with other children until it was time to go home. At my house again at the end of a long day, Lizbeth and Amy wearily took off their clothes and put on pajamas. They were quiet and serious, unlike their vivacious selves who had followed me around for weeks chattering and asking endless questions about herbs and tinctures.

They climbed into bed, and I pulled the covers up to their shoulders.

"Can you tell us a story about when you were a little girl?" Lizbeth asked.

Amy turned and snuggled close to her sister. "Yeah, can you?"

"I'm sorry, but I don't remember being a girl."

"Were you a boy?" Amy asked.

I laughed. "No. I just don't remember my childhood."

"Me, neither," Lizbeth said.

"What do you mean?" I asked.

"I don't have childhood memories either," she said, stumbling over the word "childhood."

My heart skipped a beat. I remembered Tricia saying she was having trouble with her memory before she killed herself. Stempler, too.

"Girls, I want to do a healing on you. May I?"

Both nodded.

I rubbed my hands and then laid them on Lizbeth. We connected. A wall of grief. I did not touch this: it was hers to process. I went deeper. I found a white hole. Only it did not seem as big as it had been and it was not expanding as it had in her parents. Then I moved my hands over to Amy. Same thing. Good. At least for now, they were safe.

"You're still a child," I said, moving my hands away. "You can make new childhood memories."

"Not with my parents I can't," she said.

"I know," I said. "How about a coyote story? Will that do as a bedtime story?"

The sisters smiled for the first time since their parents had leaped to their deaths.

"Tell us a coyote story," Amy said. "I like coyotes."

"Me, too," I said. "Let's see. Our coyote's name is Cosmo, and he is quite a trickster."

As I told the story, I watched the girls' intent faces and hoped their parents had felt as though they were flying when they stepped off that edge. I hoped they had soared on the thermals to whatever lay beyond, and I was grateful their children had elected to remain behind, with me.

Eight

Since the days were short, dark, and cold, I stayed close to home and the girls stayed close to me.

When the council met one evening, the girls consented to let Genevieve care for them so I could attend.

We sat around a low fire and prayed to the directions and the elements. Then I told them I could not commit to staying in Eden. "I need to find out what killed Tricia and Timothy, and what hurt the girls."

"Is it contagious?" someone asked.

"I don't believe so," I said. "You all have been living with the Booths for weeks, and no one else is ill. I do recommend, however, that no one go anywhere near a restricted area. That seems to be where it began."

"So what will you do?" Daniel asked.

"I'll see how the girls progress," I said. "If their condition remains stable, I'll either go to the governor or investigate myself."

"Are you going to leave the girls behind?" Roberto asked. "They are very attached to you."

"As a community," Paula said, "we have agreed to care for

them until they are adults, but I believe they'll want to go with you."

"I think you're right," I said.

When I got home, Lizbeth and Amy rushed me and wrapped their arms around my waist. I thanked Genevieve for watching them. She said good night and left.

I sat at the table, and Amy climbed onto my lap and laid her head against my breasts. I rocked her while she hummed quietly.

"Did they decide what to do with us?" Lizbeth asked.

"The people of Eden will care for you as long as you like," I answered.

"Can we stay with you?" Lizbeth asked.

"Do you have grandparents or any other relatives living somewhere else?"

Lizbeth put her finger on her chin and thought for a moment. "I can't remember. But if we stayed with you, we could help you out. We can pick herbs and cook and clean and help little kids when they're afraid."

I picked up the now-sleeping Amy and carried her to the bed. Lizbeth pulled down the covers, I laid her sister down, and she pulled the covers up over her. Then she climbed into her own bed.

"We could do lots of things for you," she said.

"Sweetie, you don't have to do anything. You don't have to sing for your supper. Here, get under the covers. It's just that I travel a lot, and I'm used to being alone."

"We could be very quiet."

I kissed her forehead. "No, I want you to be yourselves. I like having you here, but you need full-time parenting, and I'm not a parent."

"You're a good mother," Lizbeth said.

"I'm not a mother. Go to sleep. Sweet dreams."

She sighed, reached up, and hugged my neck, then slid down into sleep.

I dreamed of the numbers and letters again. This time they were etched on Church's forehead. He lay dead and rotting on the floor of the Grand Canyon next to Cosmo. Above them, Primer stood laughing with his arms outstretched.

In the morning, the children ate leftovers. I drank tea and wondered if I would ever be hungry again.

The day was warm and clear. I packed lunch and water and took the girls on a hike. We wandered north over the desert and up into the woodlands. From the forest floor, Amy gathered colorful leaves dropped from sumac, ash, aspen, and oak. Lizbeth ran through the woods, her arms spread wide. As I watched her, I thought of my dream and heard Primer's laugh again.

I shook away the memory and leaned against a birch and watched the girls. Had I collected leaves when I was a girl? Or whirled around the woods? Had I wept for my dead parents or had they mourned me when I disappeared?

Amy ran to me. "Don't you want to play?" she asked, holding her treasured leaves carefully and looking up at me.

"Okay," I said. "What are we playing?"

Lizbeth twirled over to us. "You pick."

I nodded: she had forgotten her childhood games.

"Let's play nymphs," I said.

"What are nymphs?" Lizbeth asked.

"Nymphs are spirits of nature," I said, "fairies or witches who have embedded their souls in part of nature so they wouldn't forget that all of nature is part of Fairyland, the Motherland."

"I know where Fairyland is," Amy said.

"Where?" Lizbeth asked.

"Here and over there," she said.

I laughed. She remembered my healing story. "That's right," I said. "So pick what part of nature you want to become and then act just like it."

Amy put her collected leaves inside the pack. Then she clapped her hands together once and said, "I want to be a rock." She ran to a large gray rock. She sat on the ground, put her back to the stone, and rested her hands on her knees.

Lizbeth ran to a tall birch whose top moved in the wind.

She stood facing it, head up, and swayed when the wind rattled its leaves and bent its branches.

I looked around. What part of nature did I want to let my spirit rest against?

I glanced up. The trees arched over my head and created a cathedral ceiling of colorful leaves. A church of leaves.

Church. He was the part of nature I wanted to embed my soul on.

But he had left me.

I would make a good coyote.

Or a fox.

Invisible. Camouflaged by stillness. No. Still I was not.

I looked south. Below us, unseen at present, the desert spread, the desert that had once been the bed to an ancient sea long dried away. I lay on the forest floor and closed my eyes. I imagined the ocean covering my body, rolling over me in waves, undulating a sea of life over me. Apart from it, a part of it.

Separate. I was always separate. From *"se"* meaning a part and *"parare"* to make ready, prepare. Did that mean to prepare to be a part of or apart from?

How could I remember cognates of words but not my own cognates, my own ancestors? My history.

I heard the rustle of leaves and felt something light fall on me. I opened my eyes. The girls stood over me, letting leaves float from their fingers down onto my body. For a moment I was reminded of Lizbeth's lock of hair falling onto her mother's breasts. Back and forth. Slowly. Falling.

I was cocooned. Cocooning. I could close my eyes and sleep and sleep.

Instead, I reached up quickly and grabbed each girl. They squealed and dropped onto me. I tickled them and they me until tears rolled down my cheeks.

"Stop! Stop!" I cried. They relented, and I lay exhausted, panting for breath.

"That was fun," Amy said.

I sat up and brushed off the leaves.

"Yes, it was," I said.

"See," Lizbeth said, pulling me up. "You remember how to be a kid."

"You do, too."

Suddenly, we all noticed a man standing away from us, watching. The girls moved behind me. I squinted.

"Benjamin?"

He walked toward us.

"It's okay, girls," I said.

Benjamin. Stay calm, I told myself, stay calm.

He smiled.

I ran to him and nearly leaped into his arms. At the same time, he dropped his walking stick and pack and wrapped his arms tightly around me.

"Where have you been?" I asked when I finally pulled away.

His eyes were full of tears. "I'd like to ask you the same thing." He looked down at the girls who were now beside us. "I remember these young ladies, Lizbeth and Amy."

"This is Benjamin," I said. "You met him when I came and healed you the first time, but you may not remember. You were pretty sick."

The girls each held out their right hand for Benjamin to shake, which he did with great seriousness.

"I am glad to see you again," he said.

I put my arm around his waist. "We were playing," I said. "Would you care to join us?"

"*You* were playing?"

"I'm a changed woman," I said.

"I need to talk to you about something."

"Okay. Girls, why don't you eat lunch. Benjamin and I will be right over here."

The girls nodded and went over to my pack and began pulling out food. Benjamin and I sat on the rock Amy had been.

"Where were you?" I asked.

"At the dances," he said. "I got back to Freedom and Coyote Creek and all hell had broken loose. My sister said you'd come by—half-gone, she described you—and told her you might be going to the Grand Canyon. So I went there. You hadn't been back. I went all over the area. Then I checked Stempler's. He's really sick. Louis and Barbara said he tried to kill himself. After the suicide attempt, he kept asking for you. He's lost a lot of his memory. Then I remembered Eden and knew you had to be here."

I glanced at the girls. They had relaxed enough to talk to each other without watching us.

"I want you to come back and see Stempler," Benjamin said.

"They fired me," I said. "Without cause. I have no obligation to any of them. Why doesn't the new healer go to him?"

"She's been. She can't do anything. Besides, he asks for you."

"I can't help him either," I said. "I already tried."

"He says he needs to speak with you."

"He's a mean old fuck."

"So?"

I shook my head. "Is someone with him now?"

"Angel."

"Angel? That dumb kid who was in love with Church?"

"Just because someone is kind does not make them stupid."

"Sorry. I didn't mean to insult your girlfriend," I said.

He clenched his jaw.

"I'm sorry," I said. My stomach balled into a knot.

"Stempler is asking for you," Benjamin said. "He doesn't have anything to do with Coyote Creek or what happened there."

"I'd like to go to Stempler, but these girls' parents just died, and they've kind of imprinted on me. Or I'm imprinted on them, however that goes."

Benjamin smiled. "They've imprinted on you? Like ducks?"

"Kind of. They lost their memory. Like Stempler and their parents. The parents killed themselves."

"And Stempler tried to kill himself. You think it's all related?"

"I don't think it's coincidence," I said. "I'll try to arrange something for the girls, and we can leave tomorrow." I hesitated. Weeks ago, Benjamin and I had parted lovers. Now? "Do you want to stay with me tonight?"

"If that would be all right," he said.

"Sure, we'd love it." I stood. "Girls, it's time to go back."

They nodded and began putting their half-eaten food back into the pack. When they finished, Lizbeth handed the pack to me, and I put it on.

"Thank you, trees," Lizbeth said.

"Thank you, rock," Amy said.

"Thank you, Earth," I said, "and sea."

They giggled. I laughed. We linked hands, and swinging our arms, we started home. Benjamin looked at me as if I were crazy, but he followed us.

At my house, Benjamin stood in the door while the girls bounced on the three beds and then chased each other outside.

"You've got quite a little family here," he said, sounding almost resentful.

I leaned over the stove, opened it, and moved the embers until a fire caught. Then Benjamin and I sat next to each other at the table.

"Are you going to tell me what's been going on?" Benjamin asked.

"It's been a terrible time," I said. "First the Coyote Creek epidemic."

"I'm sorry I wasn't there," he said. "If I'd known it was so bad, I wouldn't have left."

"After I did all those healings, something happened to me. It was like I had been struck by lightning and was melting. When I touched anyone or anyone touched me, everything got weird. We figured out everyone got sick because Primer poisoned our water. On the way to Grand Canyon to tell the governor what Primer had done, Church and I stopped by Stempler's and got snowed in."

"You and Church?"

"It's a long story." I hesitated and then said, "He's really a very nice man."

Benjamin glanced at me.

"You and Church?" he said again.

I took his hand. "It surprised me, too, but we were able to talk about so many things."

"I don't need the details," he said, pulling away his hand.

In the five years Benjamin and I had known one another, we had not been monogamous. At least I had not been. I wondered why he was upset now.

"Are you in love with him?" Benjamin asked.

"It doesn't matter anymore," I said. "He's gone, and I killed Primer."

Benjamin stared at me.

Suddenly I felt panicky. "He just died, in the middle of a healing. He killed Cosmo, and I killed him. I was furious. Raging!"

"You don't rage," Benjamin said.

"You didn't think I played either until you saw evidence to the contrary today."

"I've seen you laugh with the same kind of delight I saw today, but I have never seen you lose your temper."

"I didn't lose it. I found it! Church apparently saw the whole thing and decided I was evil incarnate and he left me. He just left."

"From what Angel told me, that doesn't sound like something he would do."

"No, I didn't think so either, but—" I stopped. But what?

"You didn't go after him?"

"By the time I got to Coyote Creek, he was gone. The council fired me because I was suddenly a danger to the community. Someone was already living in my house, and you were gone." I stopped again and took a deep breath.

Benjamin leaned over and kissed the top of my head.

"I'm sorry," he said. "You haven't had an easy time."

"You either."

"Why didn't you wait for me in Freedom?"

"I was in shock. Or I was shocked. I was stunned. I had killed someone. Cosmo was dead. I'd been kicked out of job and home. And Church. He'd left me because of the horrible thing I had done. I couldn't just stay still and wait for you, to see you look at me as if I were some kind of defective human being."

"Instead you ran away and hid out here feeling sorry for yourself."

"I've been trying to figure out what to do with the rest of my life."

He shook his head. "No. You waited here to see who would come looking for you. Who loved you best."

He sounded bitter.

Lizbeth ran into the house. "Dottie wants us to come over and play. Can we? Her parents will make dinner."

"Of course," I said, surprised.

Lizbeth kissed my cheek. "Thanks!" Then she kissed Benjamin's cheek. " 'Bye!"

I smiled. She was a sly little thing, too knowledgeable for her age. Amy dashed in, kissed me, and then Dottie, Lizbeth, and Amy ran away. Children were always in such a hurry. Had I raced away from our home when I was a child so my parents could be alone?

"They are beautiful children," Benjamin said.

"Are you hungry?"

He shook his head. "I haven't been hungry in a long time."

"Me neither."

He laughed. "That I do not believe."

I kissed his mouth. He pulled me onto his lap.

"How come you could talk to Church and not with me?" he whispered.

"I talked with you."

He shook his head, then laid it against my breasts. I put my arms around him, and we rocked each other.

After a few minutes, we got up and slowly took off our clothes and lay on my bed. Benjamin kissed my neck, my ears, my stomach: all the places he had always kissed. The more he touched me, the more adrenaline shot my stomach with fear and nausea. We kissed, and I pulled him close, so our breasts pressed against one another. His movements were tender, yet I felt pieces of my life falling away. I had thought once I found Benjamin again, once we were in each other's arms, all would be well; I would be able to let the hurt of Church's desertion go. None of it would matter. But as Benjamin's fingers stroked my skin, I felt the pain more intensely than I had before. I wanted *Church*'s fingers. *His* body. *His* voice.

Benjamin gently fit into me. We were perfect together. I loved him deeply, yet I felt numb. I looked at his eyes. His tears dropped onto my face, mingled with my own tears, then rolled down my cheeks and onto my neck.

"Do you want to stop?" he asked.

I shook my head.

He moved slowly. I watched his face and pressed my fingers against his back. If I had known making love with Church that night at Stempler's would mean losing Benjamin, I would have never done it. If I had known loving Church would mean shattering all that was familiar, I would not have loved him.

I would have tried not to love him.

Benjamin put his face in my neck. We had never made love like this: *I* had never made love like this. Without passion. I had the desire, but it was not registering in my body.

"Gloria?"

"I'm here," I whispered. "It's good just to be close."

I thought of the last time Church and I had made love in the lodge at the edge of the Grand Canyon. Up against the wall, then tumbling, laughing, to the floor.

I held Benjamin tighter. I breathed his familiar scent. His breath quickened; he pushed deeper into me. Then he gently fell against me. I wrapped my arms around him, and we held each other until we stopped crying.

Then we curled around each other.

"I love you," I said.

"I love you, too," Benjamin said.

"I didn't know this would happen," I whispered. "You always encouraged me to open up and cultivate intimacy."

"I meant with me."

I turned to face him. "Everything hurts. I've never felt like this. Like I just keep getting kicked in the face."

"Shhh. You don't have to think about anything now. Just go to sleep."

I closed my eyes and fell to sleep in Benjamin's arms.

Nine

When I awakened, it was morning. Benjamin and the girls sat at the table eating and talking quietly. They looked completely natural and at ease with one another. I wondered if this was what it was like to have a family.

Amy glanced over at me, saw I was awake, and grinned. In another second, the girls jumped out of their chairs, raced across the room, and hopped onto the bed.

"Good morning, good morning," Lizbeth said, bouncing on the bed.

"Benjamin tucked us in last night and told us a story," Amy said.

"Good for him."

"Weren't you cold with no clothes on?" Amy asked.

Oops.

"Benjamin kept her warm, silly," Lizbeth said.

The girls giggled.

"Let me get dressed now," I said.

They jumped up and ran out of the house screaming each other's names.

I got out of bed and pulled on my clothes. Benjamin watched, smiling.

"You are quite beautiful," he said.

I kissed his lips. "Thank you. So are you. Thanks for letting me sleep. The girls seem in good spirits. They must like you."

"They don't see me as a threat."

"Little do they know." I went to the door. "Girls, come in here. I want to talk with you."

They raced back inside. Breathless, they stood side by side gazing up at me. I sat at the table so my face was nearly level with theirs.

"Girls, someone is sick back where I used to live, and I need to go take care of him."

They nodded, still smiling.

"I'm leaving today."

"How long will we be gone?" Lizbeth asked.

"Sweetie, you can't come. It's a long trip, and it could snow."

Liz and Amy linked hands.

"It'd be safer if you stayed here," I said.

They stared at me. I glanced at Benjamin. He shrugged. I looked out the door. The sky was blue and clear for as far as I could see. Of course, that meant nothing about the conditions on Stempler's mountain.

"I don't know when I'll be back," I said.

Their eyes widened.

I sighed. "Benjamin?"

"Fine with me."

"Okay," I said. "We'll try it."

The girls grinned.

"Pack light. Food, water, and a couple changes of clothing. Do you have good sturdy walking shoes?"

The girls nodded and each held up a shod foot.

"All right. We're leaving in ten minutes."

They ran to their respective beds and pulled their packs from underneath.

"They've got you wrapped around their little fingers," Benjamin said.

I stuck out my tongue at him. He laughed.

"I'd feel better if they were close anyway," I said. "Maybe I can keep them from taking a flying leap."

Benjamin stood and put his arms around me. I rested my head against his chest.

When I lifted my head again, he kissed me, his tongue touching mine. I felt a flicker of desire.

Lizbeth cleared her throat. Benjamin and I moved apart.

"We're ready," Lizbeth said.

"Hang on. I need to tell Paula, and then we'll be off."

The day was clear and cool. With frequent breaks and a slower pace, the girls were able to keep up with us. At lunch, they fell asleep. Benjamin and I sat with our backs against one another and ate. I watched the girls sleep and let the autumn breeze stroke my hair until I almost went to sleep, too.

"This is very nice," I said. "I am quite contented." For this moment, the ache I had felt last night was gone. "I should have gotten a family a long time ago."

"I offered."

"I guess I never heard you," I said. "Is the offer still open now that I can provide you with two children?"

"Not until you've got all the facts."

I scooted around until we faced one another. "What facts?"

"I just think you need to wait until you see Stempler and Angel."

"Angel?" I said. "What's she got to do with my life?"

"She'll tell you when you see her."

"Benjamin!"

He sighed. "I'd rather you talk to her. But you're not going to stop pestering me until I tell you, are you?"

I shook my head.

"Angel went after Church."

"So? I knew that."

"She couldn't find him. He didn't go home like he said he

would in his letter. She met a cousin of his who had seen him, though."

"And?" This was worse than extracting a deeply embedded sliver from a mountain lion's foot, a procedure I had performed.

"Church didn't recognize his cousin."

I blinked. "What do you mean?"

"He appeared to have had a dramatic loss of memory."

I groaned. My mind raced. Church had what Stempler and the girls had. What Tricia and Timothy had before they leaped to their deaths. My heart pounded in my ears, the sound like an ocean, roaring.

"Is-is he alive?"

"We don't know. The cousin saw him for a day or two after Church left Coyote Creek, and then he disappeared."

"That was over a month ago." I closed my eyes.

Maybe this meant Church had not left me. Maybe the letter he wrote had been a mistake.

Maybe it meant he was dead.

I put my head in my hands.

"I'm sorry," Benjamin said.

"None of this is your fault," I said. "If Church has the same illness as Stempler, he's got to be found for his own safety, and he has to be found now."

My sense of urgency quickened. What had I been doing for weeks hiding out in Eden? I should have gone after Church. I had thought something was peculiar about it all, but I had done nothing.

I gently shook awake the girls. I put Amy on my back, and we continued our journey. After a while, she got down and followed Benjamin across the desert. Lizbeth was quiet next to me, perhaps sensing my need for silence. I reached for her hand and pointed out turkey vultures and hawks. She showed me faint tracks in the dirt where a coyote had walked.

We climbed Stern Mountain in darkness. Both Benjamin and I had gone up and down this path so many times we could practically do it with our eyes closed, which was the effect of the pitch-darkness. Normally I would have chastised others for doing anything so foolhardy as to climb a mountain at night, but the incline was easy and Stempler's house not far up. Barbara and Louis heard us coming and brought out a lantern to light the way. I could actually see better without the artificial illumination, but I did not say anything and accepted their help graciously. They left us at Stempler's door.

The four of us went into the firelit house. The girls stood quietly just inside, exhausted and uncomplaining.

Angel turned from the counter, smiled, and came to me. I embraced her, and she held me as if she meant it, as if she had real affection for me. I wondered how people were able to connect with others with such little effort. Maybe if I watched Angel for long enough, I would learn something.

"Angel," I said, releasing her and turning to the children, "this is Amy and Lizbeth. They are very tired."

"Hello, Amy and Lizbeth. Hi, Benjamin. I've made soup. Why don't you both eat a little of that, and I'll make up a place for you to sleep."

"Thanks, Angel," I said.

"Stempler's up in the loft," she said.

"You okay, girls?" I asked. They nodded sleepily. They would not stay awake through the soup.

I glanced at Benjamin, then climbed the steps to Stempler's bed. I could not see him, but I heard his breathing.

"Stempler?"

"Healer."

"Yes, it's me." I sat on the edge of the bed and felt his big old body next to me radiating heat. "I heard you're having a rough time."

"You heard I tried to leap into the arms of the many-breasted priestess."

I had felt the urge to dive headlong into Beauty Valley myself on occasion.

"So what happened?" I asked.

"It just feels so lonely," he said.

"Stempler, you've been alone all your life."

"Have I? I can't remember. But if it's true, that's sad."

"What else don't you remember?"

"When I was a kid," he answered.

"I don't remember when I was a child either, but I've never tried to kill myself."

"I felt like I was falling into myself," he said. "Dissolving, muddy."

"Do you want a healing?"

"First, I've got to tell you. I remembered some weird stuff."

"Like what?"

He breathed heavily. I put my hand out for a healing, and he grabbed my wrist. "Wait. I don't want to lose it. I keep getting flashes of things I'd forgotten. Like you. I remember you. Only you were different. About fifteen years ago or more. Different hair and skin. Even a different name. Sarah. I think. But I'm sure it was you. You cussed me out just like you did a few weeks ago. Only I was younger and better-looking. That's why I've been able to tolerate you so well these past years."

"Stempler, you've never been able to stand me!"

"No, no. I've always found your company tolerable. And it's because I knew you from before. Only I didn't know it."

"I don't understand," I said. "I remind you of this Sarah?"

"No. Listen to me. It's all fading. You are Sarah. Only I didn't recognize you."

"Settle down. May I?"

"Yes," he whispered, giving in to me.

I placed my hands on him. We connected. The light was devouring him. I tried to dim it, to spread comforting blackness.

I removed my hands.

"Terrifying, isn't it?" he said.

"Yes," I answered quietly. "Do you feel any better?"

"A little." He grasped my arm tightly again. "You were looking for something. Or someplace. A code."

"A code?"

"I think so. You said it would solve the problem. You were being followed. You went up north in search of some kind of enclave of soothsayers. When you didn't come back, I went looking for you. I bunked in a little cottage right at the foot of the two mountains. At the V."

That sounded like the cottage I had stayed in when I first left Coyote Creek. Wasn't life full of little coincidences?

"I even found the soothsayers, or they found me, but you weren't there."

"Stempler, I am not Sarah," I said, "and you need to sleep."

He squeezed my arm.

"Take it easy," I said.

"She kept dreaming. What was it? Numbers and letters. A sequence of numbers and letters."

I stared at Stempler's dark outline. How had he known about my dream?

"Sarah," he whispered. "Gloria, please, help me. I don't mind dying, but this is like being devoured."

"Sleep. Let me try and figure this out."

He slowly released his hold on my arm. I put my hand on his forehead and sent him healing energy. When he was asleep, I went downstairs.

The children were sleeping, too. Angel and Benjamin sat at the table, drinking something hot. The steam curled around their faces.

"Benjamin, I need that other soothsayer," I said. "Can you ask Barbara or Louis to get her from Coyote Creek?"

"Sure," he said. He got up, put on his coat, and went outside. I sat next to Angel.

"Benjamin told me Church has been spotted, and he's lost his memory," I said. "We have to find him. He's in great danger."

Her eyes flooded with tears. "I know, I know. But how?"

"We need to get word to his family to search for him. Or maybe the council in Coyote Creek will get together a search party."

"He could be anywhere."

"He was staying with someone, and then he disappeared?"

She nodded and wiped her eyes. "A cousin found him wandering near Red Bluffs and took him home. He was with them for a day or two. He seemed to get better. They even took him to the circus. Remember, he ran off with that traveling religious show when he was younger? So his cousin thought it would jog his memory. Instead, he got lost in the crowd, and they never found him again."

"Maybe he ran away with the circus again?"

"No," she said. "His cousin checked with the circus people. There's more. I don't think Church wrote that letter."

"What do you mean?"

"When I'd calmed down a little after you left," she said, "I realized I didn't really know his handwriting."

"Your note had the same handwriting as mine," I said.

"Which only means the same person wrote them both."

Benjamin was right: she was not stupid. So how come I was? Why hadn't I questioned any of this weeks ago?

"I went through his papers and journals," she said. "Things I was certain he had actually written. That resignation letter had different handwriting from his."

"So who wrote it?"

She shrugged. "The most likely person is the one who supposedly brought Church back to Coyote Creek. Terry? No one saw Church, you know. They only saw Terry, the woman sent by the governor."

I heard a fluttering of wings, a whirring sound. I rubbed my forehead.

Benjamin came in with a burst of cold air. One of the girls moaned. I glanced over; they remained asleep.

Benjamin shook off his jacket and stood, for a moment, with his hands in front of the fire. Then he sat with us.

"Benjamin," I said, "do you think the governor has something to do with all of this?"

He shrugged. "Primer poisoned the river. Church mysteriously disappeared after being with the governor. You went crazy and killed someone."

"I did not go crazy."

"Stempler was around a restricted area when he got ill, and the restricted areas are the governor's responsibility," he said.

"And the Booths got ill after an encounter in a restricted area," I said. "But why would the governor or his people want Church and me separated? Or Church gone from Coyote Creek? It doesn't make sense. I was with those people. They seemed very kind and dedicated."

"I don't care who or why," Angel said. "I just want to find Thomas."

"I agree," I said.

"Stempler came home after he got sick," Benjamin said, "and you said the Booths kept going to Eden. Wouldn't it make sense that Church would gravitate toward someplace familiar?"

"But he didn't return to Coyote Creek," I said, "or if he did, he didn't stay."

"I think he would try to find you," Angel said.

Benjamin and I looked at her.

"What do you mean?" I asked.

She glanced at Benjamin, then gazed at her hands. "He was in love with you."

"You knew that?" I said.

Benjamin laughed. Angel smiled halfheartedly. "Everyone knew."

"Except you," Benjamin said.

"And I read his journals," she said. "Just a little to see about the handwriting—and a bit more. I couldn't help it. He made it very clear he loved you."

"Where would he go to look for me?" I asked. "Not back to the Grand Canyon, I hope."

They said nothing. I listened to the fire crackle.

After a few minutes, Angel slowly got up from the table. "I'm exhausted. I've got to sleep."

I looked up at her as she passed by. She leaned down and kissed my cheek, then left us for her bedroll in the corner.

"What did Stempler say?" Benjamin asked me.

"He said he knew me fifteen years ago," I said, "only my name was Sarah, and I looked completely different. I thought he was raving until he mentioned this Sarah dreamed a sequence of numbers and letters like I do. She went up north looking for a group of soothsayers."

"Wow."

"Yeah."

"So what are you going to do?" he asked.

"What should I do? Stempler, Amy, and Lizbeth need care and supervision, and Church needs to be found."

"What will you do when you find him? You don't know how to cure this."

"Then I guess I better find a cure."

Ten

In the morning, Angel took the girls outside to play, so they would not disturb Stempler. I watched them from the house. Angel played easily and naturally with them, not having to stop and contemplate what to do next, as I often did.

"Good morning, healer," Stempler said as he came down the stairs.

"Good morning," I answered.

"Do you want something to eat?" Benjamin asked.

Stempler shook his head. "I heard laughter. It woke me."

"I brought a couple of parentless children with me," I said. "They have what you have."

"What do I have?"

"No memory."

"Wouldn't it be more accurate to say they don't have what I don't have?"

"Got me there, old man."

He shuffled outside, sat in a chair, and watched the children and Angel, a smile curling his wrinkled cheeks.

"I never would have imagined Stempler genial," Benjamin said, coming up behind me.

"Illness changes people, every time, even if it is only for the duration of the sickness."

I passed the morning waiting for the soothsayer from Coyote Creek. The others busied themselves playing or preparing food and eating it. Stempler actually showed Amy and Lizbeth some of his gadgets.

After a lunch of sandwiches, Benjamin opened the door to the soothsayer.

"Hello," she said, "I'm Clarity. Barbara said you needed me?"

Benjamin motioned her inside. She looked over at me and seemed to know me instantly. She was brown-haired, brown-eyed, medium height. I watched her and thought, "So this is what a soothsayer looks like."

"Healer Stone," she said, coming across the room with her hand extended. Our fingers touched. I quickly squeezed her hand, then let it go.

"Thank you for coming," I said. "I thought maybe the two of us could stop what is happening to Stempler."

She nodded.

Benjamin said, "Amy, Lizbeth, let's take a walk. Angel, you want to come?"

"Sure."

"Dress warm," I said. "It's getting cold."

"Yes, Mom," Benjamin said, rolling his eyes.

"I was talking to the children, but if the shoe fits."

They put on their coats. Amy ran to me and jumped up. I caught her, we kissed, and she dropped down again. Then out the door they piled.

" 'Bye," Lizbeth called.

Stempler sat in his rocking chair, quietly watching it all.

"Do you want me to go upstairs?" he asked.

"Are you comfortable here?" I asked.

"If I was, I wouldn't need you."

"Shut up, you old fart."

Clarity raised her eyebrows. Stempler chuckled.

"Let's do it," I said. I was curious to see how she healed,

but I did not want to give her a chance to take over. She had, after all, already stolen my job.

"Okay, be still, old man." I put one hand on his head, the other on his shoulder. Clarity did the same. I closed my eyes. In an instant, I connected with him and her. She was running through a field, with Queen Anne's lace snapping at her legs. Then the white hole loomed.

"I want to close this hole," I said.

"How do you know it shouldn't be opened farther?" Clarity asked.

"Because two people with bigger white lights are dead."

More light. Stempler was dissolving. And a piece of darkness. Another piece. Another. It was working! Yes. I heard Stempler sigh. Clarity seemed to have more control than I—or else we had more control together. It was like putting up a brick wall in high speed.

Then a flash of Stempler's memory. Falling into a hole. The bricks started coming off. I could almost see the hands pulling them down.

Stempler's breathing became shallow. I knew instantly what was happening. I opened my eyes and pushed Clarity away from Stempler.

"What are you doing?" she cried.

I quickly put my hands back on Stempler.

Benjamin opened the door and came in. "You need help?"

I stared at Clarity. "You put your hands on him again and help me repair the damage you've done, or I will hunt you down and kill you while you sleep."

"Don't think she won't do it," Benjamin said.

"I don't know what you're talking about," Clarity said. "I *was* helping."

"Shut up," I said. "Put your hands on him."

She hesitated, then did as she was told. I felt her connect, felt the energy swerve and bounce. I knew I could turn it all back on her and hurt her. She looked into my eyes and seemed to know it, too. The hole began to get smaller. Smaller.

"All right," I said, keeping my hands on Stempler, "get away from him."

Clarity stepped back.

After a minute or so, I dropped my hands from Stempler's body. He looked up at me and grinned.

"You are a nasty woman," he said, "but you do make me feel better!"

"You're not cured," I said, "but you're all right for now. Don't ever let this woman touch you again."

Stempler slapped his hands against the rocker and got up. "I'll start dinner. I'm starved."

"If you were starved, you'd be dead, old man," I said.

"Yeah, yeah, you got me there." He waved a hand of dismissal and went to the kitchen.

Clarity put her hands on her hips. "I demand to know what is going on here."

I folded my arms across my chest. "How did you happen to end up in Coyote Creek?"

"I was passing through," she said. "What business is that of yours?"

I laughed. "There are how many soothsayers on this entire continent, and you just happened to wander into my town while I was gone?"

"Yes. The council heard some disturbing things about you and asked me to fill in."

"You came from the Grand Canyon, didn't you? That was the last place you worked. The governor sent you to Coyote Creek."

She shook her head. "No."

"You tried to kill Stempler."

"She what?" Stempler called.

"I did no such thing!"

"You tried to sabotage his healing. It's the same thing."

"I guess they were right," she said. "You do have a few screws loose. I'm leaving."

I stepped across her path and stood inches from her face.

"If I find out you've hurt anyone in Coyote Creek, the governor will not be able to protect you. I will find you."

Suddenly, she looked frightened. She went around me, pushed past Benjamin, and was gone.

"That was an exercise in futility," Benjamin said.

"Not really," I said. "When she was cooperating, we made headway. I think if I worked with other healers, we could cure this thing."

"And when she stopped cooperating?"

"I can't explain it, but I knew she was hurting him. A shift in energies. I felt something similar when I was healing the deer—and Primer. I'm also starting to think you're right about the governor and his involvement. What did you think when you went looking for me at the lodge?"

"Everyone was cordial," Benjamin said. "The woman I talked with—Caroline?—seemed concerned about you. She asked me to let them know when I found you."

"Did you tell Gloria about the hunters?" Stempler asked, his back to us as he stirred something on the stove.

Benjamin and I sat at the table.

"Hunters?" I asked.

"When I was at the dances," Benjamin said, "there was talk about a group whose members call themselves soothhunters. They track down soothsayers, or so they say. They've been preaching that soothsayers caused the downfall of civilization and they'll be the downfall of civilization again if we're not careful."

I shook my head in disgust.

"The Mexicali government got ahold of some of them. They are now being indoctrinated in some lovely immigrant holding camp."

"When I was a boy," Stempler said, "there was a similar group. They strung up our local soothsayer."

"They killed her?" I asked. "The people allowed them to do that?"

"The soothsayer was a he and no one allowed or didn't allow. They just did it."

"The community should have protected him."

"Should have, would have, could have. You're missing the point, healer," Stempler said. "Watch your back, front, and all around."

Angel, Amy, and Lizbeth burst into the house.

"Are you better, Mr. Jones?" Lizbeth asked. "Can you take us to the many-breasted priestess now?"

"I think I could almost do that," Stempler said.

Benjamin and I glanced at each other. Stempler had never volunteered to take a child anywhere.

"Perhaps he's sicker than I thought," I said, smiling.

Angel showed the girls where the dishes were. With a little improvising, they found enough dinnerware for everyone. Stempler served some kind of stew with flat bread. Both were delicious.

"You always liked my cooking," Stempler said to me.

I had never tasted a meal of his in my life—besides his beans—but I said nothing. Afterward, Benjamin showed Amy and Lizbeth how to play cards. Angel stared out the window. I sat at the table with Stempler.

Amy looked over at me and said, "I can't remember my momma's face."

I got up and went to her. Dropping to one knee, I put my hands on her. Connected. The white light was expanding. Tumbling away. I concentrated with all the energy I could find and stopped the expansion, temporarily.

I dropped my hands and kissed her forehead. "There, sweetheart, is that better?" She nodded. Lizbeth looked from me to Amy and back to me. I squeezed her shoulder as I got up.

"Lizbeth, why don't you get Amy ready for bed."

She nodded, reached for Amy's hand, and led her little sister to their beds on the floor. Tenderly, she helped Amy out of her clothes.

When I returned to the table, Benjamin and Angel came and sat with Stempler and me.

"I've got to get help for them," I said. "I think I should try to find other healers. Maybe a concerted effort will help."

"The group of soothsayers Stempler talked about is at least two days away, isn't it?" Benjamin asked.

"Yeah," Stempler said. "With the kids, it's more like three days."

"And it could snow any minute up in the woods and mountains," Angel said.

"We'll be in desert most of the way," I said. "It's times like these I wish for quicker modes of transportation."

"Then I've got just the thing for you," Stempler said.

"What?"

"A solar buggy."

I raised my eyebrows. "You, an individual, have something as valuable as a working solar buggy!"

"You going to turn me in?"

"Not yet," I said. "I was just at that cottage you stayed in near the soothsayers. There's no road, and I am not digging up any new terrain."

"The buggy does not dig up anything," Stempler said. "Besides, there is a road. It's just not as direct so you wouldn't have noticed. It's four hundred years or more old, but it's good enough for the solar buggy."

"He's right," Benjamin said. "I know the road."

"Okay, so we could get there in half the time if the sun holds out. Hopefully, the soothsayers can help cure Stempler and the kids. Then I'll come back."

"I'll go to Coyote Creek and ask if they'll help me look for Thomas," Angel said.

I glanced over at the sleeping girls. I wanted to stay and search for Church myself, but I had to get Lizbeth and Amy help. I did not want them following in their parents' footsteps over some cliff.

Benjamin and I held each other all night. I listened to his heart and hoped wherever Church was a white hole was not eating away his brain.

"Hang on until I find you," I prayed. "Hang on."

In the morning, I did a healing on Lizbeth, Amy, and

Stempler. Then we filled our packs with food, warm clothes, and water and walked into a bright and chilly morning. Amy held my hand and looked at the house and then down at the valley, whose fingers were lined with snow. "I like it here," she said. "Can we come back someday?"

"Sure," I said. "Soon."

The walk to the desert floor was short. Stempler then pulled away some mountain scrub to reveal a battered-looking solar buggy. I had passed this way many times and never noticed it.

Stempler got into the driver's seat. He reached behind him and helped with the packs as the girls climbed in. I shook my head: would wonders never cease?

Silently, Angel and I embraced. Then I got in next to Stempler. I glanced at Benjamin, who stood next to Angel.

"Hop in," I said.

"I'm going to look for Church," he said.

My stomach knotted. No. I did not want to be alone again.

He leaned down and kissed my mouth. "I'll try to bring him to you. If not, I'll see you back here in a few days."

I grabbed his hand. "Benjamin."

"See you soon," he said, gently pulling his hand away.

Stempler started the buggy and turned it onto the path. The girls giggled. I watched Benjamin until Stempler turned onto the barely visible road and Benjamin and Angel disappeared.

After an hour, Stempler wearied, and we traded places. He fell to sleep next to me while the girls were engrossed in a world of their making populated by fairies and nymphs. I detested this way of travel. My feet did not touch the Earth, and I could barely hear the birds or insects.

All three of my passengers ate lunch halfheartedly. I gave them each a healing; these, in turn, exhausted me. I was not accustomed to such intense and high-energy work. Stempler, reinvigorated, drove for a time while I curled up in the back with Amy and Lizbeth wrapped around me.

We stayed in an abandoned cabin for the night. Part of the roof was caved in, but the fireplace worked, and the four standing walls kept out the wind. Lizbeth and Amy slept restlessly.

Their moans and swift kicks to my kidneys kept reawakening me, until finally I lay sleepless looking up at the stars and roof beams and listening to an owl. I watched the sky turn ruby in anticipation of the sun. Then I kissed the girls awake.

Amy was marginally worse than she had been the day before. I kept my hands on her a long while.

Stempler took the wheel for a couple hours, until the road ended. We hid the buggy—against my natural instincts regarding community versus individual property. Then we walked across the desert another hour toward the mountains and woodlands. Happy to be out of the buggy, Lizbeth and Amy ran ahead of us. The day was clear and warm. As we had gotten farther north, we had passed fewer and fewer saguaro. Now we walked around mountain scrub, their leaves mostly deep red. Amy skipped from one bush to another, looking for their leaves on the desert floor.

Finally, I spotted the cottage sitting at the edges of the desert, woodland, and mountains. The girls raced ahead, Lizbeth expertly dodging cholla and jumping over the smaller prickly pear. Stempler and I looked at each other and shrugged. Oh, the energy of the young.

Once at the cabin, I fired up the stove and put on beans and wild rice to cook.

"The girls and I will go get some wood," I told Stempler.

"I guess I better stay here," he said. "These stupid woodstoves need tending."

I laughed. "Come on, girls." I glanced at Stempler and hesitated, wondering if I should leave him alone. There was not anything he could jump off or into, so he would be safe. "See you in a bit," I said, and stepped outside.

I carried the wood basket and gave Lizbeth a water bucket. We wandered up the meandering path that led to the woods, picking up fallen twigs as we went. Lizbeth heard the stream before I did and ran to it. Amy followed. I stood and breathed in the aromatic pine and listened to the children's splashes and giggles: nature meeting natural.

As I looked up into the forest, I suddenly realized a person stood watching, just as Benjamin had a few days earlier at Eden. Only this time it was not Benjamin. A woman came toward me, her curly red hair billowing around her shoulders. She wore a cloak the color of the night sky. In one hand, she carried a walking stick, from which hung feathers, shells, and colorful strings. She smiled.

"Hello," she said. "My name is Zeenie, and we have been waiting for you."

Lizbeth and Amy came up behind me.

Lizbeth carefully set down the filled water bucket, stepped forward, and held out her hand.

"Hello," she said.

Zeenie took her hand and closed her eyes. Lizbeth smiled. "That feels nice."

Zeenie patted Lizbeth's hand and released it. Amy stepped forward and held out both hands. "I'm Amy." The woman took the tiny hands in hers, closed her eyes, and then a few moments later released her, too. She turned to me.

"We must get these girls to our community," Zeenie said, "as soon as possible."

"You are a soothsayer?" I asked.

"I am."

"There's a man with us," I said. "Stempler Jones."

She nodded. "We know him. Shall we get him and bring him with us?"

Lizbeth and Amy immediately turned and ran down the path, calling Stempler's name. I picked up the water bucket and followed.

"How did you know we were here?"

"We try to know what goes on around us," she said, "for our own safety, and so we can help those in need. What do you call yourself?"

What did I *call* myself?

"My name is Gloria Stone," I said.

"Then that is what I will call you, too."

The woods ended. Ahead the girls each held one of Stempler's hands and pulled the lumbering old man up the trail.

"What's all this?" he asked, trying not to smile. I wanted to laugh. The old goat really enjoyed our company.

"We're going to the other side," Amy said.

"The other side of what?" Stempler asked.

"The other side of life," she answered.

I glanced at Zeenie. She smiled at the girls.

"I'm not ready to die," Stempler said.

"No, silly," Lizbeth said. "We're going to where our memories live."

Stempler looked at me and then Zeenie.

"In that case," he said, "lead me to the promised land."

Eleven

We ate, then closed the cottage we had just opened and followed Zeenie into the woods again. We walked up through Douglas fir and ponderosa pine for a time, and then we started going down. The sides of the mountain were silver with rock, dark green from the Doug-firs, and yellow-orange with gambel oak. I heard water and realized we were following the river, though I could not presently see it.

The slope was easy, and soon we were amongst colorful deciduous trees. When we hit a patch of level ground, Amy and Lizbeth ran through it, their feet creating a wake in the brown, yellow, orange, and red leaves. Gradually, the walls grew steeper and higher on either side of us, the way narrower, forcing us closer to the water. Several seeps had surged into tiny waterfalls, and moss and ferns dangled along the plunging water like blue-green curtains.

Finally, Zeenie led us to the riverbank, where a canoe lay. Two tall sycamores covered this portage spot. As we stood under them, several leaves broke loose and floated to the ground, looking like bright yellow falling stars. Amy leaped and grabbed one by its stem.

"I caught a star!" she said, holding the leaf up to me.

"Then I guess you get your wish, sugar."

The sky was turning azure over us, salmon-colored nearer to the horizon. In the rock and trees beyond us, I sensed eyes watching. Probably a mountain lion.

"Have you canoed before?" Zeenie asked me.

I shook my head.

"I have," Stempler said.

Zeenie nodded. "Then you and I shall take the paddles. It'll be dark soon. We better be going."

We turned the canoe upright and carried it to the edge of the water. After the girls got in, we pushed the canoe into the water, waded out a bit ourselves, and got in, too. Zeenie and Stempler each took a paddle and the canoe glided silently through the black water. The riverbanks disappeared, replaced by the walls of the boxed canyon that rose higher and got darker as we traveled through. The girls looked around, their mouths and eyes opened in wonder. A jay flew over us and squawked three times.

After a time, the rock walls on our right disappeared and were replaced by a grove of cottonwoods whose leaves were such a bright yellow that the trees looked preternaturally lit, their trunks and branches like black skeleton bones holding up fuzzy glowing lights.

Zeenie and Stempler steered the canoe to shore. When it bumped land, they got out and pulled the boat up out of the water. Lizbeth and Amy grabbed their packs, and we all scrambled out. After Zeenie and Stempler turned the canoe over, Zeenie led us through the cottonwoods.

On the other side of the woods, the canyon opened out and up to reveal the soothsayer community. The sky bled onto the red-and-tan rock and created shades of pink and orange that melted together and highlighted everything, making the settlement sharp and clear for a few moments. The buildings were built up against one another and under golden rock that arched over it all like a huge natural amphitheater. As we got closer, it appeared that the buildings were partially made from the brick of the homes of the Ancient Ones. Golden-leafed and white-barked aspen framed it all.

A woman came forward just as the last of the colors of sunset ran out and the world was painted in haze. The girls grasped my hands and pulled on them wearily. Stempler put down his pack and sat on it.

"Hello," the new woman said. She wore dusk naturally and reached out to each of us without fumbling. "I am Lily. We are pleased that you have come. You must be tired. Let me show you where you'll be staying."

We followed Zeenie and Lily into one of the houses. Inside it was more spacious than it had looked outside and well lit by some kind of lantern which almost looked incandescent. We sat on blankets on the floor and were brought bowls of soup with flat bread and water. The girls fell to sleep as soon as they finished eating. I gently woke them, and Lily took them out to go to the toilet. When they returned, I unrolled their beds and covered the girls with extra blankets Zeenie gave me. I kissed them and gave them a healing.

Just as I finished, I looked up and saw Zeenie leaning over a sleeping Stempler, her hands held just above his body. I whispered "Goodnight" to the children, then returned to the blanket in the center of the room, and finished my soup. Eventually, Zeenie and Lily joined me.

"They are very ill," Zeenie said.

"That's why I came. I was hoping you could help. Their parents had it and killed themselves. Stempler tried."

"They have few memories," Zeenie said.

I nodded. She knew this without having to ask them.

"How many of you live here?" I asked.

"There are six soothsayers at this time," Zeenie said, "and about fifteen friends, family, and other healers."

"Why do you live out here so far from everyone?" I asked.

"Because it is beautiful, and it is our home."

I smiled. "Stupid question. I only meant that many communities could use healers."

"We believe we were put here for a reason," Lily said.

"We're trying to discover that reason which is unique to each of us. That does not necessarily mean we should all be healers."

"This is a religious community?" I asked.

"Spiritual," Zeenie answered. "And practical. Haven't you wondered why you can't remember your childhood? Or why you can heal the way you do?"

"Or why you have started having strange dreams," Lily said.

I shifted uneasily. I supposed this was the moment when I had to acknowledge what everyone else had always known.

"So I am a soothsayer?"

Zeenie laughed. "There was a question?"

"But I thought soothsayers came from a long line of healers, and they always told the truth. No one taught me, and I can lie as well as the next person."

"Most of us have had teachers and mentors," Zeenie said, "but some haven't, and I don't know what kind of *line* I came from. Although we don't make a practice of lying, I suppose any of us could do it in a pinch."

"Tonight, we want to bring you into the circle," Lily said, "and prepare for tomorrow's healing."

I glanced over at the children.

"Bridey will stay with them," Zeenie said, following my gaze.

As we got up and slipped outside, a tall dark man went inside.

We walked down toward the cottonwoods, now just tall shadows slightly darker than the night. Around a small fire, ten or fifteen people sat, their colorful faces different shades of gold as they reflected the flames.

We joined the circle.

"This is Gloria," Lily said. "She has brought three here to be healed. Tonight, we will ground and prepare ourselves for tomorrow's healing."

Then she called the directions and honored the elements. As she talked to the air, a breeze rattled the cottonwoods. When she called on fire, I suddenly became aware of the heat of our campfire. When she spoke to the water, I heard the river flowing over the smooth round rocks. She called out to the

Earth, and I felt the ground beneath me. I smiled to myself. Lily was a powerful woman.

"The circle is closed," Lily said.

I felt comfortable and safe and suddenly confident that the girls and Stempler could be helped.

"Feel yourselves connect with the Earth," Lily said.

I closed my eyes and breathed deeply. Someone began playing a drum. Then I heard rattles. I settled down and let the music flow into me. The rhythm quickened. Someone began reciting a sequence of letters and numbers, singing them out like a chant. Then another recited a different sequence. My body was immediately shot with anxiety; my heart raced and my fingers tingled. I wanted to jump up and run away. I tried to breathe through it, but I felt as though I was suffocating. The voices joined, each singing their own sequence until the sound reached a crescendo. I opened my eyes. The fire and faces pulsed, wobbled. I bit my lips so I would not scream.

The voices stopped. The rattles shook once more and then were silent. My heart began to slow. I gasped the chilly air.

"Great energy," Lily said. "The circle is open but unbroken."

Someone passed around a plate of bread. Overwhelmed, I stood. I still wanted to run away, to throw up.

Zeenie put her hand on my arm. The anxiety drained away.

"Are you all right?" Zeenie asked.

"Just a little off-balance," I said.

"You didn't feel comfortable chanting your sequence?"

I shook my head.

"You'll do it when it's right for you."

I wanted to ask, "Why would I want to?" As a chant, I had not found the sequences very relaxing or inspiring. Instead, I said good night and went back to Amy and Lizbeth. I lay down near them, closed my eyes, and immediately fell to sleep and dreamed of bloody rivers and exploding numbers.

When I awakened early the next morning, Lizbeth lay on one side of me, Amy on the other. I slowly sat up. I rubbed my aching head and grimaced. I could not remember the last time I had had a headache.

I looked around. An open window curtain let in ruby light. Bridey knelt next to Stempler and handed him a steaming bowl of something. Stempler nodded and slowly sipped the concoction. Bridey looked over at me and smiled.

I was tired. Too much was happening. I wanted these three to be healed, and then I wanted to find Church, quickly, and make certain he was well. Nothing else mattered.

I gently nudged the children. They awakened quickly and kissed me. I held them tight. Had I ever been as loving as they were? Had I ever opened my eyes to find my mother leaning over me? Had she kissed me?

The girls and I filed outside to the toilet. Frost made crystal patterns on the stones and tops of gravel. Near the cottonwoods, people had started to gather.

When we finished in the outhouse, we splashed our faces and hands with icy water, then hurried back to the house. The girls sat close to Stempler and eagerly ate the broth Bridey proffered.

"How are you doing, Stempler?" I asked.

"I'm feeling pretty good," he said. "What's up for today?"

"We'll have a healing circle," Bridey said. "Afterward, you'll all be able to eat more. For now, this will sustain you."

He held out a cup for me. I took it and sipped some. The liquid warmed me to my toes, and I immediately felt sleepy again.

When the girls finished their broth, I helped them put on additional layers of clothes. Then Bridey led the four of us outside. Today, the circle formed away from last night's fire.

"Good morning," Lily said.

Others greeted us, too, but I barely responded. Zeenie instructed Stempler, Amy, and Lizbeth to lie on blankets already placed at the center of the circle. The girls smiled at me and did as they were asked. It was all an adventure to them.

"Soothsayers." Zeenie motioned to the other soothsayers who came and knelt by the patients. I sat at the girls' feet. They wiggled their shoes at me and laughed. The rest of the community circled us. They began making music with drums, rattles, and their voices. Zeenie honored the directions and elements. Then she knelt with the rest of us.

I wanted to relax into the music, but the drumming made my head hurt.

"We ask Mother Earth to help us direct our energies and heal these three, Amy, Lizbeth, and Stempler."

We raised our hands and placed them on Amy, Lizbeth, and Stempler. I put one hand on Lizbeth's leg and another on Amy's. I immediately connected with them and Stempler and everyone in the circle. And beyond. It was as if I had been hit by lightning, only instead of killing me, it opened me up and bound me to all of those around me. I knew every one of them and they me. I wanted to giggle. Soon we found the gaping holes in Amy, Lizbeth, and Stempler. The soothsayers began chanting their sequences as they had the previous night. Adrenaline flooded my body. I wanted to pull away, but the holes in the girls and Stempler began filling. No, not filling: mending. They were holes in time. In their minds. Memories. Circling. Circling. I no longer heard the chanted sequences; instead, everyone in the circle was in my mind, part of my brain. Almost one mind. Building. Healing.

The light in Stempler disappeared. Then the one in Amy. Finally Lizbeth. The breach was sealed.

The chanting and music stopped suddenly. Zeenie opened the circle. Everyone cheered. The girls and Stempler sat up.

"I feel pretty good," he said.

Amy smiled shyly. Lizbeth laughed. Then she said, "I still don't remember my momma."

I looked at Zeenie.

"We can't bring the memories back," she said. "As far as I can tell, they're gone."

Stempler stood and stared at the fire Bridey had just lit a short distance away. A breeze bent the flames and shook leaves from the cottonwoods.

"At least they didn't take all my memories," Stempler said. He held his hands down to the girls. They each grabbed one, and he pulled them up. He half carried half dragged the giggling girls to the fire. Zeenie and Lily followed.

Momentarily alone, I began to come out of my terrified daze. I breathed deeply. The sun had burned off the fog. Now everything was bathed in color. People lined up at a food-laden table near the fire.

I walked down to the table and made a plate for Amy, while Lizbeth got her own. The girls sat with the other children. I took a place near Lily and Zeenie and picked at some kind of stew. The sun felt warm on my face.

"I want to thank you all for everything," I said. "It's amazing what we were able to do as a group."

"Why didn't you use your sequence?" a man asked.

I stared at him.

"That's personal, Bob," Zeenie said.

"No, it's not," another woman said. "If we are the caretakers, we need to use our abilities. It's our responsibility."

Bob laughed, and Lily smiled.

"Julia believes we are guardian angels," Lily said.

"Who are we guarding?"

"The world," Julia said. "That's why we can do the things we do."

"And who put us here to do the guarding?" I asked.

"The Earth," Julia said. "She popped us out. That's why we have no memory of a childhood. We didn't have any."

Bob shook his head. "We're a mutation, that's all, from all the toxic crap left by the people before The Fall."

"Pretty advantageous mutation," Julia said.

"Isn't everything on this planet a result of advantageous mutation?" Bob said.

Some of the listeners rolled their eyes. They had heard these arguments before.

"In both of your theories," I said, "soothsayers are welcome additions to this world. But in reality, not everyone welcomes us."

"People have always needed scapegoats," Bob said.

"And so we wander in the wilderness forever with the sins of the world on our heads," Lily said.

"Been reading the Bible again, Lily?" Bob asked.

Lily pointed to her head. "I don't need to read it. It's all up here."

Leviticus 16. I knew the passage, too.

I did seem to have a great deal in common with these people. I wondered if any of them had ever killed anyone, but I was not about to inquire.

"Whoever we are," Julia said, "I believe we are here to serve."

"I'm nobody's slave," Bob said. "I'm just here. No more meaning than that. And why are you here?" He looked at me.

"*Here*? I'm *here* to save the children," I said. "Now I have to find someone else who has the same illness."

"It's not an illness," Zeenie said. "It was some kind of trauma. A removal of some kind."

"By whom?" I asked.

Stempler wandered over with a plate full of food and sat next to me.

"I think aliens from outer space did it," Stempler said. "I remember a light. A bright light like nothing I ever saw before, then nothing."

"If it's aliens, we better get immigration on it to tighten up our borders," I said.

Everyone laughed.

"Where is this other person you have to find?" Zeenie asked.

"I don't know," I said, "but I need to find him before he gets worse. I want to start back today."

"I'd like to rest here for a while," Stempler said, "and then return home." He glanced over at the girls. "I bet they'd stay with me."

I looked at him.

"You suddenly a Good Samaritan?" I asked.

"I've seen the light," he said. "Literally."

I grinned. I might like this old man one day after all.

"You're all welcome to remain as long as you like," Zeenie said.

"Lizbeth, Amy, come here," I called.

The girls ran to us and plopped next to me. Amy pulled on my fingers.

"I need to find my friend I told you about," I said. "He might be sick, like you were."

The girls nodded.

"Mr. Jones said he'd take care of you until I can meet up with you again."

"Okay," Lizbeth said. She kissed me on the cheek.

"It may be a while," I said, "depending upon the weather."

"When we get tired of hanging out here," Stempler said, "we'll go to my house."

"Oh good!" Amy said. "I liked it there."

I laughed. The girls ran away again. We all watched them. Amy jumped into the air to catch a falling leaf; Lizbeth raced another girl to the river. Their laughter rolled over us like water over rocks, gurgling deliciously in the autumn morning.

Soon after, I filled my pack with water and food, said my good-byes, and started west along the river. I turned to wave once more, but the children had already bounced away.

I was on my own again.

It took me the rest of the day to get out of the canyon. Zeenie had told me to stay close to the river. This got to be a challenge when the river spectacularly terraced itself into a waterfall, but I managed. Soon the vegetation became more sparse, the ground leveled out, and I was heading for the desert. Although the canyons and mountains were fecund and beautiful, enveloping me in wildlife, I felt on firmer ground in the desert, less distracted. I could concentrate on a thought or a landmark or a cloud and that would become all. In the woodlands, I wanted to stop and touch everything; in the desert, so much was untouchable.

That night, I slept under a rock overhang. I dreamed of

numbers and letters. The sequence screamed at me. When I awakened, I vomited.

Then I knew where Church was. I was certain he had gone to the Grand Canyon.

Twelve

The days were clear and cool as I followed the old highway. I wanted to catch a ride, yet I felt a little paranoid. Although I did not believe aliens were dropping down on people and sucking away their memories, I did believe someone had done something to at least six unsuspecting travelers. I did not want to be the next victim. Of course, maybe I had already seen the white light: I hardly had any memories myself.

The nights were cold and lonely. Coyotes howled. I missed Cosmo, Church, and Benjamin. My home. I dreaded falling to sleep. The sequence stalked me while I dreamed, each number or letter becoming a vicious dog, a man with a knife, or a hungry cougar.

I saw few people and stopped to talk with no one. I walked, slept, dreamed, and walked. I tried to look around, to notice my surroundings as more than guideposts along my path, but I could not focus. No wonder people got so desperate when they were ill for more than a day or two.

I tried to do a healing on myself, tried to connect with myself. Nothing. As if I did not exist. I could not touch my own soul. My soul didn't matter, I tried to tell myself, it was my body that ached.

Then, after days of travel, with a storm brewing in the north, I reached the long road to the Grand Canyon. Elk watched me and did not run. I stopped for a moment and gazed at them, recalling a time when every creature of the wild ran from even the hint of a human being. We had been the pariahs of the animal kingdom for a very long time. I was glad the world had changed.

Suddenly, the sequence of numbers and letters flashed and a wicked laugh screeched in my head. The noise was so harsh I nearly dropped to my knees.

Then it stopped. One of the elk bellowed. I hurried on.

By the time I reached the lodge, it was snowing. I pounded on the door. No one came. I tried to open it, but it was locked.

"Locked! We the people own this place! How can you lock it?"

The snow fell slowly, huge fluffy flakes. I went around the back to the kitchen. That door was closed and locked, too. No light shone inside. I shook off my pack and went around the building looking for another entrance, but everything was closed down. I went to the barn and found it empty.

As I returned to the lodge to pick up my pack, I noticed a set of footprints in the snow. I pulled on another sweater beneath my coat, then put my pack on again and followed the prints.

They led me to the edge of the canyon. I looked down and saw blackness being filled up by fat snowflakes. I stepped off the edge and went down the same awful path where my friend Cosmo had died and I had killed.

I followed the trail down and down and down, hardly looking up or around, just following the prints. Snow dusted the mountain scrub, junipers, and rock. The spires within the canyon did not appear to have any snow, at first glance. I did not look again. I went down.

And down.

Until the ground leveled, or I bottomed out. I walked

through the aspen, their branches bare, the black puckers on their white bark like tiny black holes. The footprints stopped. I walked a little farther, through the trees toward what looked like a long log cabin. I walked around it until I found a door, which I easily pushed open.

I stamped my feet, shut the door, and dropped my pack.

"Hello!" I called.

No answer.

I felt a momentary giddy rush. I was at the bottom of the Grand Canyon!

I glanced around. I stood in a large room dominated by a stone fireplace and the large picture window across from it. Couches were arranged every which way. Or maybe disarranged. Deranged.

I walked through the kitchen, several bunkrooms, and two small bedrooms, then returned to the living room. Wood was stacked in the fireplace, and I easily started a fire. The room warmed quickly. I sat on one of the couches and pulled food from my pack. I chewed on dried fruit, nuts, and currants. I debated about firing up the kitchen and actually cooking a meal and decided against it.

I made myself a bed on the couch. After piling wood on the fire, I curled up and fell to sleep.

I dreamed the sequence and laughter. A woman reached for me. "Greedy," she said. "They're all greedy. It will be the end of them. Don't doubt it. And you'll help."

"Who am I?" I asked.

"Genesis, baby."

"Do you mean the beginning of life or the first book of the Old Testament?"

Then that wretched laugh.

I opened my eyes. I sat up quickly and put my fingers just under my rib cage to keep from throwing up. I breathed deeply. The nausea eventually subsided.

I got up slowly and tossed a few more logs into the fireplace. Outside, wind whistled through the eaves. I could not tell if the time was closer to dusk or to dawn.

I stared at the fire that wrapped the logs in tiny blue-red flames that would eventually grow to devour them.

Why was I here? Why did I keep doing compulsive things? I had led an organized, well-managed life until—

Until what?

Until Primer slipped and sprained his ankle on my mountain.

The windows shook.

I heard whispers. The fluttering of wings.

I looked up.

Primer stood there.

My heart pounded. I blinked. Still, he remained.

"Primer?"

"Hello, Gloria Stone." Half of him was in darkness, half rust-colored by the fire.

"You were dead."

He smiled. "Yes. You killed me. You didn't know you had it in you, did you?"

I could not move. I did not feel in shock, but dreamlike. Perhaps I was dreaming. I remembered children telling me about awakening from nightmares and being unable to move: night paralysis. This was what it must have felt like.

"How are you alive?" I asked.

"Couldn't you tell?" he said. "Didn't you know most of the people you met at the governor's are soothsayers? They healed me."

"You were dead. Soothsayers cannot bring anyone back from the dead."

He laughed and crouched near the fire.

"How do you know what soothsayers can and cannot do? You didn't believe you could kill. But you did. You know nothing about yourself or other soothsayers."

I could not argue with that.

"But I know about you," he said. "I orchestrated it all, you know. Every bit of it. My fall on the mountain. The poisoning. Your trip to the governor. You seeing me kill the coyote. My death. You not going after Church, believing he had deserted you."

"Why?"

He smiled. "I needed you to believe you had nowhere to go. Everyone had to desert you and you had to desert everyone except us."

"What are you talking about?" I tried to shake myself, to get up. I could not move.

"You're awfully stupid. To live life in such blithe innocence. Just carry on in your little villages eating off the land, thinking the grand nontechnological age has worked. You have no idea. There are places that are human garbage pits, just like before. Disease, famine. The immigration camps are packed. We only let the most desirable people into the territory, of course. The others sew clothes or farm for us." He shrugged. "Then sometimes we let them in, too."

"What does this have to do with me?" I said. "If you wanted me to help heal those people, why didn't you just ask me? Why all this other stuff?"

He looked at me.

"You know nothing."

That was an understatement.

"Does the governor know what you're doing? Does he know you're alive?"

He laughed. "Yes, of course."

"What do you want with me?" I asked.

"I want you to stay here with us. Help us bring about the world that was meant to be."

"You have a lousy way of asking."

My heartbeat was back to normal. I leaned forward and stood. Yes! My momentary panic had passed. Primer et al. had played some weird and horrible trick on me, but it was over.

I walked to the window and looked out. Snow sparkled beneath the starry sky. Everything outside was bright and milky-blue clear. A perfect winter night.

"I can help you get memories," Primer said.

I looked over at him. He moved closer; I stepped away.

"I have plenty of memories, thank you very much."

"What about your childhood? Don't you want to remember

your parents? Your siblings? How the air smelled on your tenth birthday? Your first love?"

I remembered my first love.

"Where's Church?" I asked.

"The Reverend Thomas Church you know is gone."

"If you hurt him—"

"You'll what? Kill me again? You're so stupid. You cannot hurt or stop me. Church is nothing. I have the program codes, and I can make you do anything. I can make you stay or go. I can make you piss your pants if I want."

The flutter. Suddenly, I was urinating. I stood frozen, staring down at my slacks, feeling the warm liquid soak into the cloth and spread down my legs.

"Or I can make you stop pissing."

I stopped urinating.

Panic exploded in me, nearly blinding me. I fumbled for my pack and ran down the hallway into one of the rooms. I slammed the door and then leaned against it. I tore off my slacks, poured jug water on my towel, and quickly washed my legs. I could hardly think. Think. Think.

I pulled on another pair of slacks.

Primer had not come after me. Why should he? Where could I go in the dark in the snow in unfamiliar territory?

I tried to breathe deeply, to calm the panic, but it just continued to grow, reminding me of the white lights in the girls' and Stempler's brains.

I had to get out. All of this was familiar and totally alien.

If I stayed, maybe I could find out where Church was.

"Gloria?" Primer whispered from just beyond the door.

I grabbed my pack, ran across the room, and opened the window. Without my coat or blanket, I jumped out into the snow. A startled deer leaped away. I leaped after it, running, not thinking about Church or Amy or Lizbeth or where the Colorado River was, knowing only that I had to get away.

My feet slipped on sand, slid on rock, dug into the Earth. I could not move fast enough. I startled deer, coyotes, a bobcat pouncing on a rabbit. When I could run no longer and ruby light sliced through the canyon, I walked and walked.

Then lights started flashing. Stars popping. I could barely see. I stumbled toward darkness. A cave enveloped me. All the soothsayer sequences tumbled around in my head and became attached to my sequence. I heard a flutter. Whirring. Something opened.

I curled up on the ground and saw it all. I could not stop it. It was clearer than any memory. Time stopped and went backward.

And I remembered:

Thirteen

"Do you know who you are?" the woman asked.

I opened my eyes and sat up. "No."

"You are the first, my sweet, created by a process we call abiogenesis: life from nonlife. You are affectionately called a babe. Biological artificial being."

She was not an old woman, but her hair was gray, her eyes blue. The room was large, its walls covered with glass. Several shining tables. Sun slanted through a tall narrow window. I blinked and stared at the light.

"Yes, child," she said. "That is your first sun. These are your first minutes. As a whole being. We've been growing and manufacturing parts of you for a long while."

I looked around again. Who was "we"?

"You'll stay here at the institute for a while, then be sent to your owner. Any questions?"

"Who are you?"

"Just call me Mom." She laughed. "Or Maia. Whatever."

"Why am I here?"

"You are here to serve," she said. "We live in paranoid times, dear. The net is falling, but the business leaders still have their feudal kingdoms—or busidoms—and they need information. You don't look like a computer. It'll take the average hacker forever to detect you, and assassins will just think you're another nobody."

"I'm a computer?"

"Yes. Do you know what a computer is? Of course you do." She laughed. "You know everything. You can access your engineering processes, if you like, though not all of your programming. Self-determination is not in your cards, presently. Now, we'll do a few tests."

Others came into the room. I was hooked up to machines. They took blood out of me. They tested my reflexes.

Then they told me to access the network, the web around the planet. I thought about it and was able to discern the waves, dive into it, and contact the net. Some pathways had already fallen, and I could not reconnect them. At one point I sensed another like me; it flitted away before I could catch it. I reached for satellite reflections, but many were shut down. Still, I was able to answer whatever questions Maia asked about the current market, prices, bids, etc.

"You are able to contact others like yourself," Maia told me. "You can all send and receive radio waves. You'll continue to be able to contact other babes all over the planet, until you're sold. Then we shut down that program. We wouldn't want you revealing any of your owner's secrets to other babes."

"I don't like that designation," I said.

"It's a little early to have likes and dislikes. Think of yourself as a soothing influence on the world. Business people are currently the glue that holds the world precariously together. You provide them with the truths they need to access. You are truthsayers. True soothsayers." She smiled. "But don't worry, you are more than what you appear to be. You'll be protected. When the busidoms fall—and they will fall—you all will be very vulnerable. In the event of catastrophe, I've programmed you to go into a short hibernation. In this state, your body will change, and then you'll emerge without any outward or inner signs of who you were. After the first time, this will happen to you every fifty years or so."

"No inner signs of who we are. What does that mean?"

"You'll forget who and what you are. You'd be in further danger if people figured out you're nearly immortal."

"Forget? We'll have no memory?"

"No personal memory," she said, patting my hand. "Otherwise, you might inadvertently expose yourselves."

"But won't that be like dying?"

She shook her head. "Actually you'll still have the memories. You just won't have access to them until the world is a safer place for you."

"And then what?"

Maia laughed. "I can't tell you everything, child. Now, your testing period is over. You done good."

They took me to a dormitory. I sat on one of the many empty beds and waited. I looked up at the high ceiling. It reminded me of the picture of a gymnasium I had in my memory. I stared at the long, narrow windows. The glass was filmy with grime or tint, and I could not see out.

When it got dark, I lay on top of the bed. The building squeaked and breathed. I regulated my temperature so I would not get cold before realizing I could have gotten under the covers. I scanned my systems: programmed cells able to duplicate themselves when needed. I dived into the net, did not care about stock prices or which government had been taken over by which business, swam until I found another like me.

"Where are you?" I asked.

"In a big empty room." The other opened its eyes, and I saw a dormitory like mine. Were they my own eyes I saw through?

"Are you lonely?" it asked.

"I am alone," I answered. But I did not long for the company of Maia or any of the lab coats. "No, I am not lonely."

"I envy you," it said. "Have you slept?"

"No. Why? Is it something I should do?"

"Haven't you accessed self-care? Sleep helps the body replenish itself."

"I breathe. Isn't that enough?" I asked.

"You are the first. Shouldn't you have investigated all this? Self-knowledge is a good thing," it said.

I was not sure what was good and what was not. I looked up my diagnostics. Like most living things, I needed air, water, food, and rest so my body could continue to create the proper chemicals and hormones, in order for my programming to survive. I deduced from this self-help program that I was alive.

When I finished, I closed my eyes and shut down. For a time, I monitored my systems. This did not feel restful. Interesting, but not restful. I concluded this was not sleep. I counted ceiling tiles in the dark for a while. Then I closed my eyes and went to sleep for the first time.

I opened my eyes to daylight. I was more than moderately relieved that all my systems had not shut down totally. Outside, someone was washing windows, rubbing a circle big enough to reveal his face. The man smiled and nodded.

I went to my locker and put on clean clothes. I took the used clothes and carried them to a bin marked "dirty laundry." My clothes were not particularly soiled, yet I sensed this was the right container. After I dropped the clothes inside, I walked down the wide hallway. My footsteps echoed. When I stopped and shuffled my feet, the echoes changed.

Eventually, I came to another large room filled with long tables and benches. At the front of the room was a kitchen where three people worked. From the aromas, I concluded they were food service people.

I looked around. Only one being sat at the tables. I walked to him. He glanced up from his food tray as I neared.

"You are the other," I said.

He stood and reached out his hand to me. I grasped it. We stared at each other. This was the first touch I had had with another like myself. The first touch which was not a prelude to a test.

"I can feel the lines on your palm," I said. "And your heartbeat."

He nodded. "You can turn all that down, you know. You don't have to be aware of everything."

I sat across from him. He pushed his salmon-colored tray toward me.

"I'll give you a clue," he said. "Real food doesn't taste like this."

"How do you know?"

"My keeper used to bring me things from the outside. Didn't Maia clue you in on anything?"

"She did mention I should run on automatic more."

"What a wise teacher."

"You are different from me," I said.

"Yeah, you are kind of a monotone momma. But you're nice-looking. You are supposed to cultivate a personality, so no one will guess you have access to all the secrets."

"I like your personality. Perhaps I will cultivate it."

He laughed. I had not laughed before. How did he do it?

"Huh, huh, huh," I said.

"What are you doing?"

"Laughing."

"Well, I'd work on that," he said. "What did Maia name you?"

"She didn't. Did she name you?"

He shook his head. "I named myself."

I liked that idea.

"How did you go about determining your name?"

"I delved into the classics," he said. "First I tried the moniker Prometheus. Giving light to humankind and all that. But it doesn't really roll off the tongue."

"Prometheus," I said. I looked down at my tongue.

"Access your colloquialisms program," he said. "I liked Bacchus. Pan. Dionysus. Then I thought I'd be ironic. I'd call myself Man, or Manuel. Manny for a nickname."

"I like it," I said. "I suppose then I should call myself Woman."

"You're beginning to get a sense of humor," he said. "Why don't you name yourself after a goddess?"

"You haven't accessed the tale about hubris, have you?" I asked. "I will have to think about a name."

A woman came to our table carrying a tray of food. She put it down in front of me.

"Are you finished with yours?" she asked Manuel. He did not answer.

"Sir? Are you finished?" she asked again.

"Um. Ah. Yeah, sure," he finally answered.

She smiled and took the tray.

When she was gone, I said, "You were not finished."

"I know," he said.

"You're shy. But you weren't shy with me."

"You're a truthslayer," he said, "like me."

"I thought we were soothsayers."

"To-may-to, to-mah-to."

I ate the food and could not identify most of it. Still, the feeling in my stomach was pleasant.

Afterward, Manuel and I walked. We found a door that opened to the outside. We stepped onto the porch. The institute was surrounded by lush, dense forests.

I breathed deeply and coughed. "Will my auto systems know what to do with all these microbes and pollen I'm inhaling?"

"Of course." He hopped down the steps onto the ground and twirled about.

I smiled. He was a pretty sight.

"Catch me if you can!" he called, and ran away from me.

I jumped off the steps. My feet dug into the ground, and I ran forward. I was moving the Earth! Manuel raced into the forest. I followed and was surrounded by cool green darkness.

I stopped and walked up to the nearest tree. I peered closely at the gray grooved bark. Above, light green leaves fluttered. An oak tree. I put my hand on the trunk, gasped, and pulled it quickly away.

Then I touched the tree again.

It lived and pulsed and breathed.

"Manuel!" I called.

In a moment, he was beside me.

"Put your hands on the tree," I said.

He did as I asked. His eyes widened.

"Does everything do that?" he asked.

We ran to the next tree and placed our hands on it.

"Yes!" we cried together.

Then we touched the grass. A violet. Ferns. Ivy. All of them were alive. We raced back into the institute. I ran up to the kitchen lady.

"May I touch you?" I asked. Manuel hung back.

"Well, I guess it's all right."

I reached for her hand. Same thing! Of course, cheese was causing her indigestion and her heartbeat was a little irregular. I held both her hands and adjusted her: sent a bit of energy to her stomach and a little more than a bit to her heart. I did not know precisely how I did it, but the woman smiled, took her hands from me, and walked away.

"It's the same with her!" I said. "Except I could fix her."

He nodded. "Yeah, my keeper let me touch him. I fixed his arthritis and nasal polyps. It was like tightening a screw on a loose hinge—or at least my memory indicated it was like that."

"Do you know how you did it?"

"No. Neither did my keeper. He said it was probably residual energy of some kind. Or, he said, it was magic."

Later, we lay on my bed in the darkness and looked out the long, narrow windows. We watched the moon move across the sky and change the shadows in our dormitory.

"Look, the moonlight is draped over the end of the bed like a blanket," Manuel said.

"Or a milky-white cape," I said.

"Or sunlight reflected off a sphere in the sky," he said.

I laughed. What a glorious feeling! Laughter shook my throat and lungs.

"That is what finally gets you to laugh?" he said.

"Yes, you're amusing."

"I don't want to be alone again," he said.

"Were you alone before?"

Our fingers twined.

"Yes, weren't you? All those days I came in and out of consciousness. All those hours they left me alone after testing."

"We'll stay together," I said, "until our owners pick us up. Even then we'll be in each other's thoughts."

"Literally."

The moon slowly draped us with light. How different our clothes looked. My purple shirt became blue, Manuel's blue jeans black.

"Magic," Manuel whispered.

He pulled me up off the bed. We stood on the wood floor in the light of the moon. He put his arm around my waist and held my left hand in the air and twirled me around.

"Access dance," he said.

Around and around we went.

"I don't suppose we should use the word access," he said. "It does sound rather computerized. Remember is a better word."

"Yet not technically correct. Memory is the mental faculty of retaining or recalling past experience. We have no past experience."

"It doesn't have to be *our* memory," he said. "It is past experience."

"This is true," I said. "Now, your turn." And I twirled him around our dance floor.

We slept together.

In the morning, we ate together and then wandered through the woods, holding hands and discussing philosophy. After lunch, we talked of art and poetry. After dinner, mathematics. We were left completely to ourselves.

We practiced brushing our teeth together in front of the mirror. Brushing our hair.

"We can change our bodies," he said, "become any color, size."

"Maia said something about that, but I did not understand completely. It sounded like dying to me."

"Dying? She told me that if civilization as we know it collapses, and we're in jeopardy, a survival program kicks in. She didn't mention anything about dying."

"We forget everything about our lives each time we go into hibernation."

"I would forget you?" Manuel asked.

I nodded. "Besides, why should our bodies change? I think we both look pretty nice the way we are."

Manuel turned and looked at me. "You think so?"

I touched his face. We liked touching each other.

"I think you're very pretty," I said.

"You know, Maia told us to practice all things human," he said.

"Okay." We leaned toward each other and kissed the other's lips.

"Close your eyes," I said. "They close their eyes."

"Let's try again."

Our lips met.

When we parted, we smiled at each other.

"Not bad," Manuel said.

"Agreed."

One day, others like us wandered into the dormitory. We came in all shapes, sizes, and colors. Manuel and I smiled at each other: we were the first, and they were all seconds.

"Our children," he giggled.

Maia arrived with the keepers and reminded us to do all that was human.

"Does she mean kill each other and pollute the world?" Manuel whispered.

"No. She means you should leave up the toilet seat when you urinate," I answered.

Sometimes we all spoke to one another in radio waves. Sometimes we laughed en masse, and the keepers and food service people would look askance at us and hurry back to each other to huddle and point.

Manuel and I showed the others the moon and taught them to touch the trees.

One day, Manuel and I sneaked away to the woods to be alone with each other. The moon was full and bright overhead. We crept into the woods and listened. Insects galore. An owl moaning. Wind in the trees. In the distance a dog howled.

"Where the wild things are," Manuel whispered. He began taking off his clothes. I did the same.

"Now we are truly wild!" he said.

We held hands and ran through the forest, the air sliding all over our bodies. Together we howled. I wondered if we could change our bodies into animals. If we could change our size, shape, and color why not our genus, our breed? Would we then have enough sense to change back? Or enough sense not to.

We found a spot where the moon shone through the trees onto a bed of soft cushiony moss.

We dropped onto it, our legs and arms twined.

"Do you remember that Maurice Sendak book," Manuel asked, "where the boy has been sent to his room for being too wild, so he goes to live where the wild things are?"

My memory showed me the story. I laughed. "Yes! How wonderful. Out here, amongst the trees and birds and moss and stars and moon, we are where the wild things are."

Manuel embraced me. "But the boy doesn't stay. He goes back home to the soup his mother has left for him."

"And it was still hot," I recited.

"I wonder what it was like to be that little boy? To be home."

"Don't you feel at home here?" I asked.

"I do, with you and the others, but all this will not last," he said.

I kissed him. "I want to practice all things human." He returned my kiss. Gently we stroked one another. I smiled.

"This is nicer than chocolate," I said.

"I don't think they know what they've created with us," he said. He put his hand on my pubic hair. I lay back on the moss. "We're office equipment. Why didn't Maia use her genius for something more productive? A cure for some disease. A stop to global pollution."

I put my hand on his penis and watched with a combination of fascination and horror as it grew larger and harder. He watched, too.

"It does that," he said. "Up and down all day."

His fingers found my clitoris. As he gently rubbed me, he lay down and sucked my breasts. Then, with a little maneuvering, we had his penis inside my vagina and we did what came naturally via our programming, only none of it felt programmed. We were together body and mind and moved as one. Every part of my body tingled and sweated and juiced up.

We seemed to explode together. Afterward, gasping, we held on to each other.

Then we did it again.

"You know we won't all be as connected," Manuel said, "once we go to work."

"I know."

"Doesn't that bother you?"

"Yes, but maybe once we're programmed, we'll only care about pleasing our owners."

"Maybe we'll override the programming and save the world," Manuel said.

"Who made us the saviors of the world?" I asked.

"Maia." He kissed my nose. "Let's run wild and naked through the forests."

Manuel was the first to leave. His fingers touched mine when Maia and the keepers came. We all watched him walk away, listening to their footsteps echoing. None of us moved. We watched through Manuel's eyes as they drove him down city streets, around heaps of garbage, past screaming crowds, and into a building. A busidom.

Maia looked into his eyes and said, "Who all is watching?" I heard a whisper, or a flutter, and Manuel was snapped away. We were no longer connected. I wanted to scream.

Late that night, while most of the others practiced having sex, I lay under the covers staring out the window.

"He just wants information," Manuel whispered in my head.

I grabbed onto his thoughts, twined mine with his.

"So you spent the day on the net," I answered.

"I spent the day wishing I was with you," he said.

I remembered the feel of his palm lines against mine.

"They're crashing systems on purpose," Manuel said.

"Manny," I whispered, "I'm lonely."

"We'll outlast them, you know. Then we'll find each other." We were sailing through the air without the net. "Tell the others it will be all right. Good-bye, Woman."

"Good-bye, Man."

I told the others what Manuel had said, or rather, I thought it to them.

One by one, they left the institute. One by one, we lost their thoughts.

Then they came for me. Maia was startled to see some of the others weeping as I waved good-bye. Our footsteps echoed like those of soldiers marching drills. So I shuffled my feet and danced a jig. The others cheered.

The city was not like the ones in my memory. Much was in ruins. People stared at us with hollow eyes. I reached for their thoughts and found nothing. These humans. I wanted to stop the vehicle. I knew I could ail what healed them. Heal what ailed them. Unless it was hunger. Or loss of soul. I wished Manuel could press his thoughts against mine, wished he could fit his up-and-down penis into me.

I closed my eyes, found the others, and wrapped myself around their minds.

We flew somewhere. Drove somewhere else. Maia told the driver to pull over. She opened the door and got out. I followed her. Sand undulated, peach-colored, to the horizon that dripped bloody with sunset.

An animal yipped.

Maia said, "It is falling more quickly than I thought. Remember, you are more than they think you are. You can become self-aware; there are program codes. Here." She handed me a wafer. "Take, eat, this is my body."

I ate the wafer.

"It's not my body, actually," she said, "but it is all that I know. It is all that you need to know to survive."

"I have accessed information on computer engineering, abiogenesis, and artificial intelligence."

"Yes?"

"And no one has the skill or technology to create us."

"Yet here you are," she said, smiling. "Come on, before Mr. Millanze blows a gasket."

"Maia," I asked, "will I ever meet Manuel again?"

"What makes you think I can see into the future, sugar?"

Mr. Millanze lived in a house underground. He was younger than I expected, although I don't know why I expected anything.

He shook my hand. His skin was warm.

"I work long hours, and I work on the go. Any problems with that?"

"No."

We were surrounded by cement and steel. I found another and looked through her eyes at a blue jay flying from oak to fir tree.

Maia touched me. A flutter. A whisper.

"She is yours now. She will do whatever you wish."

Then she was gone.

"I'll give you my passes and you can look up your new identity. I want you to know that stuff cold in case anyone questions you."

I helped him buy and sell in the evening. After midnight, we drove up a hill above the city and watched the heat lightning while he had me engage his mercenaries in an assassination attempt on the leader of County Newark. He kept up a running conversation with the captain of his mercs, through me, while taking off my clothes. He whispered for me to get wet and then he penetrated me. I stood still, talking in the captain's voice, while Millanze banged me up against his car.

Later, he had me whisper Tokyo's stock exchange closing numbers to him while he had sex in me again. I did not like the sound of his breathing, so I turned my hearing down. I did not like his smell, so I turned off my aural capabilities. He made me keep my eyes open. He thought I saw him, but I watched the stock market prices instead.

Some days, he lounged by his pool and stared at the sky. Those times I was allowed to roam within hearing distance. Most often, I had to be near. He would ask me to disable a satellite. Or send his mercs after border crashers. Or turn the main power grid off until the politicos in this or that borough or city "learned their lesson."

"Good thing there is only one of you, or we'd all be in trouble," he often said, laughing.

Sometimes we stayed underground because of food riots or would-be assassins. His other assistants came, too, and busied themselves in the busidom by having sex in me.

One day, they sat at the pool while I wandered in the desert, staying within earshot. I squatted next to a rattlesnake sunning herself. If she bit me, would I be poisoned? No. My body had an antidote. But Millanze and his associates did not. If I asked, perhaps she would go kill them.

My programming did not allow me to harm him. Or disobey him.

I reached for the others, but they were all gone. Sometimes when I crawled the net, I caught glimpses of their beings.

I wondered what Manuel was doing. I held my hand up to the rattlesnake; her tongue tickled my palm.

"Babe!" Millanze called me Babe. "Babe!" He roared that name.

I hurried to the pool. The men lounged bare-chested. Sweat gleamed on their chest hair.

"Babe," Millanze said, "Brent tells me there are other biological artificial beings. Maia led me to believe you were the only one. I paid a great deal for you."

"Do you have a question, sir?" I asked.

"Yes," he growled, "are you the only one?"

"No."

"That bitch!"

"You didn't really believe she would only make one when having more would be so much more lucrative," one of them said.

"Maybe not. Still, I could kill her." He glared at me. "You should have told me."

"You never asked."

"That's a sin of omission." He smiled. "Piss yourself." My bladder released urine down my legs. The men laughed.

"What else can she do?"

"Give you a blow job you wouldn't believe," one said. "She can suck dick until you think your brains will fall out."

"Dance for us," Millanze said.

I danced.

"Now vomit."

I vomited.

"Now eat it."

"Millanze, this is disgusting!"

I ate the vomit.

"We will outlast them," Manuel had said. Maybe, maybe.

When Millanze slept, I ran across the desert. Listening to the music in my head and the air whistling in my ears, I ran faster and faster. Ofttimes, a coyote ran with me, a gray ghost, urging me onward. Onward.

I would stop on the most sunbaked, parched piece of ground I could find and scream the truth as I knew it.

"You are a crazy mean bastard! You are ruthless and evil. The world is dying, and you're the reason! If they're all like you and yours, Millanze, then I hope you all die!"

Die.

During a 120-degree heat wave, Millanze instructed me to shut down the grid. I imagined the babies on incubators and old people gasping for breath. I could almost smell food rotting and people starving.

Millanze spun in his chair, laughing.

"Were you always like this?" I asked.

He stopped spinning and looked at me. "I'm just trying to keep everything from falling apart. They've got to learn to do what I want."

"What is it you want?"

"For them not to exist. They just spread disease and use up resources."

"Then you'd be alone."

"But I would be in control."

"Of what?" I asked.

"Of it all."

He did not see the fallacy of his argument.

One night I came home from my run, and Millanze lay on his chaise longue with a hole in his head.

He was dead.

I sighed with relief.

Then someone ran out of the house screaming, "It's his soothsayer. Get it!"

I jumped out of reach of the man's hands and ran back into the desert where I stayed, unfollowed, for the day.

Until Maia called me back.

Millanze and the killers were gone. Maia stood next to the pool with a woman.

"This is Millanze's sister. She has your program codes now."

She shook my hand, just as her brother had when we first met.

"I am Suzanne Millanze. I have my own business up in the Northwest. Kind of your birthplace. Would you like to come with me?"

"No," I said. "I want to find the others. I want Manuel. I do not want to do the things you make me do."

Suzanne glanced at Maia.

"I am not my brother. I only need access. I will not fuck you. I will not kill any innocents."

"Do you have mercenaries?"

"One must do what one must do."

I looked at Maia. "Please. Release me. These people kill without thought. They torture with pleasure. They never watch for moonlight or touch each other's souls."

"We are not all like Millanze," Suzanne said. She turned to Maia. "Is she self-destructive?"

"Her programming forbids it," Maia said.

"Millanze was such a sick bastard. Can't you erase her memory of him?"

"Of course."

"No!" I moaned. "Please! Leave my memory alone. It's all I am."

Suzanne shrugged. "Whatever. Come along."

I grabbed Maia's arm. "Don't you ever question the ethics of what you're doing?"

"We aren't in the business of ethics," Suzanne said.

"Is Manuel well?" I asked Maia.

"Maia, if she's going to fuss this much, I will insist you reprogram her."

I went quietly.

In Seattle, I took care of her business for many years. She was kinder than Millanze. She called me June because she had inherited me in the month of June.

"The Romans each had a spirit that kept them alive. The man's spirit was called genius, the woman's spirit was juno. You'll be my juno," she told me.

Some days she worked in the hospitals instead of turning the power off. She never touched me.

No one ever touched me.

During the winter riots one year, she got ill. She did not ask for me, and I did not go to her. I watched Seattle burn while Suzanne breathed her last.

I told no one. I packed a bag and walked away. I hid in burned-out buildings along the highways. Once I hitched a ride in a bus full of technorats.

"Technology is bringing us to our knees," one of them preached. "Now it's time for us to bring tech down!"

I thought about telling them what I was, but I knew they would probably hurt me, and my program prohibited self-destruction. Instead, I got drunk and had sex with one of them. He was young and quick, but sweet and gentle.

They dropped me in Portland, which still stood. I walked along the streets admiring Christmas decorations. Someone even waved at me from a store window. Didn't they know the world was burning down?

I stood and watched a toy train run along its tracks around a tree trimmed with colored lights and shiny bulbs. I saw in my memory that people had been celebrating the return of the sun for thousands of years. Pagans in Europe had tramped out into the woods and hung symbols of everlasting life and their wishes for the new year on evergreen trees. I smiled and touched the window.

Suddenly the lights went out all over the downtown. I drew my finger away, but the light did not return. Some head of some busidom playing with the grid, no doubt.

I wandered until I came to a large river, and I followed it east. The smells were familiar. I stayed off the highways—too many bandits. I trudged through wetland and forest, waded across rain-swollen creeks. Finally, I walked away from the river and down a long drive. The gates were opened.

Maia's institute.

I ran down the drive and went inside. It was cold and damp. And dark. I shouted. No answer.

I walked down hallways and into the empty dormitory. The beds were gone. I wandered into Maia's lab. The glass cabinets were all broken. Drawers were pulled open, their contents spilled onto the floor.

I picked up a shard of glass shaped like a crescent moon and held it up to look at my reflection. I touched my face. My cheeks were red and dirty. I wondered what Manuel looked like now.

I went outside again and into the forest where Manuel and I had run together. I hung the moon shard on a low branch of a Douglas fir.

"I wish you happiness, Manny, wherever you are."

As the moon swung on the fir branch, I wished I could find Manuel and the others, wished I knew the program codes to end our slavery.

Then I ran away.

I wandered, trying to avoid the rioting. Mobs stalked those

they accused of being soothsayers. Mostly the innocent died, hanged and burned because the people believed a soothsayer had to die twice in order to truly die. Real soothsayers were too smart to get caught, generally, and none of us spoke up for those who were falsely accused. I wanted to, but my program would not allow me to put myself in jeopardy.

Then one day, I had an urge to run away. Maybe Maia got on what was left of the net and sent us all into hiding. Or maybe our programming kicked in, deciding the world was unsafe, and sent us scurrying into hibernation. I didn't know how it happened. I only knew I had to find a safe place. I stumbled away from the ruined city where I lived and into the forest. I sobbed as I ran. To be out of control was beyond horror. I could not stop myself from blindly trudging toward my programmed fate. I found an empty cave, I sank to the ground, and a fog descended. I wailed and screamed. I tried to picture Manuel, Maia, even Suzanne and Millanze. It was my life! I wanted to remember what it was like to be loved and unloved, to run for my life. *My* life.

I howled.

And all that was me disappeared.

Until I awakened, momentarily blind and sick. I vomited and blinked. Shakily, I touched myself. My skin, hair, eyes, facial structure, and body all felt unfamiliar. Suddenly I realized I did not know who I was. I pushed myself up and out of the cave. I stood still in the forest for a few minutes, getting my bearings. Although I did not remember myself, I knew I had to be careful. And I had to survive.

A blue jay squawked as she flew over my head. I watched her coast on the thermals, and then I followed her out of the forest and into my new life.

Fourteen

The memories stopped.

I opened my eyes. I was not in the cave. I blinked, wondering if I was still remembering. I glanced at my skin. Different shade from the first me, same as the seventh me. I pulled the covers up over my shoulders and realized I was on a bed.

I felt as though I had aged a decade.

Of course, I did not truly age. I was a machine. I was technology, the technology that helped end the world. I was all that I had abhorred my entire life.

Ha! Not my entire life. *Lives.*

Now I had the answers to all of my questions. Now I knew I had no parents to remember, no childish memories to fear or embrace. I had no life except the one that had been programmed for me.

Wait until Stempler heard this story. He would laugh himself silly.

What would everyone else do?

Ostracize me? Kill me? Go after the other soothsayers? What sins were on their heads?

I remembered what I had done for Millanze.

What a disgusting human being I was.

Not human.

Just disgusting.

Me who prided myself on my techno ignorance. Above them all.

A shadow fell across me. I opened my eyes again. An elderly woman leaned over me.

"You awake?"

"Yes. Where am I?"

"You're here," she said.

"How long have I been out?"

"A long time," she said.

I slowly sat up. My stomach felt a little queasy.

"Thank you for taking care of me."

She shook her head and stepped toward the woodstove. She lifted the lid and stirred the coals.

"It wasn't us who found you. A white man sat with you every day and made certain you had food and water."

"I'll have to thank him."

What I wanted to do was run. I should not be near people. Maybe around others like myself. I could return to the community of soothsayers and tell them who and what they were. Wouldn't they all be shocked! And then what?

Suddenly I remembered Primer had said he had program codes. That was how he had controlled me. He was still out there. And Church was still missing.

Nothing had changed except now I knew what I was.

Maia said we would remember ourselves someday when the world was a safer place. Was that day now? I did not feel safe. In any event, when my sequences combined with the sequences of the other soothsayers in my brain as I raced away from Primer, I had remembered my lives. The sequences had been like the combination on a lock.

I was unlocked.

Should be locked up.

Now, I could remember at will. Or stop remembering. I had seven lives to recall. Every fifty years, more or less, I had stumbled into a cave and forgotten so that no one would ever guess I was an immortal and come after me. Not even myself.

I opened my eyes again. The old woman was gone.

I slowly got up and went to the door. Opening the curtain, I saw beautiful clear blue skies, with an occasional puffball cloud floating by. Red canyon walls rose up all around. The air was cool but not cold. How long had I been in the cave before I was found?

I stepped out. Grass pushed up through muddy ground. Cottonwood and willows edged the canyon walls and surrounded the simple homes. Behind the houses, on a promontory jutting from the cliff, two giant red pillars rose.

I heard water and walked toward the sound, down through box elders and hackberry, to a creek bloated with runoff and water bluer than any I had ever seen. Bluer than any sky.

I touched a cattail that had survived the winter and waded into the flow.

"They say the current is strong at this time of the year."

I turned around.

Church stood a few feet away, dressed in white, bearded, his blond hair long. Next to him, Cosmo sat, his tongue lolling like a dog's.

I touched my head. Was I locked in another memory or hallucinating?

"Cosmo? Church?"

Cosmo bounded toward me and leaped into my arms, knocking us both into the icy water. The shock of the cold sent us scrambling for the shore, where I flung my arms around Church.

"I'm so glad to see you! How is it possible?"

Church patted my back and pulled away from me. "You're wet. Let's go back, and you can change your clothes."

"I don't care!" I tried to kiss him, but he stepped away. My stomach lurched. What was wrong with him?

"You've just gotten better," he said.

He gently pulled me back up to the house I had just left.

Inside the dark room, he brought me clean clothes, then waited outside.

Cosmo stayed inside with me. I quickly took off my river-soaked clothes, rubbed myself and Cosmo with a blanket, and put on dry clothes. Then I sat on the floor and put my arms around Cosmo. He whimpered.

I felt along his sides for his scars, looked at his extra toes, and found a relatively new nasty-looking scar on his head.

I was absolutely certain the coyote on the trail had been dead. Unlike Primer, he could not have risen again.

I put my hands on Cosmo's head. Connected. Saw through his eyes easily. Searched his memory. Running after someone. Falling. Falling. Captured. A white light. Wandering. Not remembering. Searching. Whimpering in the cave where I lay curled.

"*You* found me? What a good friend, Cosmo."

I kissed his head, got up, and went outside. My heart skipped a beat when I saw Church. He did not seem to notice me, even when I sat in a chair next to him. Cosmo lay on my feet. Why didn't Church look at me? Maybe he really had been horrified by what I had done to Primer—by what he had believed I had done.

"I've come out of hell into paradise," I finally said. "Everyone has been looking everywhere for you. I thought Cosmo was dead. You wouldn't believe all that has happened."

Church looked at Cosmo and then at me. His eyes were so different.

"You remember me?"

"Of course I remember you," I said.

"I thought you were in a coma all the time I was with you."

My stomach tightened.

"What do you mean, Church? I've known you for a year."

He stared at me. "The coyote led me to you. We brought you up to the plateau but you didn't get well, so Nile—he's the healer—thought you might do better down here. I don't remember you from before."

I sighed. I had hoped his memory loss would not include me.

"May I touch you?" I asked. "I am a healer, too."

"Yes, if it will help you," he said.

I put a hand on Church's head and another on his chest. This was my Church, the man I loved. And he did not know me.

I connected with him. Found the white light. Only it was not expanding, just pulsing. I began to close it.

"No." He pushed away my hands.

"But it's what has taken your memory."

"It is the light I have looked for all my life," he said.

I wanted to smooth his hair off his face, take his hands in mine, kiss his mouth.

"Do you remember your life?" I asked.

"Some of it." He turned away from me and stared out at the canyon walls. "I remember as a child I had so many doubts. Now I don't. I am never in darkness. I close my eyes and there is light. I open my eyes and there is light."

"You were happy," I said. "I knew you."

"Don't trouble yourself with me," he said. "You are still healing."

I'm not healing! I wanted to scream. I'm a terrifying technological wonder who helped bring down the world as it was, and I love you and you love me!

Loved me. Past tense.

I breathed deeply. Calm down.

"Where are we?" I asked.

"Havasu Canyon. They winter on the plateau, so there are only a few others down here presently."

"Why are you here?" I asked.

He frowned and said, "This is where God put me, where I must stay."

Oh no. Not a missionary!

"You want to convert the Indians?"

"No. I want them to convert me. I am here to find the heartbeat of the Earth. To know the Mother."

He got up and walked slowly away.

My heart thudded in my ears. On some level, he remembered part of me: I was the one who talked to him about the Earth. He could be saved.

I looked around. Primer would never guess I was here. I was safe from him, and the world was safe from me.

I had been running for three hundred years, give or take a decade. I had not yet perused the memories all of my lifetimes, but I felt the weariness of age-old wandering. Maybe this was why humans did not live as long as trees or stones. We shattered ourselves with movement. Not we. Them. I was not human.

Enough thought. I was in paradise. I would stay still for now. Until I could help Church.

Cosmo and I ran alongside the river until we found Church sitting on rock, meditating. We played nearby.

"Who are you?" he asked, when he opened his eyes.

"I'm the lady you found in the cave."

He smiled. "No, who were you before?"

"You had a church in the town where I lived. My name's Gloria Stone. I was the town . . . healer."

"Was I good at what I did before?"

"You were a kind and gentle man," I said.

"I wonder if I still am."

I smiled. "I'm certain of it."

We returned to the settlement, and Church introduced me to Grandma Ellie, the healer Nile, and his son Jigs and daughter Elysia. We ate together in Grandma Ellie's home. Cosmo ran with the creek.

"Healer Nile," I said as we drank soup, "you don't need to stay down here with me. I don't want to keep you from your people. I am perfectly well."

"They will be down soon," he said. "Besides, there are other healers. I find you very interesting. They carried you out of the big canyon, you know, and then we carried you down here and you did not move! Like a fetus in a mother's womb. You were reborn again!" He grinned. He liked to talk. Church smiled at him, and I laughed. "The spirits have said little about you," he said.

How could the spirits say anything about me? I was just a piece of machinery, long outliving my purpose.

"They should have said what a pain in the butt she is," Grandma Ellie said. "It's too damn cold down here!"

The teenaged children giggled.

"Mom, it's practically spring," Nile said.

Church watched the children. He paid no attention to me. Where was our connection? Our sexual spark?

Perhaps it had been my doing all along. I had seduced him. I had known his weakness was me. I had exploited that knowledge to his detriment. If he had not wanted me, he would never have come to the Grand Canyon and had his memory ripped out.

"How'd you come across Church?" I asked Nile.

"We found him wandering the streets of Red Bluffs," he said. "He was very lost. We did a sweat and ceremony."

"Are you a soothsayer?" I asked.

Nile said, "Soothsayers do not heal with herbs or sweats or prayers to the spirits."

"Oh?"

"Soothsayers take the energy directly from the Earth," Ellie said, "and channel it through their bodies." She put down her bowl. Nile nodded to the children; they excused themselves and ran outside.

"Isn't that what you do?" Nile asked, looking into my eyes.

"Not exactly."

"Are you sure?" he asked.

Church looked at me. "You are a soothsayer?" he asked.

"Yes," I answered.

"Thank you for the meal," he said abruptly, then got up and left.

"He prays all the time," Grandma Ellie said. "Nile talks to the spirits all the time. And you're in a coma half the time. Who's got time for work then? Me! That's who!" She noisily picked up the dishes.

"Mom, we'll do it. Go count the sunsets."

Grandma Ellie made a noise; then she, too, left the house. Nile laughed.

"She hears and sees more than any of us," he said. "And you. Why don't you want to talk about your healing experiences?"

"They are not as grand as you make them out to be. I am a soothsayer, but you don't understand what that is. Some woman created us about three hundred years ago out of programmed biological cells. We're really computers created as slaves, and we helped bring about the end of civilization. I am technology. I am illegal. I am a thing."

He nodded. "That is quite a history. Someday I will tell you the history of my people."

"No, this is true."

He laughed. "Yes, I know. We have heard such tales before."

"You don't understand. I'm a machine. I'm a thing!"

I wanted him to acknowledge the horror of my existence.

He got up. "Yes, you're a computer thing, and I'm a man thing. What makes you a different thing from what I am?" he asked as he gathered up the dirty plates.

"The fact that my creator put me here to create havoc," I said, helping him. We carried the dishes to the hot water on the woodstove.

"My creator put me here to do her dishes."

I gazed at him and started to laugh. For now, my horror dissolved in a pan of soapy water. Outside, Cosmo howled at the rising moon.

For a few days, I followed Church around, waiting for recognition. Waiting for love. I started to feel like a puppy dog in heat.

"Why did you take care of me when I was ill if you didn't know me?" I finally asked Church one day.

"Because it was the right thing to do," he answered. "I could not let you starve."

"And you never felt even the slightest hint of recognition?"

"You did remind me of someone."

"Who?" I asked.

"I can't remember."

I watched him and listened whenever he had one of his rare conversations with one of the others. Sometimes it was difficult to see the good Reverend Thomas Church, who had touched me like no other in my memory. He had connected me to myself. And the world. Some days, I wandered around with Nile, telling him about my life. I felt in stasis, waiting. I now knew more than anyone else on the planet. I could answer so many questions. I also knew I could use the sequences to help the other soothsayers remember—if they wanted to remember. And, of course, they would. As frightening as much of it was, it was a tremendous relief to know who and what I was. *Even if no one wanted me again? Even if no one ever loved or trusted me again?*

One night, I crept into the house where Church lived alone. He slept soundly while I watched. It would be so easy to put my hands on him to heal the breach and hope he would come back to me.

But that would be wrong.

I left him and went out into the night. Cosmo and I dodged the moon as we ran back and forth between the willow and peach trees. When I looked up once, I thought I saw someone on top of the red pillars. A man? Leaping into a mountain lion and landing on the next pillar as a woman.

Manny and Womanny.

I laughed, blinked, and she/he/it dissolved. I went back inside my little house and slept.

Some nights, I carefully and slowly remembered parts of my life. I had loved and lost. Healed and wandered. Always wandered, looking for home, searching for that place where I could feel connected, where maybe I would remember who I was. But I never remembered. I watched people grow old while I did not. I moved on so no one would begin to question what I did not understand myself. I watched the world turn away from their longing for the world as it was, toward the world as it could be. Until amnesia would slam away all my discoveries.

One hour at a time. One day at a time I remembered

myself. I wanted to reach across the ages and embrace she who had been me. Or slap her. Wake her up. Whisper the sequences to her.

One day I helped Nile turn over the soil in the fields in preparation for planting. The day was warm. Green buds were breaking open in the trees. A bird of prey careered above.

"Let's go play," Nile said.

"Spirits talking to you again?" I asked.

"Yeah, the wind spirits." A dust tornado gently swirled around us.

"Come." He reached for my hand and I took his.

We walked mostly along the creek. Birds sang out from their perches in the blooming trees. Cosmo ran alongside us.

"How long were you lovers?" Nile asked.

"Cosmo and me? We're just good friends." I smiled. "I don't know how long Church and I were lovers. What does it matter? I was like a schoolgirl in love."

"But you never were a schoolgirl?"

"Exactly," I said.

"He is deeply troubled," Nile said.

"He believes he is being spiritual," I said.

"He has lost his soul. You could help him."

"He said no."

"Still, you could heal him."

"I don't believe in fascism," I said.

"Not ever? No matter what it means to you?"

I remembered our snowed-in night at Stempler's. Had my seduction been a form of fascism?

"No, never. Not anymore," I said.

"I guess you aren't as horrible as you believe."

When Nile stopped, we were at a waterfall, the white water dropping into terraced pools and becoming turquoise. It was the brightest, bluest water, surrounded by calcite that decorated the pools like gingerbread house trimming. Staring down at the pools was like looking into deep beautiful blue eyes. Near the edge of one pool, Ellie dangled her legs in the water—or else her legs had become water. I blinked. Or was that Maia?

"She weaves the universe into existence every day," Nile said, "and unravels it every night." He gently tapped the top of my head, and I looked at him. "That is where your thread is."

"What?" I looked back at the water, but Ellie was gone.

Nile climbed down to the pools, and I followed. We sat on a dry grassy patch on the banks.

"Are you going to stay here forever?" he asked.

"Can I?"

"If you like. But we won't give you what you need. Neither will Church."

"Quit trying to probe my psyche. I'm not human. Doesn't *psych*ology require a human mind?"

"Actually in Greek mythology doesn't Psyche represent soul?" he asked.

"The *human* soul."

He leaned back. "You want to be connected, to feel at home, yet you separate yourself. What difference does the act of creation make?"

"A lot. My . . . my kind, my kin—for lack of a better word—have done horrible things. I have done horrible things."

"But what have you done lately? Who are you now?"

"I know I am someone who can't bear to let anyone control me again."

We were silent for a few minutes. Then Nile said, "Are you going to stay here forever, following around a man who doesn't know you? Waiting for him?"

I sighed. "It is rather pathetic."

I lay back next to Nile and stared at the sky. I listened to Nile's rhythmic breathing, watched a group of crows ride the currents above us, and promptly fell to sleep.

When I opened my eyes, the moon shone on the water. The sky was still blue, although the sun was down. I could feel the ground trembling slightly as water poured into the pools. All around me giant white threads glistened as they hung from one object to the next, to the next, to me, each thread occasionally thrumming and glowing with life. I touched the top of my head and felt my connection to all things.

A cloud covered the moon. The threads disappeared.

I opened my eyes again.

"Something in these waters makes people hallucinate," I said.

Nile laughed softly. "You aren't people, so why are you affected? You're just a disconnected machine."

"Don't try to get a rise out of me. It won't work. I was either sleeping or hallucinating."

He shrugged. A cloud crossed the moon.

"You get caught in detail," he said. "Everything is an either or. You're either a computer or a woman. An evil being or a healer. And you see everything around you in those terms. The people in Coyote Creek either support you or desert you. Not everything is as black-and-white as you make it out to be."

The moon came out again. The world dripped fairy-tale color, mist, and sounds.

"There can only be one truth," I said.

"Why?"

"I know we destroyed many lives," I said.

"And how many have you saved? How do you know you weren't put here for the lives you saved or the good you can do?"

"I don't believe in fate," I said.

"How do you know soothsayers aren't guardian angels burped up from the Earth via Maia's genius?"

"Maia created us to make herself money."

"How did she explain your healing abilities?" he asked.

"She didn't." I glanced at him. "The Earth burping again?"

He laughed. "Who knows?" he said.

I gazed at the moon and then at the water draping over the travertine rocks like a turquoise cape draped over the shoulders of a strangely shaped giant. I looked at my palm and recalled Manuel's life line pressed against mine.

"Looking for love in all the wrong places," I murmured.

I lay on the ground again, sideways, and gazed at the waterfalls. Could I change myself into water and just go with the flow? *Molecules slip-sliding away. Swirling silver moonlight in my drops as I rush toward the Colorado, body sliding over ancient rocks with stories to tell, curving at the canyon walls until the sun slurps me and I well up into a thundercloud that finally bursts and spills moon drops onto the faces of Manuel, Church, Benjamin, Cosmo, Lizbeth, Amy, Stempler, and Angel, onto the faces of all my beloveds.*

I stared at the moon, and it became two shiny discs in Ellie's face.

"Acknowledge what you are and get on with it," she said.

I could see the threads again.

"I am technology," I said.

"From the Greek '*teks*,' " she said.

"Yes!" I cried. "Which means 'to weave.' How extraordinary."

"You are a weaver," she said. "Actually, you're a webster. That's another word for a female weaver."

I laughed. "Of course. Maia said we were more than we knew."

"So go out and weave, Woman."

I opened my eyes.

Dream within dream, within dream, within . . . what?

Cosmo breathed on my face, and I sat up, out of the darkness. Nile reached for my hand.

"Do you love?" he asked as he gripped my hand.

"Yes."

"Then what else do you need to know?" He pulled me up. "It's going to be cold. We better get back."

In the morning, I stepped outside to find clouds had descended to touch the Earth. As the fog began to rise and swirl, sleeping deer curled into red rock and a mountain lion jumped up and became a will-o'-the-wisp. Everything I looked at became something else. Cosmo yelped and snapped at a disappearing wolf.

Through the mist, Benjamin and Angel came. I watched to see what trick of light they were. The fog continued to rise. Benjamin waved.

I looked around for Cosmo. He watched Benjamin. I smiled: so Benjamin and Cosmo were not one and the same.

I ran to meet the newcomers. Benjamin and I embraced. Tears streamed down my face when I finally released him. Angel kissed me. She looked older, browner.

"We followed Church's trail to here," he said. "We didn't come earlier because of the weather."

I nodded. The tears continued down my cheeks.

"Are you all right?" Benjamin asked.

I grasped his hand. "I have a lot to tell you."

"Is Church here?" Angel asked.

"Yes," I said. "In the first house there." I pointed. "But he's lost a great deal of his memory." She ran ahead. Cosmo bounded over to us.

"Cosmo?" Benjamin leaned over. "I thought he was dead."

"So did I," I said. "The dead coyote had barbed-wire scars and extra toes."

Benjamin laughed. "Gloria, every coyote in the Coyote Creek area has extra toes, and every other coyote has been trapped in barbed wire."

"I didn't know."

He put his arm across my shoulders. "Are you okay?"

"I didn't kill Primer," I said. "Or if I did, he was brought back. He isn't dead. It was all some elaborate scheme to get me to go to the governor."

"You're kidding?" he said. "Well, I've got bad news from Coyote Creek. Georgia and Herb both got the memory illness. The council ran Clarity, your replacement, out of town. Then Stempler came back into town with the girls and a couple of the soothsayers. They did a healing on Herb and Georgia, and they're better, but they still have little memory."

I glanced up. Angel and Church stood outside his house, holding hands. I flinched. He allowed her to touch him.

Benjamin and I walked up to them.

"He remembers me," Angel said excitedly. "From a long time ago. I was about five when he left home with the traveling show."

"She was a golden-haired child running along behind me," he said. He smiled, and for a moment he was in his eyes, his body. He was my Church.

He looked at me, and his smile faded.

I bit my lip and squeezed Benjamin's hand. I looked away from them. The fog was gone. We were surrounded by red and green-gold. Protected in paradise.

Hiding in paradise.

Ellie had called me a webster. It was time to return to the world and find out what that meant.

Suddenly I remembered that Primer had told me he could get me memories, and while I was healing Stempler I had glimpsed a memory of Clarity's: a memory of running through a field of Queen Anne's lace. An exact replica of Tricia Booth's memory. Clarity had stolen Tricia's memory.

And Clarity had been one of the few, one of the chosen, of Governor Duncan and Primer.

I felt weak in the knees. Of course, it all came back to Primer. Had to.

"It's Primer," I said. "He's behind all of this. I have to find and stop him."

"I'm going with you," Benjamin said.

I looked for Ellie and Nile while Benjamin and Angel prepared a meal. At Ellie's house I called, but no one answered. I checked the fields and found nothing except laughter in the willows. A hawk cried out. I looked up and waved.

I went back to the others and packed my things. We ate in silence.

"Church is coming with us," Angel said, as we put on our packs.

I looked at Church.

"Is your name Sarah?" he asked.

"Gloria," I answered. "Gloria Stone."

He turned away from me.

I searched for Ellie and Nile once more, but the canyon seemed empty of human occupants except for Church, Benjamin, and Angel.

As we went up the trail, I wondered if Grandma Ellie was reweaving the universe this morning after unraveling it all night. I hoped we would not inadvertently break any of her threads on our way up out of the heart of the Earth.

Fifteen

We were lucky the weather was mild and the trail easy. Church and Angel walked behind Benjamin and me. Angel kept up a running conversation with Church. He spoke quietly, and I hoped Angel was a comfort to him.

When we got up to the plateau, I turned and looked down. Although it was not yet spring, the Havasu Canyon looked lushly green. We were leaving paradise.

We camped for the night in a red rock alcove. Benjamin told stories of his childhood. Church laughed out loud in some places. He sounded so like himself that I was certain he would reach out his hand to me and say, "Gloria, where have you been?"

But he did not.

I awoke once. The fire was out. Church moaned in his sleep. I went to him. He was shivering.

"Thomas," I whispered. "Thomas?"

He grabbed my hand and squeezed it. Immediately we connected. I was at the pulsing white light, and I knew I could close it by myself. Now that I was remembering my past, I had more control over my healing abilities. I knew what to do.

But Church had asked me not to heal him.

So I pulled away from the light and lay down behind him, spooning my body up against his. I stayed with him until he stopped shaking, then returned to my bedroll.

At breakfast, while Church and Angel took a walk, I told Benjamin about what I had remembered. "About three hundred years ago, a woman named Maia created computers that looked and acted like people—even the biology was similar, only they were programmed like computers. Do you know what programming means?"

He nodded.

"Well, I was one of those things, those computers. I was the first, Manuel was next. We lived together in this big old institution with others like us. We practiced being human. We could all be in each other's minds. We loved." I stopped and swallowed. "We loved each other. Then we were sold into service and cut off from one another. We had to do what our owners said. It was in our programming. We couldn't stop taking orders. It would be like you making yourself stop breathing. You can only hold your breath so long."

Benjamin silently watched me.

"They played with information and power and technology until it all came down. They made us do terrible things. Made *me* do things. Perform. I had to perform or things were done to me. Or withheld from me." I closed my eyes for a moment, then opened them. "Once, no one touched me for years. Years. I thought if I acted just right, did my job just right, I would be noticed—loved?" I coughed. "Another of them fucked me whenever he wanted. They controlled me." I roughly wiped away my tears. "After The Fall, a survival program kicked in, and I forgot everything. When I awakened, I used my abilities to heal. But I was always wary, always afraid I would be found out. Even though I couldn't remember what I had done."

"What a relief it must be to finally know," he said.

I glanced at him. "Yes, it is a relief. Does it—does it bother you to realize how different we are from one another?"

He laughed. "We have always been different from each

other. Now that I know your birth was not like mine doesn't change anything."

"You don't sound shocked."

He took my hand and kissed it. "I am absolutely floored. How terrible for you to have gone through all that. Yet how wonderful you have survived and that you're here."

"The thing is: Primer has access to program codes and may try to control me again."

"That would be a sight to see."

"Benjamin!"

He laughed.

That night, when Church cried out in his sleep again, I held him. His body felt warm and perfect against mine. As I waited for his shakes to subside, I wandered my own mind. I found the survival program. It contained automatic memory loss and body changes. I dismantled the memory loss. I never wanted to forget again. I switched the body changes to manual. Perhaps I should switch it to Manuel or Womanuel. I giggled.

Then I opened a few memories. All my lifetimes had not been horrible. I found my first visit to Stempler's house. Dark Sarah swearing at him as we played chess. He was younger and good-looking, but not *better*-looking, as he had said. He watched me with amusement. For me as Sarah, his house had been a refuge from the someone or the hint of someone I feared.

While rummaging through my memories, I accidentally fell to sleep.

When I awakened, it was just daylight. Church was sitting up watching me.

"Sorry," I said. "You were shivering."

"Thank you," he said.

Soon after we started that morning, we reached the road that led to the lodge and the Grand Canyon. Cosmo ran away.

"Are you sure you know the way to Red Bluffs and Church's cousin?" I asked.

Church and Angel nodded.

"I think we should go with you," Angel said.

"No. Look, even Cosmo has left. Primer is dangerous. I don't want either of you to be hurt." I kissed her. "We'll see you in Red Bluffs."

I smiled at Church. His fingers lightly touched my hand. "Good-bye," he said, as if this were the last time we would ever see one another.

Then we parted. Benjamin and I walked toward the lodge. My heart raced. I tried to breathe deeply and calm myself, but I was terrified. If I kept this up, I was going to have a computerized heart attack.

"You look sick," Benjamin said.

"I am sick! You have no idea what it's like to have someone have control over you."

"I don't, eh?"

Today, no herd of elk watched us. No snow fell.

I glanced at Benjamin. "Are you all right?"

He sighed. "I just keep wishing things were back to the way they were before. I'm not usually nostalgic. But I miss us. I thought we would grow old together, making love and traipsing through the desert until we were too old to move." He swallowed and clenched his jaw. "Of course now I see it would never have happened. You would have disappeared in thirty or forty years."

I hugged his waist.

"But I would have had those thirty or forty years," he said.

"I will always love you," I said.

"That doesn't really help," he said.

We walked in silence the rest of the way. At the door to the lodge, my heart pounded even louder. Benjamin knocked.

No one answered.

I tried the handle. It turned, and the door opened.

"Hello!" I called, stepping over the threshold into cold darkness.

"Hello!" Benjamin shouted.

He closed the door, and together we went through the lodge. We found no one.

"Primer's probably down in the canyon," I said.

"He could be anywhere," Benjamin said. "It's too late to look for him tonight. Would you feel safe staying here?"

I glanced around. "Sure, as long as one of us stays awake."

Benjamin built a fire. I crept into the kitchen, found leftovers, and brought them back into the living room.

Benjamin and I sat in front of the fire and ate.

Afterward, we started to make love.

"Are you sure you want to?" I asked. "Now that you know what I am?"

He smiled and sank into me. We made love with each other as if it were the very first time, instead of the last.

I took the first watch while Benjamin fell to sleep on the couch. I stared at the fire and listened to the building settle. I kept hearing something outside. Finally I put on my coat, locked the front door, and went to the kitchen. I looked out the kitchen window. Clear moonlit skies.

And a light in the barn window.

I glanced behind me, then stepped outside and walked to the barn. An owl hooted just as I reached the barn door. I went inside. It smelled of hay and urine.

"Hello!" I called.

"Hello."

I turned around.

Primer.

I was not surprised, but my heart jumped into my throat anyway.

"You came back," he said, leaning against the stall.

"Didn't you program me to come back?"

He smiled. "So you've caught on."

"Caught on to what? That you are an evil man using others to do your dirty work?"

"Is that how you see me?" he asked. "Ah well. All that matters is that you are here, with me."

"I am here to stop you."

He laughed. "Stop me from what?"

"From doing whatever it is you are doing. I know the governor's soothsayer Clarity took memories from Tricia Booth.

And Clarity, or someone else, did the same thing to several others."

"How could someone take someone else's memories?" he asked. He was so smug, unafraid.

"I don't know. Shall I try it with you?"

He shifted and walked to the window and looked out. "They worked so hard with the dregs of society. They saw horror every day. They just wanted some respite. None of them remembered their childhoods. None remembered much of anything. One day, one was healing an immigrant and the immigrant's memories accidentally became hers. She was radiant! She had a life. She had something to look back on."

"She stole someone else's life!"

"You of all people should understand."

"Oh? Yeah, so I wished I had memories, but it never occurred to me to steal them! How stupid of me!"

We stared at each other.

"Why was it so important to find me, Primer? Why did you make sure everyone I loved was alienated from me?"

"I had to make certain you returned, that you had no place to go but here."

"Weren't the program codes enough to get me to do your bidding?" I asked.

"Strangely enough, no."

"Why kill that poor coyote?"

"I didn't kill the coyote," he said. "He was already dead."

"How convenient."

"When Edward found the dead coyote, I thought we could use it to push you over the edge, so to speak. We had already whispered the codes to you and you almost killed that deer. But you didn't. You didn't really hurt me, either. I was looking for any way to keep you here—even guilt. We thought you were the answer to so many mysteries. Years ago I met the governor, and we became great friends. She showed me this list in her safe called program codes. According to her, the codes were spells or incantations. Or so a family legend said. When these codes were recited to the right soothsayer, the one born to be the mother of all soothsayers, it was said, she would do the bidding of the reciter. Kind of like the genie in Aladdin's Lamp. This soothsayer would change the world. When I first saw those codes, I felt like they were what I had searched for all my life—the codes and whomever the codes would work on. I tried the codes on every soothsayer I encountered, but nothing happened. I did meet a woman once who was part of this traveling circus or something. Someone said she had healing abilities, so I whispered the codes to her. She ran away, terrified. I tracked her for a while, but I never found her.

"Many years later I heard about you. When I finally met you, I sensed something about you, just like I had with the circus lady, but the codes didn't seem to work at first in Coyote Creek, until after the epidemic. Then you came to the canyon."

"But I didn't stay."

"Funny thing, isn't it? Like I said, you didn't always respond to the codes. But sometimes you did. And here you are."

"I am here to make you pay for what you've done. I'm going to make sure the restricted areas and immigration camps are investigated. And I'm going to stop you from fucking with people's brains."

A flutter. Whispers. Then Primer's voice reciting a program code.

"You will do whatever I want," Primer said.

"No, I won't."

"Cry."

"No."

He stared at me and said the code again. Not even a flutter.

I laughed. "It doesn't work anymore." I threw my hands up in the air. "You created this elaborate scheme to get me under your control, whispering secret codes, telling me what to do and not to do. And what you really did was cause me to remember. You're right, I do know the answers to many mysteries. But I am free of you and all those who are like you. I am finally free."

"Free to return to your true love who doesn't know you

from Adam? Or Eve. Who doesn't remember when he first saw you naked by the stream or what your hand first felt like on his chest?"

My eyes widened. I grabbed Primer's arm. We connected. I saw myself through his eyes as Church and I made love in Stempler's house and then at the lodge. Saw myself as I slept and Church watched. Saw myself through Church's eyes.

I roared and threw Primer to the ground, pinning him under my body.

"You bastard!" I screamed. "*You* did that to Church. You've stolen his life and mine!" Suddenly, as I felt his body beneath mine, I realized what Primer was.

"You're a soothsayer," I whispered. "Do you know what that means?"

Of course he did not. He was about to find out.

"Tell me your sequence," I said.

He shook his head

"Tell me. I can reach into your brain and take it if I want."

"No."

I wanted to rip it out of his mind just as he had driven Church out of his.

I gritted my teeth. Then I realized I knew his sequence. I knew all the program codes. Out loud, I recited his sequence and the sequences of the other soothsayers I knew, plus my own: the combination to unlock his memory. Primer squeezed his eyelids together. I repeated the sequence again and again . . .

. . . until Primer screamed. His wail was long and plaintive. Good. His memories had been unlocked. I moved off him, suddenly exhausted. He curled into a fetal position. I knew what he was feeling, what he was remembering.

I sighed and put my hands on him. Maybe my touch would help him get through it more easily, the stupid evil sonofabitch.

I connected with him. Dived into his remembering and saw when he looked up to see the other. Holding her hand and feeling her life line against his. Watching the moon drape light over their lives. Making love on the forest floor . . . separating. Separated.

Disconnected. Controlled . . . Remembering the other's hand in his, her breath on his shoulder as they slept . . . Maia giving him a wafer, just as she had given me one, only his had a different program . . . Forgetting. Desperately searching.

Stunned, I opened my eyes, and Primer opened his.

"Hello, Woman," he whispered.

"Hello, Man," I said.

He reached for me, and I put my hand in his. Tears fell down our faces.

"You did horrible things," I whispered.

"Didn't we all."

"Maia programmed me to be the key," I said, "but she programmed you to search for the codes that would awaken me."

"I kept thinking there was an answer out there to the vast emptiness I felt—that desperation to do something, even though I didn't know what it was. Maia did not make any of this easy on us." He shook his head. "Maybe we can figure out a way to give back the memories we took."

"Some of the people are dead," I said. "What about Cosmo? What happened to him?"

"Edward got ahold of him," he said. "He liked taking animal memories. After he did it, Cosmo was disoriented, naturally, and he fell into a ravine. We thought he'd died."

I shook my head. "That is really sick."

"I know," he said.

We looked at our clasped hands: we could feel the lines on the other's palms. We smiled at each other.

Hours ago he had been a monster. Now he was my friend again. Life changed in a heartbeat. Or two.

"The humans will want to exterminate us for what we've done," Primer said.

"Human history is not without shame. We tumbled the world in fifty years or more but healed it for three hundred."

"Some of us healed it," he said. He looked out into the dawn. "I am so sorry for what I've done."

"Then let's do something about it," I said. "Every person, every living thing, has the ability to heal or destroy. We are no exception. We have to choose like anyone else. Now that we've remembered, no one has control over us. The control codes are canceled!"

Primer smiled.

"What did Duncan have to do with all of this?" I asked.

"He liked soothsayers around," he said. "From stories he had heard when he was a child, he thought the soothsayers could help keep the immigrants out, or at least in line, and he is interested in technology. Power. He's fascinated with the time before The Fall. He wants comfort, information, power. Plus, he believes he can live forever with all those soothsayers around him to heal him. His mother never told him the legend of the codes, and I made certain he never saw them."

"Did Duncan encourage the soothsayers to take other people's memories?" I asked.

"He didn't care what they did as long as he was surrounded by them."

"When I visited here and met them, they all seemed so nice," I said.

"They were on their best behavior," he said. "We wanted you to stay."

"I don't think I would have done it," I said, "taken other people's memories, no matter how desperate I was." I glanced out the window. "But I guess I never thought I would try to kill anyone, and I did."

Primer shook his head. "Actually, you didn't really kill me. I just wanted it to look that way. We thought once you thought you'd killed me and that Church had left you, you'd stay here out of guilt and fear of punishment. None of us thought you'd run back to Coyote Creek and tell everyone what you had done."

"And then what? Were you just going to stay dead forever?"

"No. I'd have a miraculous rebirth, tantalizing you with the great power of soothsayers if you'd just admit what you were and agree to stay here and help us."

"That's a lot of brainpower wasted," I said. "Reminds me

of humans of old, like our former owners." I sighed. "Come on. We've got things to do."

I kissed Benjamin awake. He sat up quickly when he saw Primer.

"It's all right," I said. "Benjamin, this is Manuel. I told you about him."

Confused, Benjamin shook his hand. I sat next to him. Primer stood near the dying fire.

"He is also Primer," I said.

Benjamin looked from me to Primer and back again. "What? How?"

"He's a soothsayer just like me."

Benjamin blinked and then shook his head. "Oh no. He's nothing like you! He poisoned Coyote Creek. He was involved in some kind of elaborate plot against you."

"He won't hurt anyone now."

"Suddenly he's a different person?"

"Yes. He was looking for me, and now he's found me. The programming has ended. He won't hurt anyone else."

"How can you be so sure?" he asked.

"I just know. And I know what's been causing the memory illness. Duncan's soothsayers have been stealing memories."

"What?" Benjamin said. He looked at Primer. "You've been stealing memories?"

Primer cleared his throat.

"Actually, he has Church's memories," I said. "He is why Church is ill."

"*He* destroyed your life?"

"No," I said, "my life is not destroyed. And he will make restitution for what he has done. They all will. Now, I want to find Duncan and let him know it's all over. Will you come with me?"

He stared at Primer for a moment, then said, "Of course."

"Good. I'm exhausted," I said. "I've got to get some rest before we leave."

"You know you can adjust your bodily functions so you're

not so tired," Primer said, sounding just like he had centuries ago when we sat in the cafeteria together.

"I *want* to sleep," I said.

I left them and went to the room Church and I had shared months earlier. I pulled down the covers on the bed and got in under the cool clean sheets. I stared at the pillow next to mine and felt sick to my stomach. I wished Church was in my arms, me in his, connected to each other forever.

Or until one of us left the other.

I closed my eyes. Duncan's soothsayers were, no doubt, still stealing memories, misusing their abilities. They had to remember, and I knew how to help them remember. They might still do harm even after they knew their pasts, but odds were, like Primer, they would no longer feel the necessity. Did anyone ever feel the need to be cruel, to destroy, when all their needs were met?

I sat up. Maia's wafer had given me access to all the sequences and codes for all the soothsayers once I remembered. That meant I could prevent the other soothsayers from remembering—I could force them to do whatever I wanted. But I wouldn't. They had a right to their freedom, just as I did. Maia had told me that one day I would know all the answers. I breathed deeply. I knew a great deal, but I certainly did not have all the answers! I did know I could now turn on the sending and the receiving of the other soothsayers, which had been turned off when they were sold to their original owners.

I dipped into the airwaves. First I found Primer's mind and turned on his sending and receiving, and then we searched for the others. One by one we connected. Group by group. Through their eyes, we saw desert, delta, wetland, ruined cities, ocean.

I laughed. The net was restored! No, the web was created. We were the websters, spinning out our lives together now, connected once again.

Many of the soothsayers on this continent were already nearing Red Bluffs for the healers' gathering.

"I can show you how to remember," I whispered. "We'll meet in Red Bluffs."

I felt connected and complete for the first time in centuries. I shivered with delight, then withdrew from the other soothsayers, back to myself alone in bed near the Grand Canyon. I fell to sleep instantly and did not dream.

Primer told us Duncan was at Area 27, an immigration camp. One of his soothsayers wanted more childhood memories. The journey to Area 27 was uncomfortable. Benjamin did not understand my trust of Primer, and Primer/Manuel was still unsteady as he continued to remember his past.

We knew we had arrived at the restricted area when we came to old high barbed-wire fences. Bedraggled people within stared at us. We followed the fence to the one building with four walls and a roof which was situated near the main gates. Primer and Benjamin each pulled a gate open.

Duncan came out of the house, followed by several soothsayers: Terry, Lester, Edward, and Caroline. My false friends from the Grand Canyon. Duncan opened his arms to welcome us.

"Save the act, guv," I said. "Primer told me what you've really been doing in these immigrant camps. Not only are you using these people as slave labor, but your soothsayers have been sucking out their memories."

"Primer, she was your project," Duncan said. "You were supposed to have her under control."

Benjamin made a noise.

"As you can see," I said, "things have changed. You wanted tech, you've got it. And what this tech says is you will all turn yourselves over to the proper community authorities. Before that, however, the soothsayers are gathering in Red Bluffs. This means you."

"*You* were in our minds? You sent that message?" Terry asked.

"Yes," I answered. "You're all going to get a history lesson."

"I'm not going anywhere," Edward said.

I sighed. I wanted the soothsayers to have free choice, but they could not have free choice until they remembered. For one last time, I whispered the codes which would force Duncan's soothsayers to do what I said, and I told them to go to Red Bluffs for the gathering. They had no choice. The fascist had temporarily returned.

"Before we leave we're going to clean up this place," I said.

"You can't do that," Duncan said. "These are legitimate camps. I have free rein to do as I wish."

Duncan seemed so different now, in charge, irritated, the *patrón*. They had all fooled me so easily. Why had they wasted all that time and energy deceiving me? So I could show them the promised land of an easy life through better technology? They had way too much time on their hands already, they didn't need an easier life!

"We're going to heal these people," I said. "You all can help."

Duncan crossed his arms across his chest and stared after us. The soothsayers followed me of their own volition as I walked to the lean-tos. Healthy people, already loaded down with their things, walked past us out the gates. I stopped first to heal an elderly woman. She looked up at me with ice blue eyes and held my hands.

"May I help you feel better?" I asked.

"Honey, I'll take whatever you can give."

We connected. Her entire life rolled out before me, like a lazy spiral slowly spinning and unspinning itself. I found a cloud in her lungs and blew it away. Around me, the conniving, memory-sucking soothsayers seemed to glow as they healed. I wondered if for some it was the first time they had healed. If I had never felt the spark that connected me to each and every person each time I healed, would I have felt that restless emptiness which led them to believe it was acceptable to steal another's memories?

Who knew?

I kissed the woman and went to the cot of a teenager. She

stared up at the tattered lean-to. Her mother touched my sleeve.

"That's all she does."

"What's her name?" I asked.

"Katherine."

I knew before I touched her what I would find.

"Katherine, you need some help?"

She did not answer.

I placed a hand on her head and her shoulder. The light was all-consuming. So much memory was gone.

I felt a flicker of anger at whoever had done this. And I sensed. Some. Thing.

"Hey, kids. Get over here." I glanced around. Benjamin stood near a sullen-looking Duncan. The other soothsayers gathered around me and the girl.

"Which of you vampires took her memories?" I asked.

Lester looked at his hands.

"You?" I said. "What were you going to do with girl memories, Lester? Look back and remember fondly the first time blood flowed from your nonexistent vagina!"

"I-I just wanted to see what it was like being a girl."

Primer and I glanced at each other.

"You had no right. Put your hands on her and you try to be in that light with her."

He touched the girl. I felt him pull away as he neared the light, but I made him stay. As I forced him to be in the light, I suddenly recalled Millanze fucking me up against his car. It was too easy to be like him, to manipulate others to do what I wanted. Soon, I hoped, I would no longer be able to control anyone except myself.

I released Lester. He looked over the girl at me.

"Primer said you don't know how to fix these memory holes, that the memories are completely gone and imprinted on you. But I believe the memories are still with them. I want us to try to heal her, to bring her memories back."

We all touched Katherine. We connected, just like I had with the soothsayers in the woods, except this time, I knew what to do. I dived into the light, through it, and found what I was looking for. Her memories were not gone; she was just off track. It was like those old-time phonographs with a stylus running over the grooves of a record. Sometimes a scratch or a bump would cause the needle to play the same thing over and over. Except when Lester stole Katherine's memories, it deepened the groove and the needle was stuck just playing the empty groove over and over, unable to get out of the rut onto a memory. The other soothsayers followed me through the light, and we bumped Katherine out of the rut.

The light snapped away.

One by one, we dropped our hands from Katherine. My cheeks were wet with tears. We had healed her completely and could now heal Amy, Lizbeth, Stempler, Georgia, Herb.

And Church.

Katherine sat up and put her arms around me.

"Thank you," she whispered.

When we finished the healings, Primer, Benjamin, and I walked to the entrance to the camp. Duncan stood at the gate, his hands on his hips, trying to block our way as we left.

"You don't know what you've unleashed," he said. "You haven't the authority."

"Governor," I said, "you have a great deal to learn about governing."

We went to two more internment centers and did more healing. Then we traveled through the glorious Oak Creek Canyon area to Red Bluffs. Flowers and trees were beginning to bloom. Creeks, streams, and waterfalls overran their boundaries. Birds of every color dotted the trees and skies, calling out loudly to each other.

In the distance, we could see the red rock giants, those peculiar freestanding rock formations unique to the area. Everything was red. I felt calm and centered; Primer got edgy.

"It's all going to get out," he said. "Everyone is going to know. You remember the hangings and riots."

"It's a different time now," I told him. "It'll be all right. Most people are happy, well-fed, and comfortably lodged."

Benjamin watched us, silently, warily. I hoped I was right.

Later, Benjamin asked, "How can you be so sure Primer won't keep hurting people? He started all this—this destruction of the life we had."

"Because seeing him again is like discovering a long-lost brother."

"Everyone has relatives. Even murderers and thieves."

"I saw into his soul when he was remembering," I said. "He was lost. Now he's found."

"Isn't that an easy answer?"

"Benjamin, it really is not so complicated, and you can't blame him for everything."

Benjamin snorted. "Yes I can! If he hadn't poisoned the water, you would have come to the dances with me. You and Church would never have gone off together."

I looked at him. "I probably wouldn't have gone to the dances," I said softly. "Not then. Maybe now. But that's not the way things work. I understand it's confusing, but I'm glad I remember! I feel like the world is opening up to me for the first time. Maybe I'm being naive about the other soothsayers, but I really believe it's best for them to remember, too, and then we can get on with being who and what we are."

"I feel like I'm being ripped apart," Benjamin said, looking away from me. "You can't know what it's like."

I thought of Church wandering, mindless, somewhere with Angel. "Yes, I do know."

Once in Red Bluffs, we were led to the council. Council elder Kindra welcomed us and volunteered to take us to their meeting place. We walked down a red path bordered with twisted scrub oak and then up onto smooth pink rocks with a red rock giant towering behind us. We gathered in a circle, Kindra, Primer, Benjamin, myself, and other council members. Kindra made an offering of tobacco to the spirits. While he prayed, I gazed up at the red rock. I was an infant compared with it. Did it watch us? Was it aware of our existence?

When the ceremony was over, Kindra talked about the weather and the promise of good crops. They made a fire and cooked for us.

After they left, Benjamin, Primer, and I sat and waited.

For The Fall to begin again.

Sixteen

The soothsayers began arriving over the next few days. I climbed up onto the rock and watched as they found places on the stone and waited.

One day Amy and Lizbeth ran up the red path dressed in blue. I hopped down and swept them into my arms.

"We missed you," Amy said.

"You, too," I said, kissing her. "How's it been with Stempler?"

"Fun. He opened up a bunch of other rooms in his house," Lizbeth said, "so we had places to run when it was too cold outside."

"Running in the house, eh?" I said. "Hmmm. Just you two and that old man all winter?"

They nodded. Stempler made his way through the crowd.

"Hello, healer."

"Hello yourself, old man," I said. "You'll be pleased to know you were right. I am Sarah."

He raised his eyebrows.

"I'll tell you the whole story later. You'll like it."

"I look forward to it."

I kissed the girls again. "I love you," I said. Then Stempler took them back into the crowd of soothsayers and healers.

When the day seemed that it could not get bluer or the rocks redder and the line of people coming had stopped, I stepped up onto one of the smooth stones so that I could see all those gathered. Benjamin sat below me, Primer just off to the side. I could see Duncan's soothsayers and Zeenie, Lily, and the other soothsayers from the enclave.

I kicked off my shoes. My feet fit perfectly over the stone. I raised my arms and reached through the ether to the others. I connected and saw myself through the eyes of those present.

I spoke aloud and sent my thoughts swirling around the globe to all soothsayers.

"We are gathered here to discover who and what we are. What you are about to learn will shatter every notion you have ever had about yourself.

"First we honor the spirits and beings of this land. We honor the east and the element of air and pray for illumination. We honor the south and the element of fire and ask for the will to go forward. We honor the west and the element of water and ask for the ability to love and dive wholeheartedly into our deepest feelings. We honor the north and the element of earth which surrounds us this day and ask for peace, and the ability to be still and silent."

Benjamin smiled at me. I winked.

"Now, soothsayers, hang on! I want each of you to chant your sequence. Sing it out until you can't."

Slowly I heard one sequence, then another, and another, each flowing over the other. For those not at the red rock, I opened my ears and eyes so they could hear and I sang out the sequences they sent to me.

The sequences became a chant, a beautiful song. I opened completely. No anxiety this time. Just pure ecstasy as I was linked with the people, soothsayers, rock, air, insects, birds. All of me vibrated, molecules giggling and knocking against one another.

The rock beneath my feet began to vibrate. The music rose. For a moment, I saw an image of Maia over our heads, laughing, her gray hair slithering into snakes and then fading away into music again. Maybe Ellie was right, maybe we were conduits for the Earth. As the soothsayers linked and connected and entwined each other, I felt as if we were part of the Earth, sinking into her and out again, singing her song, being her voice, connecting with every creature on the planet. The songs of the soothsayers reached a crescendo.

Then, one by one, the sequences stopped as the soothsayers began remembering. As one slumped, another held her, until they, too, remembered. The other healers touched the soothsayers and prayed over them. When the voices stopped, the drums began, holding us all in the circle of music.

Eventually I sank down onto the vibrating rock. I leaned over and pressed my ear against the cool stone.

And listened to the heartbeat of the Earth.

Some remembered quickly, others did not. I sat cross-legged and watched. Those who came out of their memories gathered around the humans who had had their memories stolen. I closed my eyes and healed with them, pushing the needles out of the ruts, releasing the memories of Lizbeth, Amy, Georgia, Stempler, and Herb.

Later, many of us sat and talked.

"What does this mean for the world?" people asked.

"I guess as communities and individuals we'll all decide what it means," I said. "Each community will have to decide what to do with those soothsayers who stole memories. As residents of Arizona Territory, we will have to decide what to do about Governor Duncan."

We talked until after dark. There were no accusations yet, no suspicions, just fascination. I quickly grew weary of being the supposedly all-knowing sage. When my legs got cramped and tired, I excused myself. I looked for Angel and Church but did not find them, and no one knew where they were. I held the girls until they fell to sleep. Then Stempler and I carried them to Kindra's camp.

"They're pretty exhausted," Stempler said.

I nodded. "Do you care if we come stay with you for a while?"

"Does this mean you're all moving in with me?" he asked.

"You asked me to fifteen years ago. What's different now?"

He grinned. "What's different is you got two kids, which will make your company almost tolerable."

"Yeah, yeah. I really don't know what to do now, actually. Did anyone fill you in on what I remembered?"

Stempler nodded. "Kind of ironic, isn't it? When you come to visit me, I'll have the highest tech available. You don't think they'll make me take you out and shoot you, do you?"

"Of course not," I said, grinning. "We've destroyed all your guns."

I returned to those still locked in memory. My weariness disappeared. I felt the solidness of the Earth in my feet and up through my legs. I looked around at the darkness. On a ledge off the red rock, a coyote was silhouetted. He raised his head skyward and howled. Cosmo.

I raised my head and did the same. Soon, all around me, people howled. I laughed and howled again. We had become the Cosmo Clan, or the Red Rock Clan, or the family of the Earth. Whoever we were, we howled together into the night.

In the morning, we prayed our thanks to the land, then went our separate ways, knowing we were always and forever connected. Knowing we had to individually and as a collective think about the future when the reverberation of remembering ceased.

I looked for Church but did not find him. I ate breakfast with the girls and Stempler.

"Did Stempler tell you about me?" I asked, glancing at the old man.

"You mean that some lady grew you in a laboratory more than three hundred years ago?" Lizbeth asked.

I made a face at Stempler. "Well, I'm not sure I'd describe it quite like that. The important thing to know is that I was not born the way you were. I was a machine created to look like a woman."

Amy stopped chewing. "Can you have babies?"

"No," I said.

"So we could be your babies?" she asked.

I smiled.

"We're too old to be babies," Lizbeth said. "At least I am. We'd be her children. You said you were a machine. Does that mean you can break down?"

"You mean do my parts get rusty?" I said. "No. I replicate myself just like you. I just can control some of my functions more than you can."

"I can control my functions, too," Amy said, enunciating the word "functions." "Our parents taught us that a long time ago."

Stempler and I laughed.

"Does this mean you'll never die?" Lizbeth asked.

"I'll die someday, but not for a long time."

"You'll never try to fly off a cliff?" Amy asked.

I looked down at her sweet, earnest face. "Never," I said. I cleared my throat. "Stempler and I thought maybe you'd like to live in his house for a while, until we all decide what we want to do."

"With you, too?" Amy asked.

"If you still want me."

"Silly," Lizbeth said. "We love you. This means we can finally all go see the many-breasted priestess."

"Yeah," Amy said. "How many is many?"

I kissed her forehead and smoothed her hair off her face. I wondered if I would ever be able to show them how much I loved them.

"Many is more than two," I said.

"No," Stempler said. "Many is more than four."

"Oh really?" I looked over the girls' heads at him. He winked. I smiled. Perhaps life would work out after all. The girls smiled up at me. For an instant, I imagined them as old women and suddenly realized I would probably see them die one day. Lizbeth tickled Amy, and she laughed loudly. It was a lifetime too early to start thinking about loss.

"We want to see where you live," Lizbeth said.

"I don't live there any longer," I said.

"They want to see where you *lived*," Stempler said. "You all can come see me after you wrap up things in Coyote Creek."

I looked at the girls. They nodded. We belonged to each other. I guess we might as well start acting like it.

"All right. Let's get packed and get going."

Primer had asked me to return with him to Coyote Creek, where he would hand himself over to the council. Georgia and Herb agreed to take him in Coyote Creek's solar buggy, and I would follow in Stempler's. Benjamin came with us. He said little. Amy fell asleep on his lap; I fell asleep on his shoulder.

Stempler dropped us off just outside of town. The girls kissed him good-bye, and he happily endured their embraces.

"Thanks, Stempler," I said. "We'll see you soon."

"Not if I see you first, healer," he said. He waved and drove off.

The four of us walked to town. The sight of its saggy main street and Black Mountain behind it filled me with joy. Cosmo ran up to us. I rubbed his head, and he yelped as the girls screamed with delight. Benjamin rolled his eyes, and I laughed.

I looked up the mountain. Up that path was my home.

Had been my home.

Now what was it?

A crowd had gathered at the oak. The girls spotted other children and ran toward them, already at home. Benjamin sat on Millie's porch, watching them. I sat next to him.

"What are you going to do now?" I asked.

He gazed at me for a moment and then put his hand on my cheek. I kissed his palm.

"I'm going home," he said.

He stood and stretched. Then he pulled me up, and we embraced. He leaned down and kissed me.

"Be a stranger for a while," he said.

He stepped off the porch and walked away. My chest and throat hurt. I wanted to run after him and beg him to stay.

I watched until I could no longer see him.

"I love you," I whispered.

"Gloria!" Georgia called to me.

I wiped my eyes, then turned and walked to the oaks. Everyone clapped and called out "Hello!" I nodded. Primer stood between the council and the rest of the townspeople, his hands behind him.

"Gloria," Georgia said, "the council and town would like to ask you to come back and be our healer."

I looked at the council and the faces of the townspeople. I loved them all. I could live in peace with them forever.

Yet, everything was changed.

I slowly shook my head. "Thank you, but I don't think so. A lot has happened."

Georgia looked stunned. "This is your home. We want you to stay here."

I glanced around at them again.

"I worked for you for many years," I said. "I never harmed a single one of you. I was a part of this community. I took care of you, and you took care of me. And then I got sick, I had a problem, and you all turned on me. You kicked me out of my home, gave someone else my livelihood. We were supposed to be a community. You all talked the big talk until I did one thing wrong."

"That one thing was kill a person," Herb said quietly.

"As you can see," I said, pointing to Primer, "that one person is not dead."

"We didn't know," someone said.

"You should have given me more of a chance," I said. "I should have mattered more to you."

"Maybe you should have fought harder," Georgia said, "and listened to us better. We weren't throwing you out of town."

I turned to her. "You threw me out of my home, and I had no way to make a living."

The silence made my ears throb.

I sighed. "I should have waited and talked it out with you. But I need you to trust me more, especially now that we all know who I am."

"We want you to stay," Georgia said.

"Let me make a suggestion," I said. "I'm not ready to be a full-time healer again. Yet. I need to figure out some things and maybe build some trust with this community again. You need a healer. How about Primer being that healer?"

The discussion that followed was long and heated. In the end, however, Georgia said, "Mr. Primer, you have done great harm to this village. If it wasn't for Gloria, I don't know what would have happened. Gloria, do you now trust this man to care for the residents of this town?"

I looked at Primer. His eyes were Manuel's eyes.

"With my life," I said.

"Then we've agreed that you, Primer, will remain in this village as our healer until such time we believe you have discharged your debt to us. Is this agreeable to you?"

Primer looked at me and then at the council.

"Yes. Thank you."

"This meeting is adjourned," Georgia said. "We'll see you in a few days for orientation. Gloria, the house is yours for as long as you want. We hope you will remain here. Could you at least stay long enough to show Primer around?"

"Sure," I said.

Georgia embraced me. "We truly love you and want you to be a part of us again. I'm sorry we acted so hastily. We were frightened and confused."

"Me, too," I said.

I believe everyone present hugged me and the girls. A few of them even embraced Primer.

"Do we get to see your house now?" Lizbeth said, holding her sister's hand.

"It's not really my house," I said, as we started up the hill.

Cosmo raced beside us, up the hill and then down again, up and down, until he finally ran full speed up the mountain away from us.

"Actually, I heard the mayor say it was your house," Primer said.

I grinned. "Yeah, she did say that, didn't she? And I'm not even the town healer anymore. You can stay at the house for now, Primer, though it's going to be a little crowded with the four of us."

"I've never been a healer," Primer said as we climbed. The girls skipped ahead.

"Never?"

"Okay. I've healed, but not as a regular gig."

"Well, this is as regular as it gets. These people are mine. You better do a good job."

Cosmo greeted us at the juniper. My heart fluttered a bit to see the old homestead. Inside, all seemed the same. The girls ran from corner to corner. Our dinner was even waiting for us. I sighed. *And it was still hot.* Home sweet home.

"Is this our home?" Amy asked, jumping up onto me.

"For now," I said. "How's that sound?"

"I'm home wherever you are," Lizbeth said.

I kissed her forehead. "Sweetheart, it's better to be home wherever *you* are."

We took our enchiladas, beans, and salsa outside. Cosmo ran after the sun. Primer and I leaned against each other and ate, watching the saguaro shadows stretch. The girls yawned in between mouthfuls.

I took them inside before we had finished the meal. Gently, I undressed them and tucked them into my bed. We would figure out sleeping arrangements another night. I returned outside and sat with Primer.

"Do you think anyone will ever love us the way we first loved each other?" he asked.

"Of course not. We were the first," I said.

"I'm going to go by the name Manuel," he said. "I haven't gone by that since we were first together. You know how I got the name Primer? I was holed up in some underground ruin forgetting my previous life. When I woke up, I was staring at a book that was titled 'First grade primer.' First and grade seemed like stupid names. I didn't realize until later that it was pronounced 'prim-er' not 'prime-er.' What was Maia thinking anyway, having us periodically lose our memories? Talk about repeating history."

I shook my head. "I don't understand a lot of what she did. I'll call you Manuel, but don't expect me to change my name to Woman. I like Gloria."

"Did you ever find Church?" he asked.

"No."

"He sure loved you."

"Did he tell you that?"

"No. I-ah-I remember it."

I stood. "*Primer*, don't remind me what you did too often. I might have to kill you again."

"You never killed me the first time."

"Second time's the charm."

Manuel slept on the floor. I slept near him, off and on. Finally, I got up and went outside. I lay on the ground looking up at the stars.

"Thank you for giving me back my memories," I whispered. "Thanks for my home, the girls, Cosmo, Primer, and all my friends."

I went back inside the house and slept until just before dawn. Then I got up, kissed the sleeping girls, and hurried down the mountain. I had to see Church. I had to remind him of what he already knew.

The town was quiet. I went inside the church.

And was astounded. The building overflowed with trees and other greenery. The windows were wide-open, and the pews were arranged more in a U than a straight line. I walked down the aisle. The raised platform at the front was gone, along with the crucifix. Stones were arranged in a circle around items on a low altar with a figure of a woman on one side and a man on the other.

"Well, hello."

I turned around.

"Hello, Angel."

"Do you like it?" she asked, linking arms with me.

"I love it. It's beautiful."

"It is, isn't it? Now it can be a place of ceremony and worship for those times we can't be outside or we just want to be in."

"Have you changed your religion?"

She laughed. "Just expanded it. What are you going to do?"

I sighed. "I don't know yet. Perhaps I'll become a traveling soothsayer to minister to other soothsayers, help them use their abilities wisely." I laughed. "I am the first. That must mean I've got some kind of wisdom."

"I'm sure."

"I'm sorry we didn't get to know each other better," I said. "I was too busy patronizing you."

"And I was too busy desperately searching for Thomas. But there's time now."

"Speaking of Church. Where is he? I thought we were going to meet you both in Red Bluffs."

"Thomas kept saying he had lost something, and he thought he could find it here."

"Did he find it?"

She shrugged. "He helped me with this transformation of the church, but he still doesn't remember much."

"Is he around now?"

"I haven't seen him since last night. He wasn't in his room this morning. He probably went for a walk. Why don't you wait for him?"

I kissed her. "I'll come back later. I just wanted him to know that we discovered a way to bring back the memories. I could help him, or another soothsayer could do it if he doesn't want me to."

"I'll tell him," she said.

I went back up the mountain. Primer and the children still slept. I was filthy. I got a towel and clean clothes and walked down to the creek.

As soon as I took off my clothes, I realized I had forgotten what time of the year it was. Regardless, I stepped into the icy water. I seemed to be covered in red sand. When I got acclimated to the cold, I dipped my head in the water and washed my hair. I scrubbed away the red dirt and added it to our plain old gray dirt.

When I stood, I noticed someone standing across the stream from me, watching.

Church. His beard was gone, his hair short. His eyes looked less wild, more sad.

"If you wanted to see me naked," I said, softly, "I could have arranged a more convenient location."

I reached for my towel and wrapped it around me. Church plunged into the creek and sloshed over to my side.

"Sarah?"

"No, Gloria."

He reached for my hands. I felt the connection, saw the sliver of myself I had seen the first time Church and I had touched: Sarah.

"I can bring the memories back," I said, looking into his blue blue eyes.

"But the light will go away."

"Yes," I answered, "it will."

"But you will come back?"

I blinked. "Yes, I will come back."

"All right."

My heart raced. We walked out of the water to the shore. I took off my towel. Slowly, Church removed his clothes. We stood, naked, at the edge of the water.

"Are you ready?" I asked.

He nodded. I hoped I could do this by myself. I hoped I could put our lives back together.

I placed one hand on Church's head and another on his shoulder. We connected instantly. The light was all consuming. I plunged straight into it and found the groove. Suddenly I was filled with something strange and beautiful, so relaxing I wanted to fall into it, did fall into it, and splashed it all over myself. The feeling pushed Church's memories open. I wanted to laugh. How ridiculous that I had ever felt disconnected, not belonging. Every moment I had healed or made love had been overflowing with love for Lizbeth, Amy, Benjamin, Cosmo, Maia, Primer, Georgia, Church, the Earth. It did not matter that I was unlike any of them. It did not matter that I was not technically human—I was still loved. And I loved.

I reached out to the other soothsayers and they reached for me, all over the Earth, weaving a web around the planet, the connections pulsing with my discoveries and all their memories and knowledge. We were the new web, the new weavers. We were here for the planet and all her creatures. We were Gaia's websters. However we had been created, we were children of the Earth.

And then Church's memories burst upon mine, and I remembered with him and they were my memories, memories of being Sarah. Stempler's Sarah.

Church's Sarah:

"You think God is only up here," I said, touching the boy Thomas's head. "But She's in your heart, your body. She's what love is."

The boy smiled. A teenage boy in love, I knew, running away from home to join the traveling church.

"You'll be a good man, Thomas," I said. "I can tell. You've got a good heart."

"Yes, ma'am."

I laughed. "And someday you will fall in love with the woman of your dreams."

"I already have," he said.

What a beautiful boy Thomas Church had been. And I had been his first love!

The devouring white light disappeared.

I opened my eyes. Church opened his. We leaned toward one another and gently embraced.

"Gloria," he whispered. "You were right. I didn't find God in my head but in my heart the first time I met you and again the second."

"And now the third?"

He gently kissed my lips. "And now the third."

"You understand what I am?" I asked, as we pulled apart.

"I've always understood who you are."

"I've got kids now," I said.

"I've always wanted children."

"And we've all gotten pretty attached to Stempler."

"I've always wanted a cranky old grandfather with a great house."

Cosmo yelped and ran up to us.

"My old friend," Church said, rubbing the coyote's head.

I laughed, and we put on our clothes.

"You sure you're ready for all this?" I asked.

He slipped his arm around my waist.

"I've been ready my whole life."

Cosmo ran away from us toward the spring's first butterfly.

"Glo-ria!" Lizbeth and Amy called from above. Primer stood with them. They all waved wildly. Church and I waved back.

"We've made breakfast!" Primer called.

"Good, I'm starving," I said. My appetite had finally returned.

Hand in hand, Church and I walked up the mountain toward home.